Shane reached out as if to take the photo, but Elle jerked back to avoid his hand.

She reached up to snap on the light, then opened the folder. Inside it, she found a second copy of the photograph and a sheet of paper with her name printed on it, her address—both home and business—her age, marital status, even her ex-husband's name. Charlotte's name appeared at the bottom of the page. Her full name. Charlotte Michelle O'Meara. Followed by her date of birth, the hospital where she'd been born and her date of adoption.

Elle lifted her gaze very slowly to Shane, struggling to understand. Her insides were knotted, her throat so tight it was all she could do to speak. "What the hell is this? Just who are you, Shane? And why have you been spying on me and my daughter?"

Dear Reader,

I come from a large, scattered Southern family: three brothers, lots of aunts, uncles, cousins, nieces, nephews and "greats" and a dizzying array of in-laws and longtime friends who have become close as kin over the years. Our family gatherings are filled with chatter, laughter and entirely too much good food as four generations swap stories and memories. We are a widely diverse group in just about every way, but one value connects us all: the importance of family, whether by blood, marriage, adoption or simply love.

In this, my second book of the Soldiers and Single Moms trilogy, I return once again to one of my favorite story themes: the definition of *family*. Divorced single mom Elle O'Meara loves her little adopted daughter, Charlotte, with all of her heart and soul. But when Charlotte's biological family shows up in the form of the child's sexy army-veteran uncle, Shane Scanlon, Elle must confront her secret fears. In doing so, she learns that family has many facets—and that love is the ultimate bond.

I hope you enjoy meeting these two families as much as I loved getting to know them myself!

Gina

GINA
WILKINS

The Way to a
Soldier's Heart

Recycling programs
for this product may
not exist in your area.

ISBN-13: 978-0-373-64045-4

The Way to a Soldier's Heart

Printed in U.S.A.

Before she even learned to read, **Gina Wilkins** announced that she wanted to be a writer. That dream never wavered, though she worked briefly in advertising and human resources. Influenced by her mother's love of classic Harlequin romances, she knew she wanted her stories to always have happy endings. She met her husband in her first college English class and they've been married for more than thirty-five years, blessed with two daughters and a son. They also have two delightful grandchildren. After more than one hundred books with Harlequin, she will always be a fan of romance and a believer in happy endings.

Books by Gina Wilkins

HARLEQUIN SUPERROMANCE

Soldiers and Single Moms

The Soldier's Forever Family

HARLEQUIN SPECIAL EDITION

Proposals & Promises

The Boss's Marriage Plan
A Reunion and a Ring
The Bachelor's Little Bonus

Bride Mountain

Healed with a Kiss
A Proposal at the Wedding
Matched by Moonlight

A Match for the Single Dad
The Texan's Surprise Baby
The Right Twin
His Best Friend's Wife
Husband for a Weekend

Doctors in the Family

Doctors in the Wedding
A Home for the M.D.
The M.D. Next Door

Doctors in Training

Prognosis: Romance
The Doctor's Undoing
Private Partners
Diagnosis: Daddy

Visit the Author Profile page at
Harlequin.com for more titles

For my precious little grandsons—Ephraim, who showed us how to find joy in "party dots," and Malachi, the newest member of our family. Gigi loves you both!

CHAPTER ONE

UNLIKE HER IMAGINATIVE MOTHER, Elle O'Meara had never once pretended she could predict the future. Janet O'Meara's so-called talent for occasional precognition was based more on wishful thinking than reality, but most of their friends indulged the little quirk. As for Elle, almost every day brought surprises—mostly good, some bad—and she generally preferred not to try to anticipate the next development. Still, when a dark-haired, blue-eyed man in a black leather jacket, worn jeans and a gray T-shirt sauntered into her little coffee shop on a quiet Wednesday morning in late October, she was struck by the oddest sense of heightened awareness—as if something about this customer was different from the others she'd served that day. Almost momentously so.

Telling herself she'd been spending too much time with her lovable but deliberately eccentric mom, she smiled brightly as she set aside the cloth she'd used to wipe the counter and welcomed the newcomer. "Good morning. Welcome to The Perkery. What can I get for you?"

He was her sole customer at the moment and he swept the overhead menu board with a quick glance. Pastries and other baked goods were listed on the left, soups and sandwiches on the right, but he didn't spend much time studying either side. He glanced at the now-empty play corral behind the counter, a colorful area filled with toys and toddler books. Elle got the impression this guy didn't miss many details of his surroundings.

She couldn't help noticing how nicely his thick, dark lashes framed almost sapphire-blue eyes when he focused on her face again. Her jolt of reaction this time was entirely explainable. Hormones. She supposed it was nice to acknowledge that hers were still in working order, despite being pretty much ignored for the past two busy years.

"Coffee, please. And—" He motioned toward the almost-empty display stand on the counter beside her. "Are those filled doughnuts?"

"Yes, they are. Made fresh this morning. Your choice of raspberry, lemon or Bavarian cream filling. There could be a chocolate left—no, I'm afraid they're all gone," she added after a quick double check.

He ordered the raspberry. She liked his voice, she thought as she set the plated pastry on the counter in front of him, along with a big ceramic mug for him to fill at the coffee bar. Deep, rich, nicely modulated. It suited him.

The guy was definitely attractive. Early thirties, close to her own age. Slim but solid build. Square-cut face with strongly carved features. His coffee-brown hair was thick and wavy, carelessly styled in a manner that would make any warm-blooded woman want to play in it. Her fingers tingled at the thought, and she suppressed an exasperated grimace. What was up with her today?

After paying, the man thanked her and carried his plate to a tiny table by the window. He looked around with the idle curiosity of a new customer as he crossed the room in this lull between breakfast and lunch. She saw him smile faintly when he spotted a couple of whimsical plastic jack-o'-lanterns arranged on the shelves of tea-and-coffee-themed merchandise for sale. The splashes of orange and black stood out among the light woods, stainless steel fixtures and ocean-blue walls. Suited to the coastal South Carolina setting, the decor had turned out just as Elle and her business partner, Kristen Boyd, had hoped. Breezy, bright and welcoming.

Tucking her shoulder-length, honey-colored hair behind one ear, Elle reached for her cleaning cloth again. She heard Amber, her employee, clattering around in the kitchen behind her, and she assumed everything was under control in there. Appreciating the momentary quiet in the usually bustling shop, she continued tidying behind the counter, watching surreptitiously as the man filled his cup from the self-serve coffee bar. He skipped creamer and sweeteners. The no-frills type. She wasn't surprised.

He caught her looking his way after he returned to his table. His somber eyes locked for a moment with hers, causing a tingle of awareness to course through her. She felt a silly urge to fan her cheeks with her hand, but she asked merely, "Is there anything else I can get for you?"

"No, thanks. This doughnut is really good. Did you make it?"

"I did. I'm glad you like it."

"So, you're the shop owner?" he asked, lounging back in his seat to converse with her from across the room.

She very much enjoyed this part of her job, meeting and chatting with people from nearby and far away who wandered in for a break and a snack, learning a little about them, sharing a bit of herself. Carolina hospitality was always on the menu in The Perkery—a slogan spelled out right across the top of the menu board above her. Still, it wasn't often she reacted quite so intensely to a visitor—even one as attractive as this man. "I'm a co-owner. Elle O'Meara."

"Nice to meet you, Elle." She got a thrill at the sound of her name spoken in his deep voice, proving yet again that her responses to him were out of the ordinary. "I'm Shane Scanlon."

He looked at her intently as he said his name, as though she should know it. She searched his features, once again noting the details that made his face so innately appealing, but she was certain she'd never seen him before. She was sure she'd remember if she had. This was not a man who'd be easy to forget. "Hello, Shane."

He seemed to find an odd sort of satisfaction— reassurance?—in the casual tone of her reply, which made her wonder again if he'd expected a different reaction. Perhaps she was simply reading too much into his expression.

"It's my first time to visit your town. It's an interesting area."

She smiled. "Thanks. We locals agree."

Dragging her gaze from Shane's face in an attempt to regain control over those pesky hormones, Elle glanced through the big front window looking out over Salt Marsh Avenue, the main thoroughfare through the business section of Shorty's Landing. Late October wasn't prime tourist season. This little town lay close enough to the larger, better known resort communities along the South Carolina coast to benefit from their summer traffic, but just far enough to slow considerably more in the off-season. Fortunately, during the three years The Perkery had been open so far, she and Kristen had built enough local patronage to carry them through those leaner months. They weren't going to become wealthy, but they were paying the bills and enjoying the work, which was what counted. At least, as far as Elle was concerned.

Before she could dwell on worrisome thoughts about her partner's recent moodiness, the door that led into the kitchen and office area of the shop burst open behind her. A little bundle of energy rushed through the swinging door, followed more sedately by a caftan-clad woman with henna-red hair and glittery-framed glasses.

"Mommy, Mommy!"

Laughing, Elle scooped up her daughter and nuzzled into her neck, making the toddler giggle. "Hi, baby. Did you have fun at the park with Gammy?"

"Fun with Gammy."

Charlotte babbled excitedly as Elle removed her windbreaker. At twenty-five months, the toddler's vocabulary was still limited to short phrases and somewhat random words, but Elle was able to follow fairly well. Charlotte had played on the swings and in the sandbox, both favorite activities during her almost-daily park outings.

Three middle-aged women, local friends who met for coffee every Wednesday, entered the shop from the front door, laughing and chattering as the bell jingled. Elle's mother stepped up to the counter to greet the trio by names and take their orders, freeing Elle to settle Charlotte into the play corral. She dropped a kiss on her daughter's fine, curly brown hair as she set her down and handed her a toy. Charlotte was an easygoing child who was almost always smiling, happy to entertain herself for the most part, though she enjoyed being in the shop with her family around her. Elle loved having a job that allowed her to bring her daughter to work with her.

Seeing Charlotte grinning at someone, Elle glanced around, expecting to find one of the women interacting with the toddler. Instead, it was the man—Shane, she reminded herself—taking advantage of the free-refill policy and topping off his cup at the coffee bar while studying the little girl in the play area behind the counter. Something about Shane's expression caught Elle's attention. For a fleeting moment, he just looked so...well, sad, she decided. How could anyone look at her daughter's adorable blue-eyed, dimple-chinned face and still feel sad?

It took Charlotte only moments to work her magic. The little girl giggled at Shane and he smiled in response. A real smile, Elle noted. It pushed sexy, shallow dimples into his lean cheeks. Wow. Once again, she felt warmth surging.

Shane glanced at Elle then, as if sensing her

watching him, and she made an effort to compose her expression. "Cute kid you have there."

"Thank you."

Now that the other customers were seated at their customary table in a cozy corner, Elle's mom approached Shane with her characteristic curiosity about a new face in the shop. Especially, Elle thought wryly, a handsome male face.

"Well, hello there. I haven't seen you in here before. Is this your first time visiting us?" Elle's Southern-to-the-painted-toenails mother made a habit of greeting and chatting with the customers, finding it hard to imagine that some people simply wanted to place their orders and drink their coffee with a minimum amount of interaction.

Apparently familiar with regional idiosyncrasies, Shane nodded cordially. "Yes, it is."

"I hope it won't be your last. I'm Janet O'Meara." She held out one be-ringed and multi-braceleted hand.

Shane reached across the counter to take her hand. "Shane Scanlon. Nice to meet you."

He started to pull his hand away, but Janet held on. Elle almost groaned at the all-too-familiar look on her mother's face. Not this again!

"Oh, my goodness. You've led quite the adventurous life, haven't you, young man?"

Shane shot a quick, questioning glance at Elle

before saying cautiously, "I suppose I've had my share of adventures."

"I sense that you're a single man. A bachelor."

"Yes, I—"

"And a soldier," Janet mused, her expression dreamy and unfocused—deliberately so, Elle suspected. "Are you still in the military?"

"No, I— Wait. How did you—"

"I knew it!" she crowed, delighted with herself. "You were in the navy, weren't you? I see you on a submarine."

"I was army. A medic. But—"

"Of course. A healer. And now you're a doctor."

"No, I—"

"No, not a doctor," she said quickly. "A... Hmm, you're in business, aren't you?"

"Well, yes."

"Of course you are."

"Um—"

Laughing musically, Janet patted their clasped right hands with her left, making more bracelets jingle. "Oh, don't mind me, dear. Sometimes these things just come to me. I'm a little psychic."

"I see." He extricated himself quickly, though politely enough.

Janet eyed him with renewed speculation. "Don't worry, Shane, I don't know your deepest secrets. Just a few tidbits that came to me when we shook hands."

Seeing a frown suddenly darken Shane's eyes, Elle decided it was time to step in. Past time, probably. "Mom, would you mind checking on the vegetarian chili? It's been simmering for almost an hour and it's time to add the corn, in case Amber has forgotten."

"Of course, darling." With one last lingering look at Shane, her mom turned and moved into the kitchen, the swinging door closing behind her.

Elle gave Shane a rueful smile. "Sorry about that. We've chosen to humor my mother's imaginings, for the most part, but she gets carried away sometimes. It's a harmless fantasy. She really is a wonderful woman."

"So, she's not really, uh, psychic?"

Laughing softly, Elle shook her head. "No more than anyone with halfway decent intuition. She read the autobiography of a famous medium a year or so ago, and she's been convinced ever since that she has the gift. Her predictions are correct about one out of nine times, but that seems to be enough to validate her. Everyone loves her, so we don't bother arguing with her."

Shane seemed to relax a bit, though he asked, "So, how did she know I was in the military?"

"Sometimes she gets lucky. Maybe it's the way you carry yourself."

Still looking slightly doubtful, he glanced at the kitchen door before his attention was reclaimed by Charlotte, who held up a stuffed dog and announced, "Puppy!"

"Yes, Charlotte. That's your puppy," Elle responded automatically.

"Charlotte." Shane repeated the name in a low voice. She looked around at him again and he cleared his throat. "That's a nice name."

"Thank you." Again, she sensed some emotion in him she didn't quite understand, but decided she was letting herself be too strongly influenced by her mother. She'd have to be careful about that.

The bell over the door chimed again, and a couple of college students with backpacks and beeping smartphones strolled in. They, too, were regular customers, drawn to the shop by flavored coffee drinks and free Wi-Fi. It was getting close to lunchtime, so they'd probably linger long enough to order sandwiches. Elle greeted them and rang up their orders. By the time they'd settled into the deep, nautical-print armchairs at the back of the shop, Shane had slipped out.

Looking through the big street windows, Elle saw several cars, pedestrians and bikes passing by, but no sign of the man in the leather jacket. With a sigh, she wondered if she would ever see him again, or if her mom had scared him away.

Amber Carson, a college business major who,

along with several other part-timers, worked at The Perkery to supplement her scholarships, stepped out of the kitchen, smoothing the sunny yellow apron around her waist. Amber's hair was dyed a dramatic black with a bright blue streak hanging over her left eye. She had several piercings, and she favored stark black clothing and nails painted black except for her thumbs, which matched the blue hair stripe. Above all, she was smart, personable and a hard worker.

"Would you keep an eye on Charlotte for a few minutes?" Elle asked her. "I'd like to check things in the kitchen."

"Of course."

Amber smiled fondly at Charlotte, who grinned back and cooed, "Bamber!"

Leaving everything in Amber's capable hands, Elle pushed through the door into the kitchen, where her mother was just sliding the first premade salads into the industrial fridge in preparation for the lunch rush. Three varieties of soup were almost ready to serve, their aromas blending into a medley that made Elle's mouth water. Sandwiches would be assembled from prepped ingredients stored in the fridge, while cookies, pastries and other treats tempted diners from the display cases out in the shop.

Goodness, she loved this place, Elle thought

with a little pang. Now if only she could be confident her business partner still felt the same way...

Closing the refrigerator door, her mom turned to ask her, "Is that nice-looking fellow still hanging around?"

"If you mean that poor man you grabbed out there, then no, he's gone. I think you scared him away."

"I did not grab him," her mom retorted indignantly. "I simply shook his hand. He happened to have a very strong aura."

Elle could secretly agree—if, by aura, her mother meant a very attractive appearance. It didn't take any special talents to have noticed that.

"Well, anyway, maybe it would be best if you don't ambush our customers with psychic readings. Not everyone likes that sort of thing, you know." Remembering the way Shane had frowned in response to a vague allusion to his "deepest secrets," Elle winced before murmuring, "I doubt he'll be back."

"He'll be back." Her mom lifted the lid off the chili and stirred briskly with a wooden spoon, her bracelets jingling merrily. "I think you'll be seeing quite a bit of that nice young man. I told you big changes were coming for you."

"Oh, my gosh, Mom, give it a rest," Elle said with a groan. As much as she adored her mother, it was sometimes difficult to be patient—not her strength, anyway, she had to admit. "He was just a customer. Speaking of which, I've heard the bell ring a couple times, so the lunch crowd is starting to come in."

Crowd was perhaps a generous word for their average patronage this time of year, but still they'd be busy for the next couple of hours. Too busy to obsess about good-looking guys in black leather jackets, she thought with a sigh. Which didn't mean she wouldn't think of him a few times as the day wound down.

She almost wished her mother's prediction would be right this time. She wouldn't mind seeing Shane Scanlon in her shop again.

THE MAN IN question returned to the shop the next morning, just at the end of the breakfast rush. He wore his black leather jacket again, this time with a black shirt and gray pants. Though an early rain and a brisk breeze had left a chill in the air, most of Elle's customers had seemed comfortable enough in long sleeves or light windbreakers. Someone must have told Shane how very good the jacket looked on him, she decided as she stepped forward to greet him.

"Good morning," she said. "Welcome back. What can I get for you?"

"I thought I might score one of those chocolate-filled doughnuts today. I figured they must be good, as fast as you ran out yesterday."

She motioned toward the display case. "We just happen to have two chocolate-filled doughnuts available."

Shane glanced at the other end of the counter, where her mother was taking care of the only other customers, and then at the play corral, in which Charlotte played contentedly with her toys. Leaning an arm on the stainless steel counter, he asked, "Any chance you'd like to have that second doughnut and a cup of coffee with me? Unless you can't take the time."

The invitation surprised her a bit. If this was his way of flirting, he was rather serious about it. He'd given her a graceful out, and his expression made it clear he would take the hint. She wasn't in the habit of socializing much with customers, despite the occasional pickup attempt by randy tourists or bored businessmen looking for a night's entertainment. But this was as good a time as any for her to take a coffee break, and Shane did seem interesting, if only for a brief, likely enjoyable conversation.

"I'll skip the doughnut, but coffee sounds good."

He gave her a little smile, teasing out those oh-so-sexy dimples. "Great."

Silently clearing her throat, she motioned her

intentions toward her mother, who sent her an approving, not-at-all-subtle thumbs-up.

They carried their cups to the table in the window he'd chosen yesterday. Elle took a sip of her pumpkin-spice latte while Shane bit into the flaky pastry filled with a creamy chocolate ganache. "That is good," he said after swallowing. "No wonder they go so fast. You made the filling, too?"

His compliment pleased her perhaps more than it should have. "Yes. It's a fairly simple recipe, easy to whip up and pipe into the doughnuts."

He chuckled. "You make it sound too easy. You should say you slaved over it for hours."

Amused, she lifted her cup again. "Maybe I should. I do start very early every morning."

"Do you do all the cooking yourself?"

"Not all of it. My mother and several part-time employees help. My staff and I work Wednesdays through Saturdays and my business partner and her crew take over Sunday morning through Tuesday. We switch off as needed. It's a good division of labor for all of us."

"You're only open for breakfast and lunch, right?"

"We close at four," she confirmed, though the shop's hours were posted on the sign at the door.

He nodded and glanced at the play corral. "And

you bring your daughter to work with you every day?"

"Most days. Having my mom working with me here makes it easier to juggle everything."

Setting down his cup, he picked up the doughnut again. She saw his gaze sweep her left hand as it lay on the table, and she figured he noted the lack of rings—just as she was aware of his bare left hand. Not necessarily proof that he was single, of course.

"Family first," he murmured before biting into his pastry.

"Always," she agreed.

She wondered if there was something going on in this conversation she wasn't fully aware of. She was beginning to feel a bit uncomfortable with this handsome stranger's focus on her and her family, though he was probably only trying to pass the time. There was enough of a drawl in his deep voice to let her know chatting with strangers was as familiar to him as to anyone south of the Mason-Dixon Line.

"Are you in Shorty's Landing on vacation?" she asked, deciding it was time to turn the conversation to him.

He didn't seem to mind. "Mostly business. I'm making sales pitches to some of the resorts in the area."

This seemed an innocuous enough topic for

two thirtysomething professionals. "What business are you in?"

"Risk management consulting. I'm a partner in a family-owned company, Scanlon Risk Management, Inc. We're based out of Fayetteville, North Carolina, my hometown."

"Which resorts have you visited so far?" she asked while she processed that unexpected response. There were several popular resorts within a twenty-mile stretch of coastline around Shorty's Landing. Shane had a target-rich environment if he was pitching to tourist establishments.

"I arrived in the area only yesterday, so the meetings have just started," he replied. "I have an appointment with the owner of Wind Shadow Resort this afternoon."

"Trevor Farrell," she said with a smile. The luxurious Wind Shadow Resort was only about twenty minutes by car from The Perkery. In addition to having visited for various social events, she served quite a few guests from there who wandered into Shorty's Landing to explore and shop.

"I've known Trevor for several years. A very nice man. He's known particularly for hiring and working with veterans," she added, thinking of Shane's military background.

"Yes, I've heard that. It's a practice he and I have in common in our businesses."

So, she mused, Shane Scanlon worked in his family business and believed in giving back to the military community. He sounded upstanding enough, but that was accepting him only on his own words. She'd learned the hard way not to take anyone at face value.

"From the military to a risk management career. That's quite a leap. My mother was apparently right that you've led an interesting life," she said lightly. "We won't tell her, though. It would only reinforce her fantasy that she has a special sight."

He chuckled. "I'll keep that in mind. Though I'm not sure how following my family's tradition of serving a couple of hitches in the army, then joining the business my dad and uncle started would qualify as particularly exciting."

Judging by her own instinctive reactions to him, she suspected this man was considerably more interesting than he let on. Maybe more than even he realized. For some reason, he didn't strike her as the risk management type. She'd have pegged him as something much more adventurous—which only proved yet again that she was no more clairvoyant than her mother. "Was it always your plan to join the family business when you got out?"

He hesitated just long enough to make her wonder if she'd accidentally touched a nerve. Perhaps their coffee break small talk had edged into more personal territory than either of them had predicted. Still, he replied matter-of-factly, "At the time I enlisted, I was considering other options for my future. My brother, Charlie, was going to take over the family business. But he died in Afghanistan two years ago, and when Dad passed away last year, I made the choice to help keep the company going. It's been a challenge, but we're doing well now. I made the right decision."

It was more information than Elle had expected, perhaps more than Shane had intended to reveal. A lot to digest at once. He had suffered two major losses in a very short time. Though he'd spoken without inflection, she still sensed the deep emotion in him. Having lost her own much-loved father only four years ago, she knew how it felt and how the pain lingered.

She couldn't help wondering if Shane was unconsciously defending his resulting career choice as much to himself as to her. Far be it from her to criticize anyone for sacrificing for the sake of family, but she couldn't help thinking of her ex-husband's long-pent-up rebellion against following a path that hadn't felt true to him. Which didn't mean Shane was anything like Glenn, she reminded herself rather crossly. Maybe the family business was exactly what Shane wanted.

She gave him a look of apology. "I'm sorry. I wasn't interrogating you. I tend to ask too many questions sometimes when I'm getting to know someone. A habit I picked up from my mother, I'm afraid."

He wiped a dot of chocolate from his lips with a napkin. Even as that movement drew her attention to his sexy mouth, she was gratified to see that he didn't look annoyed. "How else would you get any information?"

"Right?" She was pleased he understood, despite her gaffes. "But just so you know, I don't take offense when I'm told to back off."

"I'll keep that in mind for future conversations," he murmured, those very nice lips quirking into a half smile.

He seemed to be taking for granted that there would be future conversations. She wasn't sure how she felt about that. She wasn't looking for a romantic involvement at this busy stage of her life, and certainly not a long-distance one. Still, she had to admit she was intrigued by the possibility of future interactions. As much as she'd unexpectedly learned about Shane Scanlon in the past ten minutes, she'd only scratched the surface.

A small group of employees from the pharmacy down the street entered with a burst of rather noisy laughter. Elle stood quickly. "This was nice, Shane, but I should get back to work."

Abandoning whatever he'd been about to say, Shane stood as she did. "Of course. I have to be going, anyway. Thanks for the coffee and conversation. I enjoyed it."

She smiled up at him. "Questions and all?"

"Questions and all."

Oh, those dimples were dangerous! Stifling a sigh, Elle turned to check on her daughter. Seeing that Charlotte was still playing with her toys, she glanced back to Shane. "I hope your meetings go well."

His eyes looked very blue as they locked with hers. "Thank you."

"I'll see you again?" she couldn't help asking, totally flirting.

He inclined his head just slightly. "Count on it."

Slowly rounding the counter, she watched as he left the shop and strode down the sidewalk. A little sigh escaped her.

"You see?" her mom startled her by asking from directly behind her. "I was right, wasn't I? Something exciting is about to happen for you, and I think that charming man has something to do with it."

Elle shook her head as if to physically clear it. "We have customers, Mom. And more will be in soon. Maybe you could take Charlotte for a potty break while I take orders?" Potty training was still an act-in-progress, but Charlotte was cooperating, for the most part, and Elle's mom was fully on-board with the program.

"I would be delighted." Her mom picked up the babbling toddler, but glanced meaningfully at Elle as she did so, just to make it clear she recognized the deliberate distraction.

Elle ordered herself to concentrate on her work. Her mother's prognostications notwithstanding, it remained to be seen whether Shane Scanlon was just another engaging tourist…or a man who was as interesting as he seemed.

SITTING BEHIND THE wheel of his car in a motel parking lot, Shane looked down at the printed snapshot in his hand. When he'd received the photo a week or so earlier, he'd been struck by the attractiveness of the woman in the center of the shot. Now he knew the picture didn't do full justice to the vibrant, animated woman who'd shared coffee with him that morning. Elle O'Meara.

In the photograph, she smiled brightly as she pushed a stroller through a park. The wind lifted her honey-brown hair and the sunlight glittered in her warm brown eyes as she gazed down at the laughing, pink-cheeked child. The wholesomely appealing scene could have been staged for a magazine ad. During the past few days, Shane had studied the photo enough to memorize every detail, but still he'd been startled by how strongly seeing Charlotte—and Elle—in person had affected him.

Elle had been gracious to him during their two brief encounters. Funny, encouraging. Inquisitive in a friendly, interested manner, though she'd backed off quickly when she'd stumbled into painful memories on his part. He'd seen the compassion on her face when she'd learned of his losses, but she'd obviously understood he hadn't wanted to go into details. As it was, he'd told her more than he'd intended. Elle was certainly easy to talk to. He could easily imagine having long, wide-ranging conversations with her. The fantasy was as enticing as it was unlikely.

He stuffed the photo back into its envelope, then stashed it under the passenger seat, feeling rather foolishly furtive as he did so. It wasn't as if Elle would see into the envelope if she strolled past the car. He really wasn't cut out for this undercover stuff.

He wondered how Elle's hospitable attitude toward him would change if she found out his biological connection to her daughter. He'd debated how best to approach her since he'd learned her name a few weeks ago. He still wasn't certain that telling her everything would be the best move on his part.

Judging just by his first impressions, she seemed to be family-oriented. She'd arranged her work schedule to maximize time with Charlotte, though he wasn't sure a coffee shop was the best place for a toddler to spend her days. Elle had even hired her oddball mother to work with her. So perhaps she'd at least somewhat understand the family commitments that would compel a man to hire a private investigator, to put his own life on hold, to be prepared to bargain or bribe if necessary just to track down one small child. Or maybe she wouldn't.

Elle could send him away once she learned the truth. Could refuse to even talk with him again if she found out who he was. But for both business and personal reasons, he was going to risk hanging around a little longer. For his family's sake. For his own. And most of all, for the promise he'd made to his late brother, Charlie.

Charlotte's biological father.

CHAPTER TWO

"SO WE'RE AGREED? We'll stay with the schedule we have now at least through the end of the year?"

Kristen Boyd nodded in response to Elle's question, but her faraway expression made Elle wonder if her partner had been paying attention during their Thursday afternoon business meeting. "Kristen? You're listening, right?"

"What? Oh, right. Yes, the weekend menu is fine with me."

Elle swiveled in her seat to frown at her partner, who sat next to her at the small desk they shared in the tiny office tucked into a corner of the shop, just off the kitchen. She noted that Kristen's eyes were clouded and her right hand was tangled in her thick blond curls, a sure sign Kristen's thoughts were far away.

"We weren't talking about the menu. We were discussing the weekend work schedule. DeShawn wants to work an extra hour this Sunday to make up for the time he missed during midterms last week. That's okay with you, right?"

Kristen blinked. "Oh. Of course. I'll keep him busy prepping for Monday."

After hesitating a moment, Elle asked, "You're okay, right? Should I be worried?"

Slumping a little in her chair, her partner shrugged. "I'm fine."

"Don't blow me off, Kris. I can certainly tell by now when you aren't happy."

Elle had considered herself incredibly lucky when she and her lifelong best friend had finally been able to start this business together three years ago. With Elle's then-husband, Glenn, finally finishing law school and their finances looking promising, it had seemed an ideal time to start their family, as well. And then Glenn had blindsided her by asking for a divorce.

Other than her mother, Kristen had been Elle's biggest supporter during that rough time. Elle was trying to do the same now that her friend had gone through a painful breakup, but Kristen kept pushing her away, saying she needed time to deal on her own. Which was fine, of course. Fully understandable. And yet...

Kristen's emotional turmoil was beginning to interfere with their business. Elle wondered if she should push her partner to open up to her. If Kristen wanted out of the business, she needed to say so—though the very thought of losing the shop made Elle's heart ache.

"I'd really like to know what you're planning, Kristen," she said bluntly. "I know you're still hurting over the breakup with Casey, but is there something else, too? Are you unhappy with the work schedules? With any of the decisions we've made lately? You're okay financially?"

Though Kristen supplemented her three-day-a-week coffee shop schedule by singing in a local club on Friday nights, Elle had no other income outside The Perkery. Other than their divorce settlement, she received no support from Glenn. Elle had adopted Charlotte on her own after he backed out of the proceedings, so he didn't owe her child support. He had also openly expressed his doubts that Elle and Kristen would succeed with their fledging business. Elle had been proud every single month the books had balanced, almost all of them now. It had been both a matter of vindication and of personal fulfillment for her.

Still, it would be difficult, if not impossible, for her to buy out Kristen's share. If Kristen had decided she wanted out, it was possible they'd have to sell the business. And while Elle told herself she would survive the disappointment and start over, the prospect hurt.

"I'm fine," Kristen repeated, her voice almost mechanical. "Like you said, I'm still stinging over Casey, but I'll get over it. As for money, I'm okay. Casey and I maybe overindulged in a few luxuries while we were together, but I'll get my part paid off. The club's been after me to perform on both Friday and Saturday nights. Not a lot of extra cash, but it's something."

She drew a deep breath before adding, "Maybe I get a little restless sometimes, but that's natural, right? I mean, especially after a bad breakup. I find myself thinking maybe a change of scenery would help. Maybe it would be good to start all over someplace new. But then I tell myself I'm just trying to run away from the pain, and it wouldn't really help."

Elle found little reassurance in those words. Certainly not in her friend's distant, unhappy expression. Telling herself not to dwell on potential problems, she focused instead on Kristen's pain, wanting to help in whatever way she could. "If you need some time off, you know you only have to say so. You don't have to wait until your scheduled vacation time. Mom and I are willing to work with you and your crew, and we can always add a couple of temp workers if necessary."

"I'll think about it, but I'll probably just tough it out. Thanks, Elle," Kristen added automatically. Her attempt at a smile was simply heartbreaking.

Frustration and genuine concern made Elle's tone more urgent than she intended. "Don't let it go too long, okay? Of course I worry about the business, but I'm even more concerned about you.

If you need help getting over this from a professional counselor, or just with a nice vacation, you should acknowledge it. Deal with it."

Kristen forced a smile, though there was a spark of irritation now. "Of course. But let's just get back to our meeting, okay? So, what did we decide about next week's soup choices?"

Cautioning herself not to borrow trouble, Elle reached for her tablet computer, deciding it was best to focus on business for now. Which wouldn't stop her from worrying later.

SHANE DABBED AT his mouth with a linen napkin Friday after a second meeting with Wind Shadow Resort owner Trevor Farrell. A tall and slim man in his late thirties, with light brown hair and clear blue eyes, Trevor was already quite successful with this, his first resort, and well into plans to open a couple more. After their meeting that morning, he'd invited Shane to join him and another veteran friend for lunch in the resort's upscale restaurant, Torchlight.

"That was the best lunch I've had in a long time," Shane said to his host.

"I'll pass along your compliments." Trevor looked pleased, though he probably heard rave reviews on a daily basis. "Our chef is one of the resort's greatest assets."

Walt Becker, Trevor's friend and attorney, chuckled when he set down his water glass with his right hand. Shane had noted that Walt's left hand was a prosthetic. Had he been injured in battle? It hadn't been mentioned, but Shane wouldn't be surprised if that was the case. Looking like the former marine sergeant he was, Walt was gruff, friendly and blunt-spoken. Shane liked him. Liked them both, actually.

"Trev's threatened to lock down the resort if his chef tries to leave," Walt commented. "He lost one of his most valued staff when his second-in-command, Adam Scott, left last month to follow his new bride and their son all the way to Seattle. Trev's still pouting about it."

Trevor smiled wryly. "Hardly pouting. I'm pleased for Adam and Joanna. Adam has a new management job with a luxury hotel in Seattle. He started two weeks ago. I talked with him yesterday, and he sounded happy. I'm glad about that."

"You miss having him around," Walt said. "So do I. But like you, I'm happy for them."

"Yes, well, you're practically family. After all, you are still seeing Joanna's sister," Trevor teased his friend with a wink. "And I'd be willing to lay money on there being another wedding in the near future."

Walt didn't disagree. In fact, Shane thought he looked rather smug at the prospect.

"But we're being rude." Trevor turned back to

Shane. "I hope you've been enjoying your visit, Shane. You said you're staying in Shorty's Landing?"

"Yes. Nice little town."

"It is."

Walt nodded. "Bubba's Grill on Salt Marsh Avenue has the best burgers in the area. No offense, Trev, the burgers here are great, but Bubba's, man."

Trevor grinned, obviously taking no umbrage. "They are good, I'll give you that."

Walt looked at Shane again. "If you're looking for breakfast, you'll find good pastries and coffee at The Perkery on Salt Marsh Avenue. I'd say their selection is second only to the ones you'd have here."

For some reason, Shane felt almost indignant on Elle's behalf. He couldn't imagine that Trevor's pastry chef made anything better than Elle's chocolate-filled doughnuts.

"I've stopped into The Perkery the past couple of days," he said. "Everything I had was delicious."

"So, you'd have met Elle and Janet O'Meara," Trevor commented. He laughed softly before asking, "Did Janet read your palm?"

Remembering that odd first encounter, Shane suppressed a wry grimace. "Not exactly."

"She's a sweetheart. Maybe not the most reliable prognosticator, but as kind-hearted a woman as I've met. Elle's great, too, as is her partner, Kristen Boyd. A real asset to their community. Elle spearheads several fund-raisers for local charities. I try to donate on behalf of the resort whenever I can."

It was encouraging to hear that his niece's adoptive mother was well respected in the community. Still, Shane wasn't fully convinced that Charlotte would receive everything she needed as the daughter of a busy, part-owner of a small business that probably operated on a shoestring budget. Not to mention the woman's self-proclaimed psychic mother. Having been raised by a single parent and a grandmother himself, he was hardly judging those aspects of Charlotte's life—but was a plastic-fenced play area behind the counter of a coffee shop the best place for a toddler to spend her days? Did she have other children to play with—friends, cousins, neighbors? Enough variety of routine to keep her engaged and learning?

Walt laid his napkin on the table. "I had coffee and a muffin at The Perkery one morning a couple of weeks ago. That little girl of Elle's is cute as a button. Little heartbreaker in the making, I'm thinking."

"I haven't had the pleasure of meeting Elle's daughter." Trevor reached down to pick up the crutches he'd laid beside his chair when they'd been seated. He'd explained to Shane that he'd been seriously injured in a motorcycle accident in the spring and was just now getting back on his feet after a second operation to repair the damage to his right knee.

Walt rose as their host did. "Well, she's a sweetheart."

"What's her name again?" Trevor asked idly. "I forget."

"Charlotte," Shane said before Walt could reply. "Her name is Charlotte."

It stung that he couldn't add that the child had been named after her war-hero father. These men would likely understand his pride, but it would require a lot of awkward explanations—ones he couldn't give before he told Elle. It was rather a relief when the lunch conversation was over and he and Trevor could direct their attention back to a potential business collaboration.

Later that afternoon, after an extensive tour of the resort, Shane was in his car, headed back to his motel. Though he paid attention to his driving, he still contemplated the circumstances in which he'd found himself. His professional reasons for being in the area were genuine. Once he'd tracked Charlotte down, he'd immediately scheduled presentations with local resorts both to justify his stay and because the company always needed new business.

Scanlon Risk Management, Inc., the company

started by his father twenty-five years ago, had fallen into a precarious state during his dad's illness and after his eventual death. Almost before Shane had completely unpacked his duffel after leaving the military, he'd stepped in to help his uncle get the business back onto solid ground. He was gratified that his efforts were paying off, especially if he secured the Wind Shadow Resorts account—an outcome that seemed promising after hours of discussion with Trevor Farrell.

Which brought him back to the primary purpose for his stay in Shorty's Landing...

He wished he felt better prepared for what was to come. The time had passed so quickly since he'd gotten out of the army. With so much responsibility on his shoulders, it had been difficult to find opportunity to concentrate on his search for Charlotte, though his intention to do so had never wavered.

Charlie's on-and-off girlfriend, Brittany, had learned of her pregnancy only a few weeks after Charlie had been deployed to Afghanistan. There'd been no doubt that Charlie would have stepped up as a devoted father to his child. During their last phone conversation, Shane had promised he would take care of the child if anything should happen to Charlie. A month later, Charlie had been killed in a helicopter crash in Afghanistan, leaving his family devastated and his pregnant girlfriend stunned and rootless. The grieving family had rallied around Brittany, even though she'd never been particularly receptive to any of them except Shane, whom she'd seemed to like well enough.

But then Shane had been deployed overseas, only three weeks after the birth of his niece. To the distress of his father and grandmother, Brittany had disappeared with the baby only weeks after Shane left the country. A few months later, they'd gotten word that the baby had been placed for adoption and that Brittany wanted no further contact with any member of the Scanlon family.

Shane had vowed then that he would track down his niece. It was the only way he knew to fulfill his promise to Charlie. He owed it to Charlie, to Charlotte and to his dad, who, before he'd died, had asked Shane to keep an eye out for the family in the future. Those promises had weighed heavily on Shane's shoulders, and he'd done his best to fulfill them.

Figuring it would be difficult to access adoption records, he'd decided to find Brittany and attempt to learn Charlotte's whereabouts from her. After discovering that Brittany's estranged family hadn't heard from her since before Charlotte's birth, he'd hired a private investigator.

The search had taken longer than he'd have liked. Volatile Brittany had changed her name and her appearance and lost herself in the shadowy New York nightlife, trying to escape the emotional demons that would always haunt her. Still, Shane had found her eventually. After almost a week of meetings with her, of negotiations and promises—and a generous contribution to her finances—she'd grudgingly given him the name of the woman she'd personally selected through an open adoption agency to raise her daughter. Charlie's daughter.

Shane had vacillated from the start about how to approach Elle—whether to be candid from the onset, or simply hover in the background for a few days, observing and assessing Charlotte's current circumstances. He knew there was a good chance that Elle would be angry when she learned the truth. That she'd send him on his way with firm instructions to keep his distance from both her and Charlotte. In other words, he'd been a coward—not something a thirty-one-year-old ex-soldier cared to admit.

It certainly complicated matters that his brain seemed to scramble every time Elle smiled. Even had the circumstances of their meeting been different, he would have likely tried to resist her charms. During the hectic months since he'd returned to civilian life, he'd done his best to avoid preventable complications, and a busy single mom definitely fell into that category. His increasingly urgent quest to find his niece was the exception. He'd felt pressured by his grandmother's declining health and the promises he'd made to his brother and father.

His hands tightened on the steering wheel as he thought back over these past difficult two years since Charlie died. He had to put his attraction to Elle out of his mind, keep his focus on his family. There was only so much a guy could juggle without taking a risk of having it all crash around his feet.

THE ANNUAL SHORTY'S LANDING Fall Festival was held that Friday evening at Paradise Park, located only a few blocks from The Perkery. Organized by the Chamber of Commerce and funded by donations from local businesses, the Halloween-themed celebration was always a big hit with both kids and adults. Elle's parents had brought her every year when she was growing up, and she wanted to do the same for her daughter.

Elle and her mom arrived with Charlotte only a half hour after the official 5:00 p.m. opening, and the event was already in full swing. The festival grounds were packed with kiddie rides, inflatables, games, food vendors and various other family-friendly attractions. Children in an amazing array of costumes sprinted from one trick-

or-treat station to another for candy, stickers and other goodies.

Dressed as a kitten with pink-lined cat ears attached to a headband and a fuzzy black tail pinned to her black leotard, Charlotte was wide-eyed as she clutched her plastic pumpkin bucket and took in all the activity. A smudge of pink makeup on the tip of her little nose and eyebrow-penciled whiskers on her chubby cheeks completed the costume. Her proud grandmother privately proclaimed her the most adorable child in the park. Elle couldn't disagree, though she kept the thought discreetly to herself.

Elle and her mom had also dressed for the holiday. Elle wore a long, thin black robe over her clothes with a witch's hat headband holding back her hair. Her mom, of course, was a fortune teller in a caftan and turban. Detained frequently for chats with acquaintances, they made their way slowly from one orange-and-black festooned booth to the next. Charlotte happily crowed, "Tricker Treat!" at each stop, earning more than a few "awws" from adults enchanted by her charms.

Reveling in the fun her daughter was having, Elle couldn't stop smiling. Perhaps there was a little wistfulness when she saw doting fathers with their little ghosts and goblins, but as she listened to her mom and Charlotte giggling together, she told herself she was a very lucky woman, indeed. Whatever feelings she'd once had for her ex were gone now. The jagged cracks in her heart had healed, leaving a few scars but only memories of pain. She had a family she adored and a business she loved; what more could she ask?

One of her most faithful customers waved and called out a greeting from a few yards away, and Elle smiled and waved in return. Taking advantage of the momentary distraction, Charlotte slipped her hand out of Elle's loose grasp and made a dash for a colorful fishing-for-prizes booth. Elle spun to give chase. She knew she could catch up before the short-legged two-year-old reached the attraction, but she was surprised when a man stepped into Charlotte's path to block the escape. With a hitch in her step, Elle identified him immediately. Shane Scanlon—dimples, black jacket and all.

Apparently recognizing Shane, Charlotte crowed happily and dove at him, raising her arms to be picked up. He lifted her high into the air and she giggled, wrapping her arms around his neck. Shane laughed. Elle heard every female within sight sigh appreciatively at the image of the good-looking man and the sweet little girl smiling at each other. She was fully aware that her own sigh blended with the soft chorus.

Shaking her head to clear it, she moved toward them.

Shane smiled at her. "Look what I caught."

"So I see. Hello, Shane."

"Shane," Charlotte repeated, patting his cheek with a gentle hand.

Elle would have sworn he blushed a bit, and her heart melted a little in response. *Careful, Elle.*

"Shane." Her mom approached with a flutter of her vivid orange-and-black-printed caftan, bracelets jingling as she rested a hand familiarly on his arm. "What a nice surprise. Were you looking for us?"

"Actually, I was on my way back from a business meeting when I saw the festivities going on here. I'm staying in the motel just down the street. I didn't have anything better to do, so I thought I'd stop to check it out. That's when I caught sight of this runaway kitten." He bounced the giggling toddler in his arms as he studied Elle's outfit.

Elle smiled at him. "Nice catch."

"Nice hat."

"Thank you." She reached up automatically to straighten the plastic headband. "Still enjoying your visit to our area?"

"Very much."

Tugging at Shane's collar, Charlotte pointed to

the game booth where she'd been headed when he'd scooped her up. "Fish!"

He turned his head to look. "The fishing booth? Is that where you were headed?"

She nodded emphatically. "Fish, Shane!"

"You want to catch a fish?"

She bounced again. "Fish!"

Shane looked questioningly at Elle. "Looks like I'm being invited along on your fishing excursion. Do you mind?"

"Of course not."

Perhaps Shane was feeling a bit lonely in the festive crowd of strangers. He seemed pleased to find familiar faces. Still holding Charlotte, he moved into the line waiting at the game booth where preschoolers could dangle a fishing line over an ocean-painted backboard. Hidden behind the backboard, festival volunteers attached small stuffed toys to the lines with plastic clothespins for the children to "catch." Because the area was already crowded, Elle and her mother stayed back out of the way, watching from nearby. Elle had her phone in hand to snap a photo as Charlotte obtained her prize.

"Oh, my goodness, how cute is that?" Janet clutched Charlotte's plastic pumpkin bucket to her heart as she watched Shane help Charlotte grip the toy fishing rod. "Isn't he adorable?"

Adorable might not have been the word Elle

would have chosen to describe Shane—but she couldn't take issue with it, either. He *was* cute as he made an exaggerated show of helping Charlotte cast her line over the backboard, drawing a peal of giggles from the child. The man was definitely good with kids.

"You should ask him to dinner while he's in town. I'd be happy to babysit, of course. Maybe you could take him to Bruno's tomorrow night."

Elle resisted the impulse to roll her eyes. "Mom, I'm not going to ask him out."

"Why not? It's okay for women to do that, you know."

"Yes, I know it's okay, but Shane is only in town for a few days on business. He lives in North Carolina and apparently travels quite a bit. For all I know, he could be leaving town tonight."

Her mom gave her a look. "Wouldn't hurt to ask. I have a feeling you and Shane could be just right for each other. I could tell the first time I touched him that he's a fine, upstanding young man."

Elle didn't bother to point out that her mother had thought the same about Glenn. They'd both been fooled by Glenn's practiced smiles and deliberately chosen words. Needless to say, Elle wasn't placing a lot of faith in her mom's newest "prediction."

Shane toted Charlotte over to them then. Charlotte gleefully gripped a small, stuffed black cat in one hand. "Mommy, look! Kitty!"

Had it been merely coincidence that the child's prize matched her costume? Or had the volunteer peeked around the backboard before attaching the toy to the clip on the end of the fishing line? Elle suspected the latter.

She slipped her phone in her pocket and reached for her daughter. "That's a beautiful kitty, Charlotte. Say 'thank you' to Shane for helping you at the fishing booth."

"T'ank you, Shane," the child parroted obediently.

"You're very welcome, Charlotte."

"Are you getting hungry, Charlotte?" her grandmother asked, motioning toward the other end of the park where picnic tables were surrounded by food vendors. Tempting scents from grills and fry buckets wafted from that direction. There weren't many healthy offerings, but plenty of celebrated festival foods were among the selections. "We can have hot dogs or fried chicken. You like both of those."

"Chicken," Charlotte announced immediately, squirming for Elle to put her down. "Want chicken."

Janet took the child's hand, then smiled coyly at Shane. "We'd love to have you join us for a bite, Shane. Do you like fair food?"

"Who doesn't like fair food? Okay with you, Elle?"

He turned to face her, and she noted that his hair showed even more tendency to curl now that he was wind-blown and slightly disheveled. Feeling her fingers twitch in response, she pushed her hands into her pockets and spoke cheerily. "Of course it's okay."

A few minutes later they settled at a picnic table with their guilty-pleasure Southern dinners. Charlotte and her grandmother were sharing fried chicken and waffles. Elle and Shane indulged in bowls of buttery, cheesy shrimp, and grits with andouille sausage and a dash of cayenne pepper. Elle was fully aware their group was getting some curious glances from people who knew her. Being so busy with work and family, she hadn't dated much—at all, really—since her divorce, so speculation was sure to be aroused by seeing her sharing a meal with a good-looking man.

Between the food, the cacophony of sounds surrounding them, frequent greetings from passing acquaintances and Charlotte's excitement-fueled chattering, there was little chance for real conversation among the adults at the table. Which didn't stop Elle's mom from trying to find out all she could about Shane. Elle winced a couple of times, hoping she'd been a little subtler than her mom at interrogating the interesting visitor. As he had with her, Shane answered the questions with patient tolerance, though Elle learned little about him that she hadn't already known.

Charlotte held up a gnawed chicken drumstick. "Bite, Shane?"

Such a flirt, Elle thought with an amused shake of her head even as Shane answered, "No, thank you, Charlotte. I still have some of my own dinner left."

While Elle tried to wipe her squirming child's food-smeared face with a paper napkin, her mom spoke to Shane. "You're very good with children."

"I like kids," he replied lightly.

"None of your own, though?"

Elle cleared her throat pointedly as a warning to her mother not to get too nosy, but Shane answered with a smile. "No, none of my own. I've never been married."

"Elle told me you're from Fayetteville. Do your parents still live there?"

Remembering that he'd recently lost his father, Elle winced and started to intervene, but again Shane responded evenly. "My mother died when I was only three. My dad died last year. But my grandmother, my uncle and my cousin and her family all still live in Fayetteville, so there's no shortage of family there."

Even Elle's sometimes-oblivious mother could see it was time to back away. She focused on wiping Charlotte's mouth while Elle changed the subject to something less precarious. She knew she would reflect later about this other great loss in Shane's life.

"Have your business meetings gone well, Shane? Wasn't I right about Trevor Farrell being a nice guy?"

"He is."

"And his resort is beautiful."

"Very."

"Do you think you got the account?" her mother asked, unable to resist chiming in again.

It was obvious that Shane didn't want to speculate about his ongoing discussions, but he said guardedly, "Our talks have been going well."

"I'll put in a good word for you, if you like. I can tell Trevor that I predict a very successful collaboration if he signs with you."

Shane shot a slightly alarmed look at Elle. Sighing at her mother's propensity for overstepping boundaries—even with the best of intentions—Elle interceded smoothly. "I'm sure Shane prefers to conduct his own business negotiations, Mom. You shouldn't interfere."

"Not that I don't appreciate the offer, Mrs. O'Meara," Shane said.

"Janet," she reminded him. "And I won't say anything, if you prefer. But the offer stands."

"Candy, Mommy?" Charlotte asked, pointing hopefully toward her pumpkin bucket.

Judging that her daughter had eaten enough

chicken, Elle handed her a piece of candy from the bucket. "Just one for now."

A rumble of activity from behind them drew Elle's attention to the amphitheater that anchored the south end of the park. "Oh, they're setting up for the concert. It's supposed to start at eight."

She checked her watch, surprised to note that it was already almost seven. "We'll have to leave before the concert begins. Charlotte's already drooping and she still needs her bath before bedtime."

Her mom clapped her hands together, causing her bracelets to jingle. "I have an idea, Elle. Why don't I take Charlotte home? You and Shane can stay and enjoy the concert. I'm sure you'd like it, Shane. One of the local singers performing tonight was on a national TV talent show last year! He made it all the way to the top five before he was eliminated. I just know you and Elle will have a fun evening."

Elle wondered if her "psychic" mother was aware that her daughter would like very much to pinch her. Could she be any more obvious in her matchmaking?

"It does sound like fun," Shane said before Elle could speak. He looked at her in question. His expression let her know he understood the position her mom had just placed her in, and he generously provided her with a plausible excuse. "But

I'd understand if you have other things you need to do tonight."

"No," she said on an impulse. "I mean, yes. I'd love to stay for the music."

She still doubted this would lead anywhere, but why not enjoy a rare evening with an attractive man? It was nice to get away from chores and worries for a few hours, and a public concert was a safe, pressure-free place to spend time with him, even if gossip was sure to ensue.

"Great." His dimples flashed briefly, and she couldn't resist smiling back.

He seemed genuinely nice. Maybe he was. She needed to learn to trust again.

Tonight could be just what she needed to get back out again as a single woman who could appreciate the company of a charming, handsome man, if only for a few pleasant hours. Shane Scanlon fit that description very nicely.

CHAPTER THREE

ELLE SENT HER costume home with her mom and daughter, which left her dressed in the fall tunic, slim jeans and leather boots she'd worn beneath the robe. This was an outfit more suited to a date night. Not that this was a date, exactly, she cautioned herself. Just an evening with a new friend.

She and Shane wandered through the park while waiting for the concert to start, browsing the crafts booths and watching costumed kids playing the games and collecting enough candy to support all the town's dentists for the next twelve months. With all the bustle around them, they had to keep their heads close together to talk, but Elle didn't exactly find that a hardship.

Elle's phone chimed with a text and she drew it from her pocket. "I always check my phone when I'm out," she explained, not wanting to appear rude. "I have to make sure everything's okay at home."

"Of course."

Glancing at the screen, she said, "Mom's just

letting me know that Charlotte is all tucked in and sound asleep."

She didn't add that her mom had urged her to stay out as long as she wanted. And had ended the text with a "wink" emoji.

"Does your mother live with you?" Shane asked as Elle texted a quick reply.

She slipped the phone back into her pocket. "Yes. Mom was so lonely after my dad died and I needed help with Charlotte, so she moved in. It's worked out very well for both of us."

After Elle's divorce two years after her father's death, her mother sold her own home and had been sharing mortgage and household expenses with Elle since. The house had a finished basement that they'd transformed into a cozy efficiency-style apartment into which Janet had happily settled, though she spent most of her waking hours with Elle and Charlotte.

"Your mom hardly looks old enough to be a grandmother."

Elle smiled. "If you'd said that in front of her, she'd probably have tackle-hugged you."

"She was widowed young."

"Yes." Elle sighed regretfully. "She was. Certainly young enough to remarry, even now. She's only fifty-eight, but she hasn't been interested in dating. She was totally devoted to my father. They started going out in junior high and she never had another boyfriend."

"Yet she seems happy. I don't think I've seen her once without a smile."

"That's my mom. She misses my dad deeply, but for the most part she is very happy. She loves making other people laugh. And most of all, she loves being a grandmother to Charlotte. Who utterly adores her in return, obviously."

"Yes, that is obvious."

There it was again. That fleeting sadness she'd seen in his eyes before.

"I think I'm going to indulge in dessert," he said, shaking off whatever dark thoughts had plagued him before she had time to analyze his reaction. "All these good smells are making me hungry again. What do you recommend?"

Dragging her attention from this intriguing man, she glanced at the booths around them, seeing caramel apples, funnel cakes, cotton candy, kettle popcorn and fried pies among the dessert offerings. "I don't know about you, but I'm having one of those fried pies. Apple is my favorite."

"Sounds good." He motioned with one hand for her to lead the way.

A short while later, having enjoyed flaky, crisp pastries oozing with fruit filling, they settled on a concrete riser in the amphitheater with cups of hot cider. The benches were beginning to fill, and the crowd was noisy and animated as they waited for the music to start. It was fully dark now. The artificial lights cast moving shadows around them suitable to the Halloween decorations and costumes. With no responsibilities pressing on her for the moment, Elle was having a very good time.

Shane seemed to share that sentiment. Lounging on the hard, cold bench with the disposable cup cradled between his hands, he smiled at her. "Thanks for staying with me, Elle. This is so much nicer than spending another solitary evening in that motel room."

"Do you have more business meetings this weekend?" she asked, wondering how long he planned to be in the area.

"I have a couple more items to check off my list before I leave town."

It wasn't exactly what she'd asked, but maybe his answer had been unintentionally evasive. Before he could say anything else, if he'd planned to, they were interrupted by a group of Elle's friends who swarmed around them, settling into the rapidly filling riser seating with noisy greetings and laughter. Elle introduced Shane, then rattled off names to him she doubted he would even begin to remember. The concert began a few minutes later and any further conversation was forestalled by the volume of the music from the stage.

What the performances lacked in polish, they

more than made up for in enthusiasm. Elle and her friends filled the breaks between sets with light prattle about kids, sports, festival food and the acts they'd seen. Shane fit in well with the loose-knit group, chatting easily with the other guys, deftly deflecting questions that crept toward the overly personal.

Elle had almost forgotten what it was like to spend an evening with adults, to laugh and flirt and feel young and attractive. As much as she adored being a mother, this impromptu concert was still a pleasant break. Maybe it was time to date again, at least occasionally, now that Charlotte was a little older and Elle's mom was so happily available to babysit. She wasn't ready for anything serious—but it wouldn't hurt to have a little grown-up fun every once in a while.

A cool night breeze swirled through the amphitheater, ruffling her hair and slipping down the loose opening of her tunic. She shivered, thinking she should have worn a light cardigan.

Shane started to shrug out of his leather jacket. "Are you cold? You want to wear this?"

"No, that's okay, I—"

But he'd already draped the jacket over her shoulders. "Sounds like the next act is starting."

Aware of a couple of her friends watching, she smiled and kept the jacket wrapped around her rather than arguing. It did feel good. And it held just a hint of spicy scent. Aftershave? Nice.

She looked up at him, finding him gazing back at her as she unconsciously stroked the soft leather with her free hand. Turning toward the stage, she pretended to focus on the band wailing into their microphones.

Maybe if Shane asked her out on a real date, she'd say yes. He'd probably be in town occasionally if he got the Wind Shadow account. She wasn't expecting anything serious to develop, but she'd be lying if she said she wasn't strongly attracted to him. She sensed the attraction wasn't one-sided. So...why not?

The concert ended at ten with the mayor thanking everyone for their attendance and wishing them all a happy and safe Halloween.

"And starting November 1, all the jack-o'-lanterns and orange-and-black bunting here in the park will be replaced by snowflakes and candy canes and red-and-green ribbons."

Lori Malloy, owner of a gift and souvenir shop located a few doors down from The Perkery, laughed lightly as she made the prediction to Elle and their other friends. "Actually, my staff and I started putting out some of our new holiday merchandise two weeks ago."

Pragmatic accountant Bob Hodgkin groaned.

"It's too soon to be talking about Christmas! We're still over three weeks away from Thanksgiving."

"It's never too soon for Christmas," his wife piped in. "I love every minute of it."

While the others fell into a spirited discussion about the proper date to put up Christmas decorations, Elle glanced up at Shane with a smile. "I've had a nice time," she said quietly, "but I really should be getting home now. I have to get a very early start in the morning."

"Of course."

"You need a lift home, Elle?"

"Thank you, Lori, but Shane has already offered me a ride." It wasn't all that far to her house, but would have required crossing a couple of busy streets on foot in the dark and in post-festival traffic, so she would take him up on that offer.

Six pairs of eyes turned immediately to the outsider in their midst. Though he'd been graciously welcomed, it was obvious he was still being assessed. Elle bit back a smile at the clear warning being implicitly sent: *We watch out for our own.*

Judging by the way Shane blinked, he got the message.

He walked with her to his car, which he'd parked close to the north entrance of the park. She handed him his jacket before climbing in, then buckled her seat belt as Shane slid into the driver's seat and started the engine. "Turn left out of the parking lot, then right at the next intersection."

He put the car into gear. "Got it."

What should have been a ten-minute drive came to an abrupt stop on Salt Marsh Avenue, where both lanes of post-festival traffic were brought to a complete stop by a three-car wreck not far ahead. Craning her neck to peer around the vehicles in front of them, Elle could see flashing lights just arriving to the scene. "This could take a while," she said with a groan.

"I hope no one's hurt."

She could see shadowy figures climbing out of all three crumpled cars, illuminated by streetlamps and headlights from the cars idling around them. "From what I can tell, it looks like everyone's okay. I think a couple of those cars are going to have to be towed out of the way, though. Unfortunately, there's no alternate route from where we're sitting. If we'd turned right out of the park instead of left…"

Shane shrugged. "So we'll wait. Maybe they'll get a lane cleared quickly."

She gave him a rueful smile. "Traffic jams aren't exactly common in our sleepy little town. Even during peak season. I could walk from here if you—"

"No reason for that. Obviously, I'm not going

anywhere soon. This gives us a chance to talk a bit more, anyway. What did you think of the concert?"

"It was fun. Not my type of music for everyday listening, but I enjoyed it tonight."

They chatted about music for a few minutes, finding common ground in a fondness for smooth jazz combined with good wine. Elle spent a pleasant moment privately fantasizing about sitting by an outdoor fire pit with Shane, wineglasses in hand, softly wailing sax playing from hidden speakers—the type of daydream she hadn't allowed herself to indulge in for a while.

Headed toward the blocked intersection, a police car equipped with strobing lights and a whooping siren threaded carefully through the line of unmoving vehicles, giving Elle hope that an officer would soon be directing the flow of traffic. Shane waited until the noise had died down before speaking again. "You said your mom moved in with you after your divorce. Do you mind my asking how long that's been?"

"I've been divorced a little more than two years."

"Does your ex-husband see Charlotte often?"

It made sense, of course, that Shane would assume her ex was Charlotte's father. And though she owed no explanations, Shane had been candid with her when she'd asked about his family.

Besides, she had never planned to hide how Charlotte had come into her life.

"Glenn wasn't Charlotte's father," she said a bit more bluntly than she'd intended. "I adopted her on my own shortly after the divorce. He's never seen her."

After a moment, Shane commented, "Definitely his loss."

She nodded. "Very much so."

"He wasn't interested in fatherhood, I take it."

She shrugged. "I thought he was. We talked about it a lot during our marriage, while he attended law school. He was even involved in the initial steps toward finding a reputable adoption agency and beginning the registration process. But then he suddenly announced that he wasn't daddy material. And, by the way, he no longer wanted to be a husband, either. He left the law firm he worked for here and moved to California to live a single attorney's life on the west coast. Maybe he watched a few too many *Baywatch* reruns."

She'd spoken lightly to gloss over the emotional turmoil Glenn had put her through, but Shane didn't smile. "Sounds like sort of a jerk."

Her smile felt decidedly rueful. "Turned out he sort of was. He was just very good at hiding it for a while."

"I don't know much about adoption, but I've

heard that's easier to adopt as a single parent than it was in the past."

"Fortunately, the agency I used was open to single-parent adoption, as was Charlotte's birth mother. Charlotte was five months old when she came to me, and she had a few special issues, so my application to adopt her was pushed through as soon as my background checks cleared."

"Um—special issues?"

She saw his hands flex on the steering wheel and figured he was getting restless with the extended delay. Perhaps he kept the conversation going to pass the time—or maybe he was genuinely interested. Regardless, she was always open to chatting about her wonderful daughter, who had already faced so many challenges in her short life and still woke each morning with an eager smile.

"She had surgery for infantile esotropia—basically, crossed eyes—three months after I brought her home. It was nerve-racking and, frankly, expensive, but she came through like a trooper and has done remarkably well since the surgery. Most people would probably never know she'd had an issue with her eyes just by looking at her now, though it was pronounced in the few early photos that were provided to me."

"I certainly haven't noticed anything. Was this something she was born with?"

Elle was a little surprised by the gravity of his tone. "Yes. But because newborns don't focus well, anyway, it probably wasn't clearly noticeable until she was several weeks old. The surgery isn't medically necessary, but many studies have shown that the earlier it takes place, the better the outcome in most cases. Believe me, I read all the literature and consulted with several pediatric ophthalmologists before I consented."

"Will she need follow-up surgeries? Is her vision impaired?"

"In most cases, no follow-up surgery is required, though occasionally some adjustment is needed later. In Charlotte's case, the procedure seems to have corrected the condition. She's had age-appropriate vision and depth perception tests during the past year and a half and it looks good so far. Maybe she'll need corrective lenses at some point, but that's not such a big problem."

Shane kept his gaze on the cars ahead, but his attention was obviously still focused on her daughter. "Did you ever meet Charlotte's birth mother?"

It occurred to her that the conversation was getting personal again, as she and Shane seemed prone to do. She could rationalize her own curiosity with the excuse that a single mom should know as much as she could about the men she brought into her life—if that was even a possibility in this budding friendship.

As for Shane—well, maybe it was understandable that he had questions about the adoption process. She didn't mind answering a few more. Being Charlotte's mom was the most important part of her identity. Any man, whether friend or potentially more, who came into her life should be made aware of that.

"No. Though we used an open adoption agency, she didn't want to meet. I was just grateful she chose me to raise her child after studying the application, personal statement, references and videos I submitted."

"Did you ever worry that she might—uh…"

Maybe he realized he was being too intrusive. He stopped himself before finishing the question, but she guessed what he'd started to ask. "That she might change her mind? I suppose every adoptive parent has that concern. I can't imagine how devastating it would be."

She swallowed hard, then shrugged and deliberately lightened her tone. "Anyway, I've gotten beyond that. I'm Charlotte's mother and nothing can change that now."

She was prepared for Charlotte to ask questions someday, of course, and she would answer them as truthfully as she could. She would even help if Charlotte wanted to try to track down her biological relatives after she turned eighteen. But she had to admit she was in no hurry for that day to arrive.

A tow truck with an amber light bar flashing on top made its way past them toward the crumpled cars blocking the intersection.

Shane spoke again as he watched the wrecker go by. "Was it difficult? Bonding with a baby already five months old, I mean. Did she—"

Again, she filled in the rest of the question. "Did Charlotte miss her birth mother?"

He shot her a quick glance. "Yeah, I guess that was what I was asking."

"I was told her birth mother had some personal issues, so Charlotte had a few different caregivers before me. Whether because she missed her mother or because her life had been so unsettled to that point, Charlotte was fussy and seemed anxious the first few days she was with me. I was just yet another adult in her life at that point."

Having adored Charlotte from the moment she'd first seen her, Elle had worried about that at first—along with all the other anxieties involved in becoming a new single mother. "Fortunately, within a couple of weeks, she seemed to understand that I wasn't going anywhere. That I would be the one who answered every time she cried. I was with her every minute during her surgery prep and recuperation. Mine was one of the first faces she saw when she woke up afterward. I think she understands by now in her innocent way that I would give my life for her."

Clearing her throat, she told herself to ease up on the drama, genuine as her sentiment had been. She spoke more casually when she said, "Charlotte and my mom hit it off immediately. They've become almost inseparable since. Charlotte adores her Gammy and vice versa. Now it's as if we've all been together since the day Charlotte was born. She's ours."

"She is definitely yours." Shane looked out the windshield as he spoke.

The car ahead of them moved forward and he followed at a cautious distance. "Looks like they've cleared one lane," he said, his tone brisk now. "Should have you home in a few minutes."

His attention was claimed then by the signals of the police officer directing traffic. They didn't speak for the rest of the ride except for Elle telling him where to turn. She laced her fingers in her lap, mentally replaying their conversation and wondering if Shane had satisfied his curiosity— or if he'd been trying to learn more about her as someone he might want to get to know better in the future. Now that she thought back over the exchange, it felt almost like an interview.

That absurd thought showed she must be more tired than she'd realized after a busy week, and she still had to be up early in the morning to crank out doughnuts.

"Nice place," Shane said when he parked in her driveway.

The yellow frame house was trimmed in white with hunter green shutters and a tidy small yard. Elle had always loved it. Especially now that it was where she was raising her daughter.

"Thank you. And thanks for the ride."

Shane half turned in his seat to look at her. He drew a deep breath, and she had the feeling he was bolstering his courage. The possibility that he was getting up the nerve to ask her out flitted through her mind, but why would he need to brace himself for that, even with the possibility that she would turn him down? Not that she would, but she supposed he couldn't be sure of that.

"Elle, there's something—" He broke off with a sigh when her phone beeped with another incoming text. "I know you need to check that."

With an apologetic half smile, she drew out the phone and read the screen. "Mom says she's sorry to interrupt, but she can't find the antacids. I knew she'd regret that second piece of fried chicken."

He unbuckled his seat belt. "You should go in to her. I'll walk you to the door."

She rested a hand lightly on his arm. "Don't

bother getting out. I'm sure Mom's fine, but I'll go in and check on her. I have to be at the shop early tomorrow, anyway. I have chocolate-filled doughnuts to make," she added with a wink.

He nodded, his answering smile looking a little strained as he covered her hand with his. "Do me a favor, okay? Put one of those aside for me. I'm having a breakfast meeting with a potential client in the morning, so it could be midafternoon before I get a chance to come in."

The warmth from their linked hands flooded pleasantly through her. She'd thought the two glasses of wine she'd imbibed earlier had mostly worn off, but maybe not entirely. "I'll save you one, all wrapped up so it will stay fresh until you get there."

He chuckled. "I appreciate that."

"So…I'll see you tomorrow?"

"You'll see me tomorrow."

They sat there for another long moment, hands joined, gazes locked. His eyes glittered in the shadowed car, and she was sure he was thinking about kissing her. Or was she projecting her own curiosity?

Because she wasn't the kind of woman who coyly waited for a man to make the first move, she leaned forward and took hold of the soft leather lapel of his jacket. She wasn't even going to blame it on the wine. "Let's chalk this up to curiosity," she murmured, then pressed her lips to his.

His startled chuckle was smothered by the kiss that he returned with satisfying enthusiasm after only a heartbeat's hesitation.

She'd intended the kiss to be brief. Lightly teasing. As she'd said, it had been motivated as much by curiosity as by the attraction she'd felt for him from the start. But what had started as a friendly gesture quickly flared into more. Her fingers tightened on his jacket when his left arm went around her to hold her closer.

Their lips softened, parted, molded together. She felt the slight roughness of evening beard, the heat radiating off him, the strength of the arm holding her. And she was so very tempted to allow the kiss to deepen, to dive in for an even more thorough taste of him. She was only human, and it had been much too long since she'd felt like this…

Shane came to his senses before she did. Drawing back into his seat, he disentangled her hand gently from his coat. "Good night, Elle. We'll talk tomorrow."

She blinked a couple of times, bringing his face into focus. He wore a faint smile, but his eyes were too shadowed for her to see if the smile spread that far. She honestly had no idea how he felt about her kissing him.

"Good night, Shane." Rather shaken by the unexpected intensity of what she'd started, she climbed out of the car and walked briskly toward her door, digging in her bag for her keys. She knew she'd recall the taste and feel of him long into the night ahead.

Shane didn't back out of the driveway until she had her front door open. He lifted a hand in a wave as he drove away. She stood in the open doorway until his red taillights had faded out of sight. Only then did she close the door with a sigh that sounded wistful even to her own ears.

"WHEN ARE YOU coming home, Shane? You don't have any more meetings lined up for this weekend, do you?"

"No, there's nothing scheduled," Shane told his uncle during a Saturday afternoon phone conversation. Shane sat in his car outside The Perkery, having parked just as his phone rang. He'd already given his uncle a report on the seemingly successful sales pitch that morning, and he was getting impatient to head inside for coffee and the promised chocolate doughnut. "I'd just like to spend a little more time here. I'll call you when I get back in town. I'll probably stop by your place on my way home to see Dottie. And I'll be at the office all day Monday."

"Guess I can't blame you for wanting a little

time to yourself," Raymond Scanlon conceded. "You haven't had more than a handful of days off since you got out of the army, have you?"

Shane wasn't sure he'd had even that many, not if he counted all the days he'd felt compelled to handle family issues in addition to his work obligations. Which was most days. "Everything's okay there, right?"

"Oh, sure. We'll get by until you're back."

Shane wished his uncle could sound more confident. "How's Dottie?" he asked, using the nickname everyone, even her grandchildren, called his grandmother, Dorothy Scanlon.

"She's feeling better today, I think. She's been barking orders all morning. You know. The usual."

"And Parker?"

His uncle's sigh sounded clearly enough through their connection. "She's still fretting about anything and everything, but I keep telling her it will all be okay. Still, she'll feel more relaxed when you're back. You've always had a knack for reassuring her."

Raymond's daughter, Parker, worked for the family business and was a part-time dance instructor with plans to open her own studio eventually. She and her musician husband, Adrian Mendel, were the parents of a six-month-old boy, Aubrey. They'd recently moved into their first house, which was in need of a few repairs. Shane acknowledged ruefully that he and his younger cousin shared the bad habit of taking on too much and then worrying about how to get it done.

Shane hadn't yet told his family that he'd located Charlie's daughter. When he got home, he'd have to figure out a way to let them know that the child was healthy and seemed happy, though he doubted it would be easy to convince them they had no place in the life she had now. Parker and Adrian were still openly disappointed that Brittany hadn't given them the chance to raise Charlotte as their own. Had that happened, they'd lamented, she'd have grown up knowing her great-grandmother, her uncles, her biological family history.

As loving as Elle and Janet were toward the child, as much as she belonged with them now, the fact was that Charlotte had been born a Scanlon. That meant something to Shane's family. And, he had to admit, to him. He accepted that Elle was Charlotte's mother, but he couldn't help thinking occasionally of what might have been, had Charlie lived or Brittany made different choices.

Putting those thoughts out of his mind for the moment, he said, "You know you can reach me at any time if you need me for anything."

"Enjoy the break, Shane. Get some rest, walk on the beach, whatever you need to do to recharge. You deserve it after getting Wind Shadow Resorts for us."

"Trevor hasn't signed anything yet," Shane cautioned his uncle. "But it does look promising."

"I'm sure you got it. I have full faith in you. We all do."

"Thanks, Raymond."

It had been a compliment, Shane thought as he slid his phone back into his pocket. A sincere one. So why had it left him feeling more stressed than ever? He could only imagine how much more pressure the family would put on him if they knew he was in contact with the child they'd all grieved since Brittany had disappeared with her.

He couldn't help wondering if it was really the family piling on that pressure—or if he was doing it to himself. The weight of the promises he'd made to his brother and father sometimes pressed more heavily on his shoulders than he suspected either of them would have intended. Which didn't mean he wouldn't do everything within his power to honor those assurances.

He reached for the door handle and slid out of the car. It was a warmish day for the last week of October, so he left his leather jacket in the back seat. He was comfortable enough in his pullover and jeans as he walked into The Perkery.

He was probably playing with fire by showing up here again, but he kept being drawn back. And while he tried to convince himself he wanted to spend as much time as possible with his niece, he suspected he was equally unable to resist spending more time with Elle.

This would all be much easier if he wasn't so damned attracted to her. Despite the complicating circumstances, he'd had a hard time keeping his eyes off her last night—not to mention his hands. Spending the evening at the park with her and her friends had been the most fun and relaxing couple of hours he'd managed during the past few months. There'd been a moment of connection when he'd parked in front of her house that had made his body tense with awareness of her, but he'd warned himself to remember why he couldn't act on the attraction.

And then she'd kissed him.

He'd lain awake half aroused for quite a while last night, staring at the motel room ceiling and mentally listing all the reasons that kiss had been a big mistake. As much as he'd enjoyed it, as secretly pleased as he was that she'd wanted to kiss him, he shouldn't have let it happen while she was still unaware of his connection to her daughter. Of his reason for spending time with her—or at least, the reason he'd initially looked her up.

Maybe it had been too long since he'd been involved with anyone. The only semi-serious relationship he'd had since getting out of the service had ended when the woman said he spent too much time working and taking care of his family, leaving no time for her. Fair accusation, he supposed. As he'd reminded himself before, he had more than enough on his plate for now; he certainly didn't need to take on a single mom with her own business and an emotionally dependent widowed mother.

Not that there'd have been much chance of that, anyway. Not once Elle found out that he'd deceived her, if only by omission, from the first time they'd met. She'd made it clear last night that she'd always dreaded the possibility of one of Charlotte's biological relatives making contact. He had no plans to interfere with the perfectly legal adoption, but she couldn't be sure of that. She would have to wonder why he'd been hanging around.

At this point, he wasn't sure he could answer her. He was beginning to question it himself.

CHAPTER FOUR

SHANE FOUND THE shop more crowded than he'd seen it before. Customers chatted around the little tables and stood in line at the counter where Elle, Janet and Amber bustled to take orders and serve everyone. At first he figured he must have misjudged the peak of Saturday rush hour. After a second glance, he realized that many of the customers wore matching bright pink shirts promoting a charity marathon that had apparently taken place that morning. Must be time for post-run carbs-and-caffeine, he decided.

He thought about turning around and heading back out to return later, but Elle spotted him then with a smile and a little wave of greeting. Giving in, he threaded through milling pink shirts toward the counter. Elle had a coffee mug and a plated chocolate-filled doughnut waiting for him by the time he got there.

"You didn't change your mind about wanting one of these, did you?" she asked, looking remarkably at ease despite the chaos. In fact, she seemed to thrive on it.

"I've been looking forward to that doughnut since I woke up this morning."

She laughed and nudged the plate closer. "Then I'm happy to be of service. Enjoy."

Damn. Something about the sound of Elle's laughter erased every cautious, coherent thought from his head. When he looked at her bright smile, he found himself hungrier for a taste of her lips than for chocolate and pastry. She glanced at his mouth, and he had no doubt that she, too, was thinking of the kiss they'd shared.

Maybe he really did need a vacation. But he had to keep in mind that this wasn't one. His reasons for being in Shorty's Landing were serious and pressing.

Looking up from her toys in the play corral, Charlotte spotted him. She tossed a toy truck aside and sprang to her feet, clutching the plastic railing for balance with one hand while reaching out to him with the other. "Shane! Shane!"

He smiled at her from across the counter, his chest tightening. Her eyes were so much like Charlie's. Very much like little Aubrey's. Charlotte and Aubrey could have passed for siblings. "Hi there, Charlotte."

Bouncing on her feet, she opened and closed her outstretched hand in appeal. "Shane! Want Shane!"

So she did get tired of being in that plastic

fence-thing. He looked inquiringly at Elle. "I think she'd like to come out and sit with me for a while. Do you mind?"

Her hesitation was only natural, he supposed. After all, they still hardly knew each other. Truth was, he wouldn't want her handing off the child to just any friendly stranger who wandered in. But maybe watching him with Charlotte at the festival, in addition to their very public surroundings, gave her some reassurance. "Of course not, if it wouldn't interfere with your snack."

"I'll enjoy the company."

He claimed a two-seat table just being vacated, set down his coffee and doughnut and then returned for Charlotte. Elle passed her over. The child gripped a picture book in one hand, refusing to leave it behind. "Just bring her back when you're ready for a break. She's perfectly happy with her toys most of the time."

Elle turned then to take an order from another customer. Hoisting his niece onto his hip, Shane carried her to his table and sat with her on his knee. Still clutching her book, she watched him with big blue eyes as he took a bite of his doughnut.

With a grin, he broke off a small piece and offered it to her. She accepted it with a sweet, "T'ank you, Shane," then crammed it into her mouth, leaving a smear of chocolate on her soft cheek.

"Good?" he asked.

"Good," she agreed with a fervent nod.

They shared the doughnut as they leafed slowly through Charlotte's picture book. She pointed out the drawings on each page, naming every item with a familiarity that proved she knew this book very well. He watched her closely as she scanned the pages. Her eyes seemed to be tracking fine as far as he could tell, though granted he was no expert.

"Horsey," Charlotte pronounced, poking a finger at the book.

"Yes. That's a horse. A big brown horse," he said, reading the caption.

He'd noticed Charlotte rarely used complete sentences, but he was confident it wouldn't be long before she was chattering a mile a minute. Her dad had been quite the conversationalist, always the life of a party, rarely at a loss for amusing banter or a quick quip.

God, he missed his brother.

He swallowed painfully, then forced a smile when Charlotte pointed to a big-eyed cow and said, "Cow. Moo."

"Yes, Charlotte, a cow says moo."

She pointed again. "Big."

"Pig," he corrected her with a smile. "That's a pig."

"Big."

"Pig. Puh-pig."

"Puh-pig," she repeated carefully. "Oink."

He chuckled, then made piggy sounds that elicited giggles from her.

"Silly Shane," she said with a shake of her head, making him laugh again.

Charlie would have adored this cute little girl. And Shane had no doubt the feeling would have been mutual. Everyone had loved Charlie.

Brittany had claimed to love Charlie, too—and Shane tended to believe her. Yet she'd given away his child without even offering to let Charlie's close-knit family raise her, as she must have known they would have been happy to do. The sting of that rejection had hurt them all, especially after they'd gone to such great lengths to assure her of their willingness to help, to provide whatever she needed, to take her in as part of the family even after Charlie died.

Shane didn't blame Brittany for giving up her parental rights; if anything, he admired her for making the best choice for the child's welfare. He had no issues with adoption, considered it as valid a route to parenthood as biological pregnancy. But for Brittany to give her child to a stranger without even considering her family had been unjustified, in his opinion. Her choice, which he still didn't entirely understand, had hurt them badly at a time when they were still grieving Charlie's loss. It had been especially painful for Charlie's father and grandmother, who'd have given anything for more time with his child.

"You two seem to be having fun," Elle said from behind him.

Shane looked up in response to her voice. "We are. Charlotte's been reading her book to me."

"Puh-pig, Mommy."

Elle reached down to smooth Charlotte's tumbled curls. "Yes, sweetie. That's a pig. What does a pig say?"

"Oink, oink."

"Very good. Do you want your snack now? Gammy has bananas and yogurt for you in the kitchen."

Shane checked his watch, surprised to see that it was almost two thirty. He glanced around the shop as Elle took Charlotte from him. Most of the pink shirts had disappeared while he'd been occupied with his niece. Only a few quiet customers were still settled in with their coffees and pastries.

He waited until Elle stepped back out of the kitchen with a tray of cookies for the display case before he moved to stand on the other side of the counter. He watched as she unloaded the tray into a waiting basket. "Those look good."

"White chocolate and cranberry. Want to try one?"

"Sounds delicious, but since I just ate a chocolate doughnut, I should probably hold off on sweets until after I've had some real food."

Elle slanted a smile up at him. "From the amount of chocolate on Charlotte's face, I'm not sure you had much of that doughnut."

"She might've had a bite or two," he said, relieved that she didn't seem perturbed. "I hope you don't mind."

"No, it's fine. She had a good serving of vegetable soup for lunch and she's having a healthy afternoon snack, so it's okay if she had a little treat." Elle closed the display case and straightened, setting the empty tray aside. "You're very good with Charlotte. You really like kids, huh?"

It occurred to him that maybe she was a little wary of his interest in Charlotte. Understandable.

He drew a deep breath, thinking it was past time for him to level with her. "Elle, there's something I should probably—"

He almost groaned when Janet burst through the kitchen door. This was the second time he'd been interrupted before he could come clean. "Elle, we need you back here now!"

Shane tensed, his flash of frustration dissolving into concern at Janet's expression. Was something wrong with Charlotte?

The same question must have crossed Elle's mind. She moved quickly toward her mother. "What's wrong?"

Janet had spotted Shane. "You said you were a medic, didn't you? You should come, too. We need you."

Shane didn't hesitate before rounding the end of the counter toward the kitchen, a vivid image of Charlotte's sweetly trusting face in his mind.

HER HEART POUNDING in her throat, Elle surged into the kitchen with Shane close behind her. The urgency of her mother's summons had scared her. Of course her first thought had been of Charlotte.

One quick visual sweep of the industrial kitchen let her know what had happened. Amber stood at the sink, a dishtowel wrapped around her right hand, blood soaking through the fabric. Staring at Amber with huge, worried eyes, Charlotte sat in a booster seat on a chair at the small table positioned at one end of the room, her snack forgotten in front of her. Her lower lip quivered.

While her mother moved to reassure Charlotte, Elle rushed to Amber's side. "How bad is it?"

Looking pale but calm, Amber shook her head. "I'm sure it'll be fine. I was prepping vegetables for tomorrow's soups and I cut my hand. I just need to stick a bandage on it and cover that with a glove while I'm working in the kitchen."

"I just knew something bad was going to happen today."

Elle shot her fretting mother a look. "Don't start, Mom. How deep is the cut, Amber?"

"I'm not sure. It's probably fine."

"Do you mind if I take a look?" Shane asked, stepping closer. "I've had some first-aid training."

Elle figured that as an army medic in a war zone, Shane had more than "some" training, but it seemed characteristic of him to downplay his proficiency. She watched while he unwrapped the towel from Amber's hand, and then she winced when she saw the gash he'd revealed. Blood still flowed freely from the wound in the heel of Amber's right hand. With the mandolin slicer and raw vegetables still scattered on the counter, it didn't take much imagination to mentally recreate the accident.

"Yeah, this is probably going to need a couple of stitches." Shane looked at Amber with almost apologetic sympathy. "A bandage isn't going to be enough."

Amber winced. "Are you sure?"

He was already pressing the towel against the bleeding cut again. "Pretty sure. Hold this tight until we can get you to an urgent care center. I can drive you."

"No." Giving Charlotte a reassuring pat, Elle's mom stepped forward. "It would be easier if I drive her since I know the way. And the shop will be responsible for the cost, right, Elle?"

"Yes, of course."

"We can't leave Elle here to run the shop by herself," Amber protested, her face pale but calm.

Elle was already untying Amber's apron. "I can handle it. Now that the post-marathon rush is over, it will probably be slow here for the rest of the day. We'll only be open for another hour and a half. I can call Kristen or DeShawn if I need more help. I'm sure one of them would come."

"I can help here until closing," Shane suggested. "I take orders pretty well," he added with a smile for Elle.

It seemed ungracious to decline his offer, though it was becoming increasingly difficult to think of Shane as merely a nice customer just passing through town. In the few days she'd known him, he'd made an impact on her, her mother, even her daughter. And that was starting to make her nervous.

Just why was he hanging around them so much? Was he really that attracted to her, that lonely in an unfamiliar town? He seemed harmless enough—other than to her long-denied hormones—but should she be more concerned? Or was the stress of Amber's injury simply making her paranoid again?

Maybe his notable attention had to do with his business? It occurred to her that perhaps he wanted her to put in a good word with some of the more prominent area business owners. She hoped that wasn't his intention.

"I have to get back out to the counter," she said as her mother bustled Amber through the back exit. She quickly wiped Charlotte's face then helped her down from the booster seat to take her out to the play corral in the shop.

Shane looked around the kitchen. "Is there something I can be doing in here to help?"

She motioned toward the counter where Amber had been working. "If you really want to help, you could clean that area."

"I'm on it," he said cheerfully, turning on the hot water and reaching for a clean kitchen towel and the bottle of disinfectant by the sink.

She turned toward the swinging door into the shop, then paused with the door half open, looking back at him. "You were starting to say something when we were interrupted?"

He was already scrubbing at scattered spots of blood. "Later. You'd better tend to your customers now."

She carried Charlotte out of the kitchen, letting the door swing shut behind them.

Fortunately for Elle's composure, if not for her profits, business was slow for the next hour, easy enough for her to handle on her own, especially with Shane's surprisingly efficient assistance. She didn't bother calling Kristen, figuring her partner would prefer not to work on her day off.

Two young couples entered together with a jingle of the door bells shortly before closing time. They dawdled awhile over their menu choices while Elle waited patiently with her hand hovering over the register. She heard Charlotte laughing and glanced toward the play corral. Shane was making silly faces at the child while he refilled clearly marked coffee station carafes with cream and skim milk from the kitchen. Charlotte followed his every move with obvious fascination. It was clear she'd fallen hard for her new friend Shane, which made Elle bite her lip for a moment before forcing a smile as her customers finally decided what they wanted.

Maybe Charlotte was too young to have her heart broken by a charming stranger who'd disappear from her life as quickly and unexpectedly as he'd appeared, but Elle wasn't quite as resilient. She rather envied her daughter's open, trusting nature, and the two-year-old's ability to savor the moment and Shane's attention, unencumbered by worry about the future. It bothered Elle to think that she couldn't at least enjoy an attractive man's company, even if only temporary, without questioning his every action.

The group of four didn't linger over their drinks and snacks. Tidily bussing their own table, they left with smiles and waves. Elle wiped down the table, taking the opportunity to relax and just breathe for a few blessed minutes, then turned to move behind the counter again.

Shane stood in the kitchen doorway, his shoulder braced against the jamb as he watched her stow away the cleaning cloth. "Eventful day, huh?"

"A long one so far," she agreed with a tired smile. "I hate that Amber cut herself. She downplayed it, but I know it must have hurt like crazy."

"I'm sure it did. But it should heal quickly now that she's having it tended to."

Elle reached into the play corral to pick up Charlotte and give her a little snuggle, making the child giggle. Holding her daughter on one hip, she tilted her head toward Shane then. "You seemed very comfortable handling all that blood and panic. You calmed everyone down and assessed the wound very quickly. I was impressed. Did you ever consider going into a medical career after your military service?"

He looked down to adjust the rolled-up sleeve of the pale blue shirt he wore with dark jeans. She wondered if he was avoiding her eyes when he replied lightly. "Yeah, that was one of the options I considered when I went in, but after Dad died, my uncle really needed my help to keep the family business going. I don't regret my choice," he concluded as he'd assured her once before.

Didn't he? As she had the last time, she couldn't help wondering if this had been the career he'd wanted. She'd bet he'd have made a wonderful doctor. He was certainly still young enough to attend medical school. Had he put aside a lifelong dream because of his family obligations? "How many employees does your company have?"

"Six, not counting my uncle and me. Two have been there since Dad and Uncle Raymond started the company almost twenty-five years ago."

She suspected from his tone that he felt almost as strong an obligation to those employees as to his family. She hoped they all appreciated Shane's efforts on their behalf.

"My cousin, Parker, works with us, too," he added. "She handles social media and most of our correspondence. She's really good at that. She also teaches dance—tap, ballet, jazz, that sort of thing—to kids, though she's been on maternity leave for the past few months."

"She's a dancer? Is she good?"

He nodded. "She could have danced professionally, but she chose to teach, instead. She wants to open her own studio eventually."

"Quite an ambition. You said she's been on maternity leave?"

"Yeah, though she's about ready to get back to

it. Their little boy, Aubrey, is six months old. Everyone says he looks just like me at that age. Not to brag, but he's cute as a floppy-eared puppy."

She laughed softly. "You sound more like a proud uncle than a cousin."

"I, uh—yeah." Shane pushed a hand through his hair, his expression suddenly hard to read. "Parker and I were raised almost like siblings, so I feel that way about her. What do you need me to do now?"

"You can keep an eye on the counter while I finish up in the kitchen, if you like. Just let me know if someone comes in and I'll come back out."

"You got it, boss."

Grinning at his teasing, she pushed through the kitchen door.

Her mother called shortly afterward to let her know that following a long wait to be seen by a doctor, Amber had been stitched up and cleared for duty. Elle told her mom there was no need for either of them to come back in today. She advised her mother to take Amber home, saying she could easily close up on her own.

"Is Shane still there?" her mom asked in an exaggeratedly nonchalant tone.

"He's still here. He's been very helpful."

"Such a nice man," her mother said with an appreciative sigh.

"Mom…"

"Just saying, Elle."

Shaking her head, Elle disconnected the call.

The final patron was one of her regulars, an older man who stopped by every Saturday just before closing. Elle always sold him a few of the leftover pastries from the day at a discount price, and he carted them out happily in a paper bag after lingering for a few minutes of humorously outrageous flirting.

"New employee?" he demanded, looking Shane up and down while Elle wrapped up three doughnuts and an éclair for him.

She smiled and moved to the register. "No, just a friend who's helping out. Bo, this is Shane Scanlon. Shane, Bo Meadows."

"Hmmph." Bo beetled his thick white brows at the younger man. "Just so you know, this one's spoken for. I'm going to marry her soon as she gets old enough."

Shane grinned. "Can't fault your taste."

"Darn straight." Bo winked at Elle as he paid for his order, then blew her a noisy kiss from the door when he exited, making her laugh.

"Quite a character," Shane commented.

"Yes, he is. He's also offered to marry my mother. And to adopt Amber. He's fickle."

Shane's smile faded as he glanced toward the play corral where Charlotte was doing a little dance to the music of a wind-up toy. "So, do you think you will ever remarry?"

The question took her aback, especially on the heels of her recent doubts about his reasons for hanging around.

"Not Bo, of course—unless he's your type," he added with a lame attempt to turn the query into a joke when she shot him a startled look.

She thought about giving him only a joking reply, but decided to answer candidly. He should know right up front that she looked out for herself. "My divorce left me pretty gun-shy. I'm not looking to get seriously involved with anyone again. I'm content with my life as it is now. I'm not opposed to having fun on an informal basis when there's a mutual attraction. My only requirement is that anyone I spend time with has to be completely honest with me. No hidden agendas. No passive-aggressive mind games."

His eyebrows rose. "Um—"

A little embarrassed now, she shook her head with a sheepish laugh. "I know. Too much information. Like I said, gun-shy."

She thought about turning the tables, asking if he'd ever gotten close to marriage himself, but decided this was neither the time nor place. He already looked a bit bemused by the vehemence of her reply to what he'd probably intended as merely an idle question in response to Bo's teasing. So maybe she'd made a bit of a fool of herself—but it was just as well that she'd gotten all this out in the open, anyway. If there was any chance of something developing between her and Shane, whether temporary or potentially more, she had to be up front about her expectations. No lies. No games. And no empty promises.

That was all she asked.

"I think I'll go ahead and close up," she said, turning toward the door. "I don't expect any more customers in the next five minutes. There's no need for you to hang around while I put things away and lock up. Charlotte and I can handle it from here."

He reached down to pat Charlotte's head, making her bounce enthusiastically again. "You're sure?"

"I'm sure. Thank you for all your help today, Shane. It was very kind of you."

"My pleasure."

He hesitated, his serious expression making her think there was something more he wanted to say, but then he gave Charlotte one final pat and took a step back. "I'm heading back home to Fayetteville today, but I'll probably be back in town soon for some follow-up meetings. Tell your mom I enjoyed meeting her, will you? And my thanks to both of you for making me feel welcome in town."

Elle bit her lip, her steps faltering in response to his unexpected announcement. There was no reason at all for her to be disappointed that Shane was leaving town, especially after she'd just fretted that he was showing up too frequently. She'd known from the start that he was only a visitor to Shorty's Landing, likely just filling spare time with her and her family.

Maybe he'd stop in for coffee and doughnuts the next time he passed through town, but that would probably be the extent of their interactions, and she was fine with that. Right?

"Have a safe drive home," was all she said.

Their eyes met and held, and then Shane's gaze lowered slowly to her mouth. Was he thinking he'd like to kiss her goodbye? Or was she merely projecting her own secret wish?

His phone rang, jarring in the stillness of the closed shop.

Drawn abruptly out of a fleeting fantasy, Elle blinked and looked away from Shane as he pulled his phone from his pocket and checked the screen.

"I should go," he said. "I'll answer this outside."

"Okay. See you, Shane."

"See you, Elle."

He was already lifting the phone to his ear when he opened the door. He left without looking back. She suspected he knew she watched him as he walked out.

"Did I hear you making a date?"

Elle jumped, putting a hand to her chest as she turned toward the kitchen door through which her mother had just entered. She hadn't heard her mom come into the shop, so had been unaware she and Shane had been overheard as they'd exchanged goodbyes. Her mom didn't even look embarrassed to admit to snooping, Elle thought with a slight shake of her head.

"No, we weren't making a date. Shane's leaving town this afternoon."

"Oh." Her mom made no attempt to hide her disappointment. "When you both said, 'See you,' I thought…"

"Just a figure of speech, Mom."

"I bet he wants to ask you out. Maybe he just didn't want to do it here in the shop."

Elle didn't want to talk about this now. Certainly not here. "Give it a rest, okay? It's been a very long day."

"Fine," her mother replied with a little huff. "Just give him a chance if he does call, will you?"

Elle turned toward the kitchen without responding to that. "I'm going to take care of a few things in the kitchen for tomorrow. You and Charlotte can head on home, if you want. I won't be much longer."

"Of course." Though her tone was thoughtful, Janet reached out to pick up the toddler, whose eager expression proved she knew they were getting ready to leave for the day.

As far as Elle was concerned, it was time to put Shane Scanlon out of her mind and get back to her own happy life.

ELLE'S MOTHER HAD just left with Charlotte when Elle heard someone moving around in the kitchen. She paused in the process of sweeping the floor in the front of the shop, her head cocked as she listened for another sound. Her mom was usually obsessive about locking the back door when she left Elle alone here. Had she returned for some reason?

"Hello?" she called out.

Kristen stepped out of the kitchen with an apologetic look. "Sorry, Elle, I didn't mean to startle you. I was just going to let you know I'm here."

Elle's grip on the broom relaxed. "I wasn't expecting you this afternoon."

"I know. I was just passing by on the way home from an appointment. I saw you in here through the window, so I thought I'd stop in to see if you need help. I heard about Amber, by the way. She called me to double-check her hours for tomorrow and she told me about her accident. She said it isn't painful and it won't interfere with her work."

"Yes, she'll be fine, thank goodness. She just needed a couple of stitches to close the wound.

And I'm pretty much done for the day. Everything's prepped for you to open in the morning."

Kristen pushed her fair hair out of her face and studied Elle closely. "So, want to tell me about the guy you went to the concert with last night?"

Elle supposed she shouldn't be surprised that Kristen had already heard about that. Gossip raced swiftly through their circle of mutual friends. "Okay, what did you hear?"

"That he's cute, seemed friendly and couldn't take his eyes off you. How come I'm hearing about him through other people and not you, hmm?"

Hearing a hint of hurt feelings in the question, Elle answered quickly, deliberately downplaying the report. "Because there wasn't anything to tell. He's just a guy who was in town for business. Came into the shop for coffee and doughnuts on Wednesday and he's been back every day since. We ran into him at the festival and he hung around to attend the concert with me, probably because he didn't have anything better to do on a Friday night in a strange town."

"And what are his plans for Saturday night?"

"I have no idea. He's leaving town today."

"Going to see him again?"

"Only if he's in town on business again and in the mood for coffee and doughnuts." Elle put away the broom and dustpan, then brushed off her hands and turned to her partner. "I'm not keeping secrets from you, Kristen. There was nothing going on between me and Shane. I barely know the guy, for heaven's sake."

After a moment, Kristen sighed. "I sounded kind of cranky, didn't I?"

"Yeah, a little."

"I guess I sound that way a lot these days."

Elle decided she'd rather have her friend cranky than dispirited. "Don't worry about it. Everyone feels that way after a bad breakup. You remember what a pain I was during the divorce, right? And you were always there for me. I'm here for you, too. Whatever you need, okay?"

"Thanks, Elle. I just...I just miss Casey, you know?"

"I know." Remembering her own dark days, Elle bit her lip in sympathy. She'd found solace in the work she loved, her devoted mother and her supportive friends. And then Charlotte had come along to make her already blessed life feel complete. She was both content and fulfilled being a single, working mom. She wished Kristen could soon find a way to get to that stage in her own recovery. "What can I do?"

"Nothing," Kristen said with a shrug. "I'll have to get through this on my own. But thank you. I know you're here for me."

"Absolutely. Are you sure you don't need some

time off? I can work tomorrow, if you want. The next three days, for that matter. You can spend a few days just being self-indulgent. Maybe make an appointment with a counselor who deals with the grief of a break-up. At least take a spa day."

Kristen shook her head. "No. I might as well work. I know you want to spend time with Charlotte. I'll call if I need you."

"Promise?"

Making a show of crossing her heart, Kristen nodded. "Promise."

Elle wasn't entirely reassured, but she accepted that Kristen should know what she needed. "Okay. Well, I'm finished here for the day. We could hang out for a couple hours if you like. Maybe check out Lori's new shipment of Christmas decorations we could use here in the shop? Or Barb's having a one-day sale at the boutique. Maybe she has some cute things left?"

"Thanks, but I think I'll just head on home. I'm sort of tired, and not in the mood to think about the holidays just yet. If you see any decorations you like for the shop, just get them, okay? I'm sure I'll like them, too."

Elle rubbed her aching temples as she unlocked her car door and climbed behind the steering wheel a short while later. She didn't know if her headache was due more to her worry about her partner or her complicated feelings about whether Shane Scanlon would saunter into her shop again. She suspected her heart would trip again if she looked up to see him there—and that anticipation alone was enough to make her worry that this particular man could be hazardous to the safe, even-keeled, comfortably predictable life she'd crafted for herself and her daughter. It didn't take her mother's imaginary "gifts" to make that prediction.

CHAPTER FIVE

AFTER PACKING AND checking out of his motel, Shane made the drive home to Fayetteville, arriving some four hours after he'd left Elle and Charlotte. He didn't even have a chance to stop by his place. He'd barely passed the city limit sign exiting Shorty's Landing when his uncle had called to say that Dottie had fallen and was being taken to an emergency room. Because he wanted to get there as quickly as safely possible to see her, Shane hadn't stopped for a break during the remainder of the drive.

Having stayed in touch with his family since that first call, he'd learned that Dottie had been brought back home after being checked out and released from the emergency room. He drove straight to his uncle's house, where Dottie now lived, needing to see for himself that she was okay before he headed to his own place for the night.

He would have to say goodbye to his beloved grandmother one day—but he wasn't ready to do so yet.

His uncle Raymond, a tall, distinguished-looking man in his early sixties with thin gray hair and kind blue eyes, met him just inside the door. "She's in the den. We got home about twenty minutes ago. I tried to get her to go to bed for a while, but she insisted she wanted to watch the game. I warn you, she's cranky."

Shane's smile was genuine, fueled by relief. "I'm glad to hear it. That must mean she's okay."

"She's fine, just shaken up. As were we all. There were no broken bones, though she has a mildly sprained ankle and some bruises. She's quite annoyed with us for making her go to the hospital when she told us all along she wasn't hurt."

"I don't care what she says. If she falls again, she goes right back for X-rays."

His uncle chuckled. "Absolutely. Even if I have to pick her up and carry her. Which I threatened to do this time, by the way."

Raymond motioned toward the den. "I'll let you say hello while I brew her some tea. You look tired, Shane. I'll make you a cup, too."

"Thanks, Raymond. I am a little tired." Between worrying about his grandmother and fretting about what, if anything, to tell the family about Charlotte, it had been a long drive. Not to mention his physical discomfort every time he thought about that frozen moment of parting from Elle, when he'd been sure that she was thinking of their kiss. Just as he'd been. He couldn't help wondering if she'd been even half as hungry for another, despite all the reasons against it.

Not that he would tell the family about any of that.

His grandmother was ensconced in her favorite chair, her tiny body wrapped in an afghan she'd crocheted several years earlier. Her attention was focused on the television screen on which the UNC Tar Heels were in a fierce competition for a win—Dottie was a fierce Tar Heels fan. The wheelchair she'd used grudgingly for the past few months sat beside her recliner.

She peered around when she heard him enter the room, looking irritated at the interruption. But then she recognized him and her frown changed to a semi-smile. "Shane! About time you got home, young man. I was beginning to wonder what was keeping you away."

"It's only been four days, Dottie," he said indulgently, leaning over to kiss her cheek. "And you knew I was on a business trip."

"You aren't riding that horrible motorcycle, I hope."

"No, ma'am," he said with a chuckle. "I brought my car."

"Good. You should sell that thing. I hate them, you know."

"You've made that perfectly clear."

"I missed you this week," she said, her tone softening.

"I missed you, too. What's this falling business?"

She sighed heavily. "I tripped when I bent down to pick up something I'd dropped, that's all. Lost my balance and fell with my leg twisted. No big deal. I knew I wasn't hurt more than a few bruises but Raymond had himself a hissy fit and called an ambulance before I could set myself right. Wouldn't do but for them to haul me up to the ER and work me over. I'm in a lot more pain from all that than from the fall."

"You have to be more careful, Dottie. Like Dad always said, the most precious treasures are the most fragile."

She patted his cheek with a hand that looked almost heartbreakingly frail, though he considered her one of the strongest, most resilient, most capable women he'd ever known. "Silly boy. You know full well I've never been the delicate-flower type, but both you and Charlie were always so sweet to me. Even when I was mad as a hornet at the two of you for some of the mischief you got into."

He chuckled, catching her fingers gently in his.

"As tiny as you've always been, you could still have us shaking in our boots when you got your mad on," he teased her.

"Not my Charlie," she murmured with a shake of her silver head. "He knew he could charm the mad out of me with a smile and an apology for whatever he'd done."

"You always said Charlie could smile the spots off a leopard."

Her laugh sounded wistful. "He could at that. I miss him so much, Shane. I miss all of them."

He stroked her hair, a lump in his throat. She looked tired. Dispirited by the events of the day. "I know you do, Dottie. I miss them, too."

She drew a deep breath and straightened her thin shoulders beneath the white afghan. Her voice was gruff when she spoke again, signaling that she was pushing the melancholy away. "You're interrupting my game, and it's a close one. Run and find out what's keeping your uncle with my tea, will you? He said he'd be right back with it."

"I'll check." He straightened and moved toward the door, where he paused to look back. His grandmother was focused fiercely on the television screen now, leaning forward a bit to watch the progress of a long punt.

Thinking of her feeling sad and discouraged made his chest ache. He was tempted to tell her he'd found the great-granddaughter she'd mourned and fretted about since Brittany had taken off when the baby was only a few weeks old, almost immediately after Shane had been deployed. Perhaps Dottie would find encouragement in the news that Charlie's daughter was healthy, happy and loved. Or maybe she'd fret even more at the thought of Charlotte living only a few hours away and yet so separated from their family.

He'd started the search for his niece to satisfy his own need to reassure himself and to fulfill those solemn promises that rested so heavily on him. He realized now that he hadn't thought beyond locating her. Hadn't considered what he would say to her adoptive family, what he would tell his own. Whether any of them would truly be content just to know where she was without any further contact.

It wasn't like him to be so unprepared. Had he become so distracted by everything else going on in his life that he'd dropped the ball? Or had he subconsciously thought that just the act of locating the child would be enough?

He hadn't expected to take one look at the child and see Charlie's eyes looking back at him. Hadn't anticipated that she'd steal his heart with only a smile, that she'd wrap him around her little finger by saying his name with such delight.

Most of all, he hadn't predicted his sledgehammerto-the-chest reaction when Charlotte's captivating adoptive mother had impulsively kissed him in his shadowed car. Definitely a complication he'd neither anticipated nor needed.

Would he ever spend time with either of them again? Should he take that risk—or tell himself he'd accomplished his mission and now needed to focus on all his many other responsibilities?

His uncle was on his phone when Shane entered the kitchen. A teapot and cups sat on a tray in front of him, alongside a plate and an unopened bag of Dottie's favorite cookies. Shane entered the room just in time to hear his uncle say into the phone, "Yes, I'll tell him, Parker. I'm sure he'll be happy to stop by your place after he leaves here. He'll look at it for you and give you some advice."

Shane had no doubt he was the person his uncle referred to. Apparently he would be heading to his cousin's house after he left here, though he hadn't even made it to his own home yet. He wasn't sure what he'd be looking at; whatever it was, he was obviously supposed to know what to do about it.

Somehow during the past few trying years, he'd become the one in the family who was expected to have all the answers, even when he didn't yet know the questions. He couldn't explain exactly how that had come about—whether he'd subconsciously stepped in to fill the voids left by the deaths of his father and brother, or whether the family had nominated him for the role—but here he was. And it galled him deeply that he was so uncertain about what his next move should be.

ELLE HAD JUST refilled the coffee carafes after the Wednesday breakfast rush when her mother beckoned her to the shop telephone. "It's Shane," her mom reported smugly, her face wreathed in a broad smile. "I told you he would call today!"

Because her mom had been "predicting" that call every day of the almost two weeks that had passed since Shane left town, Elle wasn't particularly impressed. Still, she couldn't deny that her heart rate increased as she moved toward the office to take the call, leaving her mother to watch the counter and Charlotte while Amber worked the kitchen.

"I hope this isn't a bad time," Shane said when she spoke into the business phone. "Janet said the shop isn't very busy, but I wouldn't want to interrupt your work, but I realized I didn't have your home or cell number."

Her mother would have summoned her to the phone for this call even if a line of customers stretched out the door and down the street, Elle thought wryly. "No, it's okay. How are you, Shane?"

"I'm well, thanks. And you?"

"Fine, thank you."

As proper and formal as they were being, she was still aware of a more personal undertone to the conversation. She could tell herself repeatedly that Shane was nothing more than a friendly customer who'd drifted through her life—and she *had* repeated that caveat to herself at least a half dozen times a day since he'd left when he'd drifted unbidden into her thoughts. Yet she still all too clearly remembered the taste of his lips. The feel of his strong arms around her.

"How's Charlotte?"

Forcing herself to keep her tone relaxed, she replied. "She found one of Mom's red lipsticks yesterday. Painted her whole face before Mom could grab it back. She looked like a baby Bozo."

Shane's deep chuckle reverberated through the line, and she could almost believe that a ripple of feminine response coursed through her hand that held the phone. "I hope you got a picture of that."

"Oh, I did. I'm hanging on to it for future blackmail."

He laughed again. "Never a dull moment with a toddler, huh?"

"You can say that again."

"So, I guess you're wondering why I called."

She'd figured it hadn't been just to hear her voice. She felt her muscles tense as she asked, "What can I do for you, Shane?"

"My company got the Wind Shadow account.

All the contracts have been drawn up and signed, so it's official."

"Congratulations. I'm sure you'll enjoy working with Trevor."

"No doubt."

"So, your visit here was quite successful, wasn't it?"

"Yes, it was."

She thought he'd hesitated a beat before he answered, though maybe she'd imagined it. "Your uncle must have been very pleased."

"Oh, he is—though he's the type that always wants to know when we'll be getting the next account."

"The hard-to-satisfy type?"

"Not really. He's just like a sports fan, always eager for the next win."

And Shane was apparently committed to providing those victories for his uncle's sake. For his family's sake, she mused. Did he find as much personal satisfaction in the challenges?

"Anyway, the reason I called. Trevor is having some sort of social bash at the resort Saturday."

"The Lighting Gala," she clarified, guessing where this was leading. "He hosts it every year before Thanksgiving. It's his way of unveiling the resort's holiday decorations while raising money for several South Carolina veterans' and children's charities."

"Have you ever attended?"

"It's been a few years," she admitted, thinking back. Last year she'd been busy with Charlotte and with work, her mother having contracted a bad cold just before Thanksgiving. The year before that had been not long after she and Glenn had split up, leaving her in no mood for a fancy party. Had she and Glenn attended the prior year? She couldn't remember.

She heard Shane clear his throat before saying, "I was wondering if you'd like to go as my guest. If you're free, that is. I know it's sort of short notice, but I've only just gotten the invitation."

She couldn't help smiling weakly, even as her fingers tightened on the receiver. She wasn't sure she'd had such an awkward date invitation since high school. But then, she hadn't reacted to an invitation quite so nervously since then, either.

She moistened her lips, trying to decide what to say. No need to ask her mom's advice, of course. No doubt her mom would be happy to babysit. So, really, there was no reason not to go. None that came to her, anyway.

Telling herself to get a grip, she said, "That sounds nice. I'd be happy to accompany you."

It would, after all, be a good professional networking opportunity for her. Quite a few business owners, particularly in the tourist industry, would be in attendance, and it never hurt to keep The Perkery on their radar.

Yeah. Keep telling yourself that, Elle.

"Great." He sounded genuinely pleased, which somewhat eased her second-guessing. "So, I'll pick you up at your house?"

"Sure." She gave him her cell number so he could contact her if needed, and he returned the courtesy. And then, telling her he didn't want to keep her from her work any longer, he disconnected with a, "See you Saturday, Elle."

She set down the phone, then lingered a moment to file a few invoices before returning to the counter. She knew she was procrastinating, putting off for a bit longer the moment when she'd have to explain to her mother why Shane had called. Her mom would be downright giddy that Shane had invited Elle to the gala. Not to mention she'd probably go into "psychic mode" again and brag about having known all along he would call.

Unable to put off her responsibilities any longer, she drew a deep breath and moved toward the door. Perhaps she'd pop into her friend Barb's boutique on her way home from the shop this afternoon. It wouldn't hurt to buy a new dress— for the networking opportunity, of course, she assured herself hastily.

Even as he disconnected the call to Elle, Shane wasn't sure inviting her to the gala had been wise. Spending more time with her without telling her everything seemed like a recipe for a potential fiasco.

He pushed aside a stack of contracts demanding his attention on the desk in his office, turning his chair to stare out the window at his not-particularly-inspiring view of other office buildings. He'd spent most of the morning trying to focus on work while debating making that call, until he'd finally given in to overwhelming impulse and picked up the phone.

Hearing Elle's voice had sent a charge through him that let him know his attraction to her hadn't waned in the weeks since he'd left her. Just hearing a hint of her musical laugh in her tone when she'd shared the amusing story had left him half-aroused, restless in his desk chair. Which made him even less certain that he'd made the right call to ask her to join him at the gala.

In trying to analyze his own actions, he'd come up with several excuses. Elle knew quite a few of the local business leaders, so she could introduce him to some of them. He wasn't crazy about social events, so it would be nice to have another familiar face among the crowd of strangers. It was a way to subtly check on Charlotte again, maybe work a few more questions about her into their conversations. Maybe he could even find a good time to tell Elle who he really was.

All good reasons. None of them the full story. He wanted to see Elle again for reasons that seemed to have little to do with any of those logical justifications. He'd thought of her entirely too often during these passing days, caught himself on too many occasions imagining what it would be like if they'd met without any obstacles between them. Remembering the taste and feel of her—and allowing himself to carry those memories into daydreams that had left him uncomfortable and grouchy. Only to find himself fantasizing again a few hours later...

Which was exactly why he should have taken his uncle with him to the gala and stayed far away from the alluring Elle O'Meara, he told himself with a hard shake of his head. He spun the chair and reached again for the contracts, telling himself he would waste no more time on pointless daydreams. Knowing even as he made the resolution that it wouldn't be long before he'd break it.

ELLE STEPPED OUT of her house and closed the door behind her before Shane had a chance to ring the bell Saturday evening. He looked a little startled as he dropped his hand and moved back from the door.

Had he really gotten even better-looking since the last time she'd seen him? Or had she merely tried to convince herself during the past two weeks that she'd only imagined how attractive he was?

"I didn't want Charlotte to see you," she explained in case he wondered why she'd been watching at the window for his arrival. "She's playing happily in her room with Mom and a set of building blocks right now, but if she saw you, she'd want you to stay and play with her. It's almost her bedtime, so I don't want to get her stirred up and then leave."

"I'd be sorely tempted to stay and play with blocks rather than to attend this gala thing," Shane admitted. "I'm not very good at these events."

She smiled. "I find that hard to believe."

"I'm sure having you there with me will make it much more pleasant. You look very nice tonight."

She glanced automatically down at the cranberry-colored dress she'd bought from the boutique, worn with a pair of blessedly comfortable black heels she'd owned for much longer. A lightweight black coat was sufficient for the weather, clear and cool with a predicted low in the midfifties. She'd fussed a bit more with her appearance than usual, and she couldn't help but be pleased that he'd noticed. "Thank you. So do you."

This was the first time she'd seen him in a suit.
He wore it well. The dark blue jacket and crisp
white shirt looked good with his coloring, and she
appreciated the touch of individuality in his jewel-
tone tie. Still, she missed the black leather jacket,
she thought with a stifled smile as he opened the
car door for her.

"Did you drive down today?" she asked when
they were on the road toward the resort.

"Yes. I had a meeting in Fayetteville this morning, so I just had time to make the drive, check
into my room and change before coming to get
you."

She smiled in sympathy. "Busy day. Are you
staying in the same place as last time?"

"No. Trevor provided a suite at the resort for
me for tonight. Gotta admit, it's fancier digs than
I'm used to. A hell of a lot nicer than a mom-and-
pop motel or an army cot. Maybe even a little
plusher than my apartment in Fayetteville. I don't
have a chandelier in my bathroom at home."

She laughed. "I've never been in one of those
suites, but I've heard they're beautiful."

"You've heard correctly."

Frowning a little, she thought of how tired he
must be already, having worked that morning before making such a long drive to the resort. "You
didn't have to come get me and then take me

home and drive back to the resort later. I assumed you were staying in Shorty's Landing again. I could have met you at the gala and then driven myself home afterward."

He shrugged. "I don't mind driving. Gives us a little extra time to talk. So, how was your day? You had the shop today, didn't you?"

"Yes. And it was busy. Which is always good, of course, except that I was a bit short-handed this afternoon."

"Oh?"

"Charlotte was invited to a birthday party for one of her playdate friends," she explained. "Mom took her and said Charlotte had a great time. Amber and I had to scramble a bit on our own because we were busier than usual for a Saturday afternoon, but we managed."

Late Saturday shifts were usually easily handled by two, but a large group of college students had stopped by unexpectedly for coffee and some sort of social planning meeting, surrounding the tables and flooding the shop with chatter and laughter. Elle had been aware of a familiar, bittersweet dichotomy of loving where she was and wishing she could be someplace else at the same time—with her daughter at the party.

"So Charlotte has friends."

Her left eyebrow rose as she swiveled her head

to look at Shane's profile. What a strange comment! "Of course she has friends. Why wouldn't she?"

"Well…you both seem to spend a lot of time at the shop," he said a bit lamely.

"I'm at the shop four days a week on average, though on rare occasions I have to pop in during the other three days. I'm in the kitchen by four thirty in the mornings and I usually leave no later than five in the afternoons. Mom brings Charlotte later and we all entertain her and keep an eye on her. I keep a crib in the office for her naps, so we can stick to a regular schedule. When the weather's nice, Mom takes Charlotte to the little park a couple blocks down from the shop for fresh air and exercise."

She forged on without giving him a chance to respond. "On the days I'm not working, I spend as much quality time as possible with Charlotte. We go on outings and picnics, meet other moms and kids for playdates, run errands together. We have dinner together every evening, and this is the first night since the Fall Festival that I won't be the one to bathe Charlotte, read her a story and tuck her in. As a working single mother, I do the best I can to give her a full, well-rounded life, and I think it's working out pretty damned well."

Shane didn't seem to take offense at her fiercer-than-she'd-intended tone. He merely glanced her way and murmured, "Seems that way."

It was probably best that he didn't try to justify his questioning. Only slightly mollified, she nodded. Maybe she'd overreacted a bit with her impassioned recital of her work-and-family schedule, but it had annoyed her that he'd even asked if her daughter had friends. She reminded herself that he had no children of his own, so probably couldn't understand quite how difficult it was to balance parenting and career. Besides, this wasn't the way she wanted the evening to start out.

"I'm sorry, Elle. I didn't mean to sound critical. I was being tactless."

Because she didn't want to be churlish, especially considering that he was probably more tired than he'd admitted, she nodded and redirected the conversation. "How is your family?"

He sounded grateful for the implied forgiveness when he replied. "They're all well, thanks. Though my grandmother fell the same day I left here last time. I'd just driven out of Shorty's Landing when I got the call."

"Oh, no. I hope she wasn't badly hurt."

"She was shaken up and sore for a few days, but she's doing much better now. Just scared us all."

"I'm sure. And I'm glad to hear she's okay. You said she helped raise you, didn't you?"

He nodded. "I don't remember my mother. Dottie stepped into that role. She was—and still is—amazing."

"Dottie?" she asked, wondering if that was really what he called his grandmother.

He chuckled. "Her name is Dorothy. My grandfather called her Dottie and Charlie picked up the nickname as soon as he could talk. He liked saying it better than Grandma. Because I pretty much copied everything my big brother did, she became Dottie to all of us."

"That's sweet." It was obvious he'd had a close family, despite—or perhaps as a response to—their losses. "I can tell you love her very much."

He nodded, but his expression was somber. "Her health is failing. We expect this to be our last holiday season with her, though of course we hope there will be more. Dottie loves Thanksgiving and Christmas, so my uncle and cousin and I want to make this year as special as we can for her."

The last of her irritation with him faded as he turned the car through the gates of Wind Shadow Resort. Maybe his seemingly judgmental questions had simply been badly phrased. Surely a man who loved his grandmother this much would realize that to Elle, as well, family always came first.

TYPICAL OF WHAT Elle knew of Trevor Farrell, the Lighting Gala was comfortable, low-key and welcoming, each attendee treated as a VIP by their charming host. Though the ballroom was festively decorated and the guests dressed in party clothes, the atmosphere was informal, with cheery musical performances, overflowing snack tables and easy laughter. The decor wasn't over-the-top Christmas, since it was still only mid-November, nor stereotypically wintry considering the temperate coastal setting. Instead, silver and glittering ocean-blue ornaments had been combined with multiple groupings of flickering flameless candles and torches as a nod to the rapidly approaching season.

Elle knew quite a few of the others in attendance, and she made a point to introduce Shane to as many people as possible, casually working in the name of his company to give him equal networking opportunity. Though Shane had claimed not to be good at small talk, he proved himself well versed in the skill, mingling easily among the guests, sharing funny quips, swapping service stories with fellow veterans. Elle couldn't help watching him surreptitiously, charmed by him all over again. And she was well aware she wasn't the only woman in the room who had this reaction.

"Hey, you two. Come join us."

The hearty invitation had come from a man Elle recognized as one of Trevor's closest friends, attorney Walt Becker. Walt was a frequent patron of Elle's shop and she had always liked him. He sat at a little table in an uncrowded corner of the ballroom beside an attractive woman with flame-red hair, dramatically highlighted features and a stunning figure shown to perfection by a short, body-hugging emerald slip dress. Maddie Zie-linski. Walt had brought her into The Perkery a few times to share his penchant for Elle's blue-berry muffins.

At first glance the stocky ex-marine sergeant and the unconventional public defender several years his junior seemed an unlikely match. Yet Elle had realized the first time Walt had brought Maddie into the shop for introductions that this couple was very much in love, despite their dif-ferences.

Carrying their champagne and snack plates to the table, Elle and Shane swapped greetings with the other couple. The women exchanged friendly hugs while the men shook hands, and then Walt introduced Shane to Maddie.

Walt waved them into chairs on the other side of the prettily decorated table. "You have to try these little pumpkin tart things," he told them, holding one up. "Man, oh, man, they're good."

Maddie laughed. "That's like his fifth one,"

she confided with a roll of her lively blue-green eyes. "I'm going to have to wheel him out of here if he keeps this up."

Walt chuckled, looking down at his stocky, but muscled form. "Last one, I promise. Probably."

Elle laughed and made a mental note to add pumpkin tarts to her fall recipes. Maybe with a little more cinnamon? she thought, taking an assessing bite.

"How's that sweet little girl of yours?" Walt asked her. "And your mother?"

She wiped her mouth and then reached for her champagne glass as she replied. "They're both well, thank you. I'm sure Mom would love to see you again soon."

She slanted a wry look at Shane. "Walt always lets Mom practice palm reading on him. I'm not sure she's ever gotten anything right, but she enjoys playing with him."

Walt grinned. "I've been tempted to let her practice on this one," he said, holding up his prosthetic left hand. "I'm not sure it would make much difference in her accuracy record. She's a sweetheart, though."

It had always struck Elle how unselfconscious Walt was about his partially missing arm. He'd told her he'd lost it to an explosive in a Middle Eastern war zone. She knew he was a tireless proponent of veterans' causes now, devoting many unpaid hours in his legal capacity to the cause. And she suspected he still carried many scars that weren't as apparent as that one. He was, as far as she was concerned, a true hero. She was honored to have met him and become friendly with him through his legal work for her.

Within a few minutes of conversation, she realized that Walt had much the same regard for Shane. "I mentioned that he was an army corpsman, didn't I?" Walt asked Maddie. "I've got nothing but respect for the medics serving in war zones. Let me tell you, it's a hard, brutal job, and I don't know if I could have done it. But I wouldn't be here today without a couple of brave corpsmen pulling me out under fire, so here's to you, pal."

Shane looked embarrassed as both Walt and Maddie lifted their glasses to him. Elle snatched up her own to add to the salute, touched by his faint blush. "To Shane."

"So, how long have you been out, Shane?" Maddie asked after lowering her glass.

"Just over a year."

"How's it been for you?" Walt asked and while his tone was easy, Elle noted he searched Shane's face rather closely. "Adjusting okay?"

She suspected Walt was fairly skilled at spotting signs of postwar stress, since he spent so many hours volunteering with those affected. Had likely fought those battles himself in his months of recuperation, though he'd never spoken of it more than in passing to her.

To give him credit, Shane didn't brush off the question. He merely smiled at the older man with obvious respect and answered quietly, "For the most part. To be honest, I've been too busy with family matters since I got home to have much time to dwell on it. Which is probably a good thing."

"Being busy and making meaningful contributions are both good," Walt agreed, "but make sure you're paying attention to your own needs, too, my friend. Those demons can sneak up on you sometimes when you least expect them if you try too hard to ignore them."

"Thanks, Walt. I've got a good support system in my veteran uncle and a loosely connected group of vet friends. I appreciate the counsel, though."

"Yeah, well, you've got a couple new friends in Trevor and me. Keep that in mind, okay?"

"I will, thanks, Walt. And let me know when you hold another of your veterans' charity events. Scanlon Risk Management will be happy to contribute."

"Appreciate that."

Perhaps Maddie decided a change in conversation was in order. "Did Charlotte have a good time at Halloween, Elle? Do you have a picture of her in her costume? I'd love to see it. This was the first time I haven't been with my nephew, Simon, at Halloween," she added as Elle pulled out her phone. "They did a video chat with me from Seattle so I could see him in his superhero costume. He was so cute. I know he and my sister and brother-in-law are totally happy out there, but it's not quite the same as spending the special days together, you know?"

Elle heard Shane cough and thought he must have swallowed something the wrong way, but he merely shook his head when she glanced at him.

Maddie cooed appropriately over the photos of Charlotte and then turned to Walt after returning Elle's phone. "Okay," she said, distinct challenge in her tone. "Time to work off those tarts. Let's dance."

Walt groaned heartily. "Aw, Mads."

She stood and looked down at him with a lifted, perfectly arched brow. "You promised. And you don't want to break your promise, do you, Sarge?"

With a gusty sigh belied by his smile, he rose and took her hand. "Fine. The hoops you make me jump through just to keep you happy…"

Elle heard Maddie murmur something about keeping him happy, and noticed with a smile that Walt's steps were much lighter as he proceeded to the dance floor.

She glanced at Shane, then moistened her lips when she found him looking back at her.

"Would you like to dance, Elle?" he asked, motioning to the small dance floor. "I can't say I'm particularly good at it, but you shouldn't have to worry about broken toes."

She laughed and rested a hand on his arm, appreciating the vibrant strength she felt there. "I'd appreciate that. And yes, I'd love to dance."

A thrill of excitement rippled through her when Shane held out his arms to her on the dance floor. She stepped into them eagerly, resting her left hand on his shoulder as her right was swallowed in his bigger, stronger left hand. The music was a leisurely arrangement of one of her favorite soft pop songs, which made the moment all the better.

"I didn't realize there would be dancing when I invited you," he murmured, smiling down at her.

Could he feel her heart racing? She didn't care if he did. Why should she try to hide how much she enjoyed being this close to him?

Looking up at him through her lashes, she gave him a gentle smile. "Trevor likes to provide something for everyone at his parties. Food, entertainment and dancing."

He shifted her a bit closer. "The food is now my second favorite part of the evening," he murmured, those devastating dimples making an appearance.

"Charmer." The bedroom quality of her soft

laugh surprised even her as she heard it. His answering chuckle was a husky rumble that made her insides tighten.

How long had it been since she'd done this? Danced. Flirted. Seduced and been seduced in return? She couldn't even remember. Something about Shane's smile drove the memories straight from her mind.

As for what else she hadn't done in much too long…

She had to swallow a hum of appreciation when another dancing couple bumped into her and pushed her more fully against Shane's long, hard, oh-so-warm body.

Shane's gaze traveled slowly from her eyes to her slightly parted lips, then back up to meet hers again. She felt almost as if she'd been kissed. Which only made her hungry for the real thing.

It took her a moment to realize the music had ended. Shane brought her back to the present by releasing her hand and taking a step back. And then another step, as though he didn't quite trust himself to remain so close. Or was she merely projecting her own yearning?

"I need another drink," he said, his voice tight. "I think I saw some nonalcoholic cider being served on one of the tables. Want to try it?"

She wasn't at all thirsty, but she needed the distraction. "Sure. That sounds great."

Without touching her, he motioned for her to precede him. She left the dance floor with only one quick, wistful look over her shoulder.

"HAVE YOU HAD a good time?" Shane asked Elle as the event drew to a close.

"Very," she replied, holding her half-finished cider and trying not to read too much into the one cozy dance they'd shared. "How about you?"

"Surprisingly—yes."

She laughed. "Why the surprise?"

"Cocktail parties are typically stuffy and dull. Somehow Trevor's managed to make this one almost fun."

"I'll take that as a compliment." Balancing on his crutches, Trevor had still managed to seemingly materialize out of the crowd to stand in front of them, smiling. "But I'd take a wild guess that your lovely companion has a great deal to do with that."

"As Grandma O'Meara would've said, you're full of blarney, Trevor Farrell." Elle patted his arm before adding, "That's one of the things I've always liked about you."

He winked at her. "Your grandmother would not have been the first to accuse me of that."

"I have no doubt."

Shane cleared his throat and shifted his weight. "So, when is the big tree lighting?" he asked Trevor.

"Fifteen more minutes. I'm on my way to make the announcement now that everyone should be putting on their coats and getting ready to move the party out to lakeside."

"Sounds like fun."

"Here's hoping." Moving with admirable grace, Trevor disappeared into the crowd again as smoothly as he'd appeared.

"I wonder how much longer he'll have to use the crutches," Elle mused aloud.

"He told me he hopes to be off them in another week. Physical therapy for a few weeks more after that and then he should be pretty much back to the condition he was in before his accident."

She looked back at Shane with a slight shudder. "From what I've heard, it was a wonder he survived that accident. I hate motorcycles."

Shane shrugged. "They aren't so bad. Trevor said he was hit by a distracted driver. He was wearing safety gear, which probably kept him alive. Can't blame the bike for the actions of an idiot."

"Let me guess. You own a motorcycle."

His crooked smile did very specific things to her nerve endings. "I do," he confessed. "Don't often have a chance to ride, but I enjoy it when I do. And my grandmother hates it."

She shook her head. "Boys and their toys," she murmured.

Shane laughed and slung an arm around her shoulder, seemingly without stopping to think about the gesture. "We should claim our coats and get ready for this lighting thing."

The way heat flooded through her in response to his closeness, Elle wasn't sure she'd need a coat. Still, she forced a smile and turned with him to collect their things.

CHAPTER SIX

THE LIGHTING CEREMONY was as impressive as advertised, and even more dazzling than Elle remembered from previous years. Trevor made a brief speech about the upcoming holiday tourist season and the warm, friendly atmosphere waiting to welcome winter visitors to the South Carolina coast. He talked about the active duty service members who wouldn't be home with their families. And then he introduced a special veteran and honored guest—a double-limb amputee—to throw the switch on this year's holiday lights.

Soaring from a platform in the center of the man-made lake, the glittering tree appeared to float on the dark water. The lake reflected the hundreds of white lights covering the tree, looking almost as if the water itself had been filled with tiny bulbs. The audience oohed and aahed appropriately, then burst into applause when, moments after the tree lights came on, the entire resort came to life with lights strung from nearly every available surface. Palmettos and awnings, bushes and railings, walkways and doorways—

everywhere Elle looked she saw glittering pin-points of white light.

"Wow," Shane murmured, his head close to hers so she could hear him over the excited bab-bling surrounding them.

"No kidding." She noted the way the lights re-flected in his dark hair and deep blue eyes that looked almost black in the shadows, and she had to suppress a sigh of appreciation. "This reminds me, we should start decorating the shop this weekend. We usually put up a couple of strands of lights and a tabletop tree covered with seashell-themed ornaments. Nothing anywhere near this elaborate, of course."

He laughed at her ironic tone. "I'm sure it looks great. Not every place needs to go over-the-top, though I'll admit this looks amazing. I'm sure Trevor's decorations pull in quite a few winter guests."

"Oh, they do. His resort is almost always filled, no matter what the season. I'm sure his new prop-erties will be just as successful."

"I agree."

The guests who weren't staying at the resort were beginning to disperse toward the parking lots, though some hung around for drinks and dancing in the resort club.

"Would you like to listen to some music for a while?" Shane asked her. "I'd suggest a walk on the beach, but I'm not sure those shoes you're wearing are suited to sand."

"Definitely not. But I wouldn't mind an Irish coffee and some music." Her mom had texted her that Charlotte was tucked snugly into bed and all was well at home, so there was no need to hurry back. It was still quite early for a Saturday night out for most singles, she thought with a rueful smile, even if her own typical Saturday evening involved herbal tea and a good book.

Shane looked pleased that she wasn't in a hurry to end their evening. "Sounds good. I—"

He sighed when a muted buzz came from his pocket. "I'm sorry. It's probably my uncle. I have to answer," he said in apology, pulling out his phone to consult the caller ID. "It could be something with my grandmother."

"Look who you're talking to," she reminded him with a smile, tapping her own pocket. "Check on your family."

She turned away to give him some privacy, admiring the resort surroundings while he answered the call. "Hi, Raymond, what's up?"

After a moment, she heard him say, "The numbers are in my suite. Why don't I text them to you later this…Really? You need them now? But… Fine. I'll get them to you in a few minutes."

He shoved the phone back into his pocket as Elle turned back to him. "Do you mind if I run up to my suite before we have that coffee?" he asked. "It should just take me a couple of minutes to find the information my uncle thinks he must have immediately. I could meet you in the club after, or you could come up and see the place…?"

He added the latter option tentatively, as if unsure how she would respond to being invited up to his room, even for such an innocuous reason.

She smiled reassuringly. "I'll come up. As I said earlier, I've never seen the suites here. This gives me a chance to satisfy my curiosity."

It was no big deal, she reminded herself. It wasn't as if he'd invited her up for private drinks or…anything else.

The suite was as nice as she'd expected, with a sitting room, kitchenette with a seating bar and an ocean-view balcony accessible from both the sitting room and the bedroom. The bedroom door stood open, giving her a glimpse of the big bed already turned down for the night. She quickly averted her gaze and shoved her hands into her coat pockets.

Shane pulled out his laptop and a thick file folder, then called his uncle to relay the requested information. Elle motioned that she was moving out to the balcony to admire the view, both to give him privacy for his call and to give her a chance to cool her warm cheeks.

Pulling up her coat collar against the night air,

she walked around the bistro table and chairs to stand by the railing and look out over the resort. It was like a fairyland with all the white lights and swaying palmettos, ocean waves in the distance glinting beneath a sliver of moon. She saw people walking on the paths below, and heard faint strains of music coming from the direction of the lake, but for the most part the guest quarters area was quiet. Though the resort was advertised as a place for family vacations and weekend getaways, she could see why it was popular as a honeymoon destination. She couldn't imagine a more romantic setting.

"Great view, isn't it?"

She looked up in response to Shane's question as he moved beside her at the railing. "It's breathtaking."

"I spent a couple days with Trevor and his team at the new resort on the Texas Gulf Coast last weekend. It'll open in about six months, and it's every bit as nice as this one. The guy knows what he's doing. He said his family's been in the hospitality business for several generations, and that's pretty apparent in his resorts."

She was surprised, for some reason, to hear that Shane had been in Texas since she'd last seen him. She focused on the conversation, instead. "Trevor's accomplished a lot at such a young age. Not even forty yet. His family and financial

GINA WILKINS 141

partners helped him establish the resorts, but he's been responsible for making the business thrive. I don't doubt that the new resort in Texas and the one in the works in Florida will be equally profitable."

"Agreed. And Scanlon Risk Management will make sure he's covered all the bases as far as liability and insurance are concerned."

She laughed. "Smooth plug."

With a charmingly roguish grin, Shane replied, "Thanks. I thought so."

She turned to face him, leaning one arm against the railing as she grew serious again. "Trevor's not the only one who's been very successful in a short time. It sounds as though you've done quite a lot for your family business since you got out of the service."

He shrugged. "I've worked hard, but so has everyone else in the company. We're certainly not on a scale like this, but we're proud of what we've accomplished."

It seemed typical of him to brush off her praise. To smoothly shift "I" to "we." He appeared to be all about the family and the business, and not so much about himself. From what Elle had observed, she couldn't help wondering if maybe he went a bit too far in that direction. Was his whole life dedicated now to his family and his responsibilities? Did he ever just do what *he* wanted, pursuing goals and desires of his own?

"Trevor doesn't talk about himself or his family much," Shane commented, turning the topic away from himself again. "Other than mentioning his family's business background, he and I have mostly discussed his risk management needs. We've shared a little about our respective military experiences, but that's about it when it comes to our pasts. Still, he seems like a great guy. I like him."

She thought he studied her face as he made the light comment, and she remembered the way he'd watched when she and Trevor had flirted teasingly before the lighting ceremony. "He is a great guy," she agreed. "I wouldn't say I know him well, but we've been acquainted for several years. His late wife grew up in Shorty's Landing. She was a few years ahead of me in school, but I knew her a little and I always liked her."

"His...late wife?" This was obviously the first he'd heard of her.

Elle nodded somberly. "Her name was Lindsey. She died in a car accident, sadly while Trevor was deployed. He was in Kuwait, I think. A non-combat deployment, from what I heard. That would have been...nine? Ten years ago, maybe."

"Damn. I didn't know. That's rough." Shane

looked shaken. Perhaps this information reminded him of his own losses.

"It was so sad," she murmured, thinking of how shocked she'd been to hear the news. She'd been a starry-eyed college student, and the tragedy had haunted her.

"And Trevor's never remarried?"

"No. I know he's dated, but I guess he's been too wrapped up in his ambitious plans to focus on marrying again."

Elle could identify with that. And while her heart had been badly bruised by Glenn's betrayal, she doubted it had been as shattered as Trevor's must have been. Maybe he would meet someone else with whom to settle down and start a family now that he was accomplishing some of his career goals. She hoped he did find love again... but she had no aspirations toward him herself. As she'd said, Trevor was a nice guy. Just not the one for her.

She looked up at the only man who had made her pulse race in quite some time, and moistened her lips before saying quietly, "I've had a really nice time tonight, Shane. Thank you for inviting me."

"I was just going to thank you for coming with me. Having you there made the socializing much easier."

She wrinkled her nose. "After watching you

tonight, I don't believe you're nearly as bad at mingling as you think you are."

"I didn't say I was bad at it. Just that there are other things I'd rather be doing. Usually."

A strong gust of wind made the treetops around them sway and blew Elle's hair into her face. She reached up automatically to push it away. Shane lifted a hand to brush back a strand she'd missed over her eyes. His fingers lingered for a moment against her skin. Just long enough to unleash a cascade of tingles.

Their faces were suddenly close together. If he wanted to kiss her, she certainly wouldn't protest. It didn't hurt that the more she learned about him, the more time she spent with this nice, seemingly conscientious and caring man, the more she liked him. The more she admired him. And maybe that made her nervous—which wasn't necessarily a bad thing. She felt her lips curve into a soft smile of anticipation as she tilted her head, offering access.

Shane's hand froze against her face, and she could feel the sudden tension in his fingers. His eyes glittered in the shadows. Neither of them moved for several long, taut heartbeats. She waited, holding her breath. Already feeling him, tasting him against her lips. Her pulse already racing in reaction.

She realized that the whole evening had been

building toward this moment—or maybe since the morning he'd strolled into her shop with his leather jacket, tumbled hair and shallow dimples. All he had to do was lean a little…bit…closer.

Her eyelids were just beginning to grow heavy when he drew back, clearing his throat loudly enough to make her jump.

"It's getting late," he said gruffly. "I should probably take you home now."

Her eyes widened and she felt her heart drop with a thud when he turned away to hide his face from her. What the…?

Hadn't he said something about having coffee? Listening to music? But suddenly he was ready to take her home, just when everything had been getting so cozy between them?

"I have a little more work I have to do before I can sleep tonight," he said by way of apology. "Those figures my uncle wanted…it's something I need to tend to. You don't mind, do you?"

She drew a deep breath and straightened her shoulders. "Of course not." Her voice was a bit cooler than she'd intended, but she tried to mask her bewilderment with a smile. "You really should have let me bring my own car. Then you wouldn't have to take time out to drive me home before you get back to work."

"It's no trouble," he assured her, his tone almost formal now. "Do you have everything? Is there anything I can get for you before we go?"

"No, I'm ready." She moved past him into the suite, scooping up her purse as she passed the table where she'd dropped it earlier. She neither stopped nor looked back until she reached the door. Shane followed her silently.

She wasn't angry that he'd drawn away from her when she'd made it very clear he didn't have to. If he wasn't interested, so be it.

She certainly wasn't hurt. She didn't know him well enough for him to hurt her, she told herself.

Still, she had to admit, if only to herself, that she was utterly confused. She'd been looking straight into his eyes during that brief interlude, and she knew that he'd come close to kissing her. That he'd damned well wanted to kiss her. What she didn't understand was what had made him suddenly change his mind.

Her carefully composed exit was marred when the long strap of her bag caught on the doorknob as she walked past it. She hadn't had time to change bags when she'd dressed for the party earlier, and had settled for carrying the black leather crossbody she'd toted to work that day. The strap, which had already been showing signs of wear from heavy use, snapped when she tugged at it. The bag fell to the floor, its closure popping open as it landed. Her wallet, keys, a lip balm and one of Charlotte's toys spilled out at their feet with a clatter.

Embarrassed, she knelt with a swallowed grumble to scoop up her possessions. Shane bent at the same time to help. Their heads were close together when he handed her a bright pink plastic cell phone. "Your phone?"

She tried to chuckle, just to show him she was unfazed by that awkward scene on the balcony. She hoped the careless laugh sounded a bit more genuine than it felt. "That would be Charlotte's."

Their hands brushed when she took the toy. All too aware of that point of contact, she moistened her lips. As if drawn by the movement, his gaze lowered to her mouth. Held for a moment. And then he straightened and reached down to help her to her feet.

Holding the bag with its dangling handle tightly, she straightened on her own, pretending not to see his hand. Still, she was close enough now to spot the interesting specks of gray in his dark blue eyes. The slight indention of the dimples that deepened when he smiled, though he wasn't smiling now.

Shane cleared his throat. "At least we didn't bump heads," he murmured, his voice a sexy rumble that vibrated through her. "I try to avoid slapstick when possible."

She managed another smile and turned again

to walk out, clutching both her broken bag and her dented dignity in a tight grip.

It was going to be a long ride home.

SHANE HAD JUST driven out of the resort parking lot and headed for Elle's house when her phone beeped with a text. She checked the screen, then gave a little huff of annoyance after reading the words.

I'm sorry, I'm just not feeling it tomorrow. I think a migraine's coming on. Is your offer to fill in for a day still open?

"Everything okay?" Shane asked, glancing away from the road for a moment to look at her face in the glow of her phone screen.

She sighed as she tapped in a reply. "It's Kristen, my business partner. She's taking the day off tomorrow and wants me to fill in."

"Wow. Short notice, huh? Don't you have to be there before daybreak?"

She nodded. "I'm usually in the kitchen by four thirty. At least when I left today I had a lot of prep work done for her for tomorrow."

"Does she do this sort of thing often?"

"No, never. She'd just been going through a rough time lately after a bad breakup. Normally she's bubbly and cheerful and utterly dependable."

Though those words described her partner less and less lately, she thought with a swallow.

"I'm sorry to hear that. Breakups can be hard to get past."

"Tell me about it," she muttered, then glanced at him with a curiosity she couldn't quite mask. "What about you, Shane? You're not involved with anyone now, right?"

Was that the reason he'd drawn away? Was there someone else? And if so, why had he asked her to the party—just for the networking assistance?

He shot her another look, and she thought she saw a slight reprimand in his expression. "No, there isn't anyone special in my life. I was seeing someone recently," he added, sounding a little reluctant, "but that ended when she decided my obligations to family and business didn't leave enough time for her."

"You don't exactly sound heartbroken about it."

He looked back at the road with a wry smile. "Truth is, I probably could have made it work if I'd tried a little harder. We just weren't a good fit. It was best to make that clear before anything too serious developed."

"Probably." She toyed absently with the broken strap of her purse as she asked, "She really resented your family obligations?"

He shrugged as he gazed at the road ahead.

"As I told you before, my grandmother is in poor health. I spend as much time with her as I can. She lives with my uncle, and even with the household help he employs, she keeps him hopping, so he needs an occasional break. Parker goes by when she can, but the baby keeps her busy, so I try to pitch in when I'm not too tied up with company business. The usual family-type stuff."

It sounded like more than the usual "stuff"—and also like Shane took his family responsibilities very seriously. Apparently he'd given up medical school and lost a girlfriend because of those obligations. Was he really as unperturbed about the sacrifices as he implied?

"Your partner—will she be okay?" he asked, seeming to grope for the right way to ask. "Her problems aren't affecting your business, are they?"

Elle supposed it was natural that he'd think of that, considering his career and the text she'd just answered. Maybe she hesitated a fraction too long before assuring him—and herself, "Everything's fine. She'll snap out of it soon."

He turned into her driveway and parked the car, though he didn't immediately shut off the engine. His hands on the steering wheel, he looked through the windshield. He'd parked beneath the security lamp at the corner of her drive, so there was enough light in the car for her to see his profile. He seemed lost in his thoughts. She wasn't sure he was even seeing her house in front of them.

She spoke tentatively when it felt as though the silence had stretched too long. "Um, so, thanks again, Shane. It was—"

As though he hadn't even heard her, he spoke at the same time. "Elle, there's something I need to tell you. I've been trying to figure out how to bring it up—or if I even should."

Growing more puzzled by the moment, she shifted in the passenger seat so she could see him better. She muttered in exasperation when her purse fell from her lap and onto the floor. Charlotte's toy tumbled out again with an incongruously merry jingle. Shaking her head, she bent to collect it. She was going to have to change purses tonight before she—

She froze in shock, her gaze caught by the photograph she'd just spotted beneath her seat. She glimpsed just enough of it to recognize the subject. She heard Shane mutter a curse as she made a grab for the photo and the folder it had slipped out of, pulling them out from under her seat to confirm her impression.

"Oh, crap, I forgot that was… Elle, I can explain."

Ignoring his words for the moment, she stared in mounting dismay at the image of herself and

Charlotte in the park. This snapshot hadn't been taken since she'd met Shane. She remembered the day in the photo. She and Charlotte had met a couple of other mothers and their toddlers for a park playdate on a Monday afternoon when Kristen was at the shop, freeing Elle for family time. That had been at least a week, if not more, before Shane had arrived.

Shane reached out as if to take the photo, but she jerked it back. She reached up to turn on the interior dome light, then opened the folder. Inside it, she found a second copy of the photograph and a sheet of paper on which was printed her name, her address—both home and business—her age, marital status, even her ex-husband's name. Charlotte's name appeared at the bottom of the page. Her full name. Charlotte Michelle O'Meara. Followed by her date of birth, the hospital in which she'd been born and her date of adoption.

Elle lifted her gaze very slowly to Shane, struggling to understand. Her insides were knotted now, her throat so tight it was all she could do to force out angry questions. "What the hell is this? Just who are you, Shane? And why have you been spying on me and my daughter?"

CHAPTER SEVEN

"YOU KNOW WHO I am." Twisting to face her, Shane spread his hands where Elle could see them, a gesture he probably intended as reassuring. "I haven't tried to deceive you, Elle. I just haven't told you everything. I was about to level with you when you—well, when you found that file."

Her initial stunned paralysis was swiftly simmering into outrage. Finding her own information on that page was bad enough, but seeing Charlotte's statistics spelled out so dispassionately made her blood boil. "You've been researching us? Stalking us?"

"I didn't take that photo," he denied quickly. "I hired a private investigator to find you."

Was that supposed to make her feel *better*? The thought of having someone digging into the intimate details of her life without her knowledge was enough to turn her stomach.

Why? The question reverberated desperately as she struggled to understand. Fear swirled beneath the anger, making her skin chill even as heat bubbled beneath it. Why had Shane—a man she'd met only weeks earlier—hired a private investigator to report on her? On her daughter? What did he want from them? Whatever it was, she would fight back if he proved to be a threat to her family.

She gripped the photos and information sheet tightly, refusing to leave them with Shane when she grabbed for the door handle. "Stay away from me and stay away from my daughter," she warned furiously. "If you come near us again, I'll call the police. I will file for a restraining order if necessary. Is that clear?"

He caught her arm to keep her from leaping out. "Elle, listen to me. I can explain."

She shook him off with a growl. "You invaded my privacy and you pretended to be a random customer. What makes you think I'd believe anything you tell me now?"

Wincing, he shook his head. "I haven't lied to you. I never will. The time just never seemed right to blurt out why I looked you up. If you'll just give me two minutes…"

She was torn between bolting from the car and staying back to demand answers. The latter won out, at least for the moment, though she kept her grip on the door handle. "Fine. You've got two minutes to talk me out of calling the cops the second I get inside."

He drew a deep breath, making an obvious effort to keep his tone even and unthreatening.

"I've told you how important family is to me. Perhaps you can understand how close I was with my brother, Charlie."

Her frown deepened. "I don't know what that has to do with—"

"I'm trying to tell you." Inhaling again, probably to hold on to his patience, he continued, "Charlie called me during his last deployment. Before we disconnected, he asked me to take care of the family if anything happened to him. Maybe he had a bad feeling, I don't know. Anyway, he made me promise to take care of Dottie and Dad, and to make sure his girlfriend had everything she needed. Most important, I promised him I'd always look out for the baby he and his girlfriend had learned about only days after Charlie left the country."

"The baby? I don't—" She stopped as the obvious explanation hit her. "Charlotte? You're talking about Charlotte?"

His gaze locked on her face, Shane nodded. "She's Charlie's daughter. She was born only a few months after he died in that helicopter crash."

Elle moistened her lips, struggling to process this new information. "You're absolutely sure she's the right child?"

"Yes. The investigator I hired finally located Brittany. Charlotte's biological mother. I tracked you down through her."

Remembering the questions Shane had asked about the adoption, Elle felt betrayed all over again at the realization that he'd already known the answers. He'd been playing her—or testing her in some way.

Resentment seethed in her. "She had no right to give you my information. We did an open adoption, but I haven't heard from her since it was finalized. She said she didn't want to be involved in Charlotte's future."

"And she still doesn't," he assured her. "Brittany has issues with responsibility and obligations. She's always been a rebel and a restless soul in search of the next party, but she tried to change when she and Charlie fell in love. The pregnancy was accidental. Neither of them were ready for that level of commitment. My brother thought he could help her deal with everything when he came back from his last mission. Of course, he never came back and that was too much for her to handle. After Charlotte was born, Brittany suffered from postpartum depression on top of her grief, and it was all more than she could handle. She knew she'd never be content to settle into the routines of parenthood, and she wanted more for her daughter than she felt able to give. She told me that's when she decided to put her up for adoption."

All Elle had been told was that Charlotte's biological mother had been single and unprepared for motherhood. Something in Elle's personal statement and video had convinced the woman that Elle was the best choice for Charlotte's new family. For that, Elle would always be grateful.

As she sat in unmoving silence, Shane continued, "Brittany has been estranged from her own relatives for years. My family reached out to her during her pregnancy, but she never really seemed to trust them. We would have done whatever we could to help her, to make it possible for her to raise Charlotte. Failing that, Parker and Adrian would have happily taken the baby, of course, and they'd have been great parents for her, despite Brittany's irrational wariness of them."

Elle instinctively shook her head, not wanting to hear that.

Shane didn't seem to notice. "The whole family was at the hospital the night Charlotte was born. Including me. I had to ship out just a couple of weeks after, but Brittany promised me before I left that she'd let them help her if she needed them. Everyone was devastated when Brittany dropped off the radar with Charlotte just after I shipped out, and we were even more disturbed when we found out she'd placed the baby for adoption."

He cleared his throat. "No one blamed me for leaving, of course," he said. The fervency of his

tone made Elle wonder if he still blamed himself.
"But Brittany and I always got along well. If I'd
had any idea…"

His voice trailed off, but it wasn't hard for Elle
to fill in the rest of that sentence. If he'd known
of Brittany's plans, he'd have found a way to stop
her. To make sure Charlotte stayed with his family. And whether he realized it or not, Shane felt
guilty for not having been here to ensure that outcome. What was he trying to accomplish? Just
how did he hope to assuage that guilt?

A shaft of fear shot through her, perhaps un-
warranted but agonizing, nonetheless. "You are
not taking my daughter," she said fiercely. "I have
a lawyer. I'll fight you tooth and—"

"Elle, stop." He caught her arm again, holding
her more firmly this time. "I would never try to
take Charlotte away from you, even if I could.
That's not why I'm here."

Drawing a breath, she eyed him suspiciously.
"The adoption was completely legal. My lawyer
made sure every *i* was dotted and every *t* was
crossed."

She saw no need to add just then that he'd just
spent time at a party with her very competent attorney.

"I don't doubt that. Brittany assured me she
worked with a legitimate adoption service. I

promised her, as I'm promising you, that I'll respect her wishes."

"Then why are you here?" she asked, still suspicious.

"I needed to see for myself that my niece is okay," he answered simply. "I needed to know Charlie's daughter has a good life."

His niece. Charlie's daughter. Just hearing the words brought a lump to Elle's throat.

For almost two years, she'd thought of Charlotte as her daughter. Only hers. Her mother was Charlotte's grandmother. The few extended relatives on Elle's maternal side with whom they gathered for holidays had accepted Charlotte as one of their own. Her paternal cousins in Georgia had thrown a baby shower for her, just as they had for the other relatives. It was a scattered family, certainly, but it was a supportive one. A happy one.

And now another family had popped up—people who shared Charlotte's genes and knew more about her heritage than Elle ever could. She couldn't even describe how that made her feel.

She hadn't been ready for this—not yet, anyway. She'd always thought when it happened—if it happened—she'd have had more time to prepare, for herself and her daughter. That Charlotte would have tracked them down, not the other way around. She did know how she felt about Shane hiding the reason he'd sought her out. Why he'd been so nice and attentive to her. That hurt. More than it should have, considering she thought she'd been so careful not to get too attached.

"Okay, fine," she said, avoiding his gaze as she clutched her bag more tightly and inched toward her door. "You've satisfied yourself that Charlotte is safe and loved. That she's happy. You can go home now and report to your family that all is well. And then you can stay the hell away from us."

Even though she wasn't looking directly at him, she was aware of his wince before he said, "I understand why you're angry, and you have every right to be. I handled this badly from the start. I should have sent a letter before I came, or at least told you who I was from the beginning. Since I arrived here, I let myself get distracted by—well, things I shouldn't have. I'm sorry."

She was far from mollified by his self-blame. "Yes, you should have told me. I still wouldn't have liked that you tracked me down the way you did, but I suppose I'd have understood. As soon as you'd satisfied your curiosity about Charlotte's welfare, it should have been my decision whether to let you meet her."

"I know. And even though you weren't aware of why I was here, I still appreciate the time I got to spend with Charlotte. She's a special kid. You're doing a great job with her."

Was he trying to soften her up with compliments? It wasn't going to work.

Elle tugged at the door handle to open the car door. "Goodbye, Shane."

She hadn't forgotten he was still holding her arm, but she thought he'd let go when she made it clear this conversation was over. Instead, his grip tightened as he spoke again in a low voice. "There's still one favor I'd like to ask of you before you go."

She shot him a look of disbelief. "Seriously?"

He nodded, his expression somber. "Just hear me out—and then take time to think about it before giving your answer, okay?"

As tempting as it was to run into her house before he could play her again, she had to ask, "What on earth do you want from me now?"

"I haven't yet told anyone in my family that I've found Charlotte. When I do tell them, I wish you would consider bringing her to see my grandmother, her great-grandmother."

"Are you—"

He rushed on, speaking over her. "I know what you'd probably like to say, but it would mean the world for Dottie—for my grandmother to see Charlie's daughter just once more before she dies. Her health is deteriorating. I mean, the whole family would love to meet Charlotte, but if you'd agree to just let my grandmother see her, I'd ask nothing more of you."

She stared at him. "You want me to bring Charlotte to North Carolina?"

"Yes. My grandmother isn't up to traveling, even for a three-hour drive, so I can't bring her here. I know that's a long trip for Charlotte, but maybe your mom could come along to help keep her entertained? I would pay any expenses, of course. Or I can drive while you and your mother sit back and enjoy the ride. Hell, I'll rent a limo if that would make it easier for you to accept."

She saw his throat work with a swallow, and heard the depth of emotion in his voice when he added quietly, "Dottie won't be with us much longer. It would make her so happy to see Charlotte."

"Don't do this, Shane," she asked in little more than a whisper. "That's not fair."

"I know," he replied candidly. "I'm putting you in a tough spot and I'm sorry. What would you do for your own grandmother? Your mother?"

Elle had been quite close to her maternal grandmother, who'd died only a few years ago. She couldn't help thinking of how much she'd have loved for her Meemaw to have met Charlotte.

Shane gave her a moment before speaking again. "I'm not asking for an answer now. I'm sure you need space to try to make sense of all this. Why don't I give you a call after you've had some time to think?"

She swiveled to slide out of the car, finally tugging free of his hand. "You can call."

She wasn't promising to answer when he did. She suspected he was aware of that, but she didn't give him a chance to say anything more. She shut the car door with a sharp snap and marched toward her house without looking back, the purse and the unsettling folder gripped tightly in hand.

She refused to admit exactly how close she was to tears.

"GOODNESS, ELLE, STOP PACING. You're wearing a path in the floor. Not to mention wearing yourself out."

In response to her mother's admonition, Elle paused in her restless rambling around the kitchen. She picked up the cup of tepid herbal tea she'd set on the counter earlier and took a sip, though she couldn't say she even tasted it. In the almost two hours that had passed since she'd jumped out of Shane's car, she'd hardly been able to sit, let alone relax. Hovering at the back of her mind the entire time had been the nagging echo of Shane's voice. *My niece. Charlie's daughter.*

Charlie Scanlon. Charlotte's late father, an honorable soldier, loving son, brother, grandson, nephew—a man Shane had described as beloved by everyone who knew him.

Charlotte had the right to know those things about the man she'd most likely been named after. She should know that her biological mother had done what she thought was best to provide a secure future for her child. Elle had always intended to be open and honest with her daughter, had planned to pass along the little information she had, but not like this.

As she'd acknowledged to Shane, for the first few months after Charlotte had come to her, Elle had gone through the typical adoptive parent's worries. Would the birth mother change her mind? Would a biological father show up demanding access to his child? Would Charlotte someday resent being adopted or have to deal with unexpected genetic medical issues? But as the months had passed and she and Charlotte had grown so close that it was hard to believe they hadn't always been together, those concerns had slipped to the back of her mind. At least until she'd seen that photo and investigator's report in Shane's car.

"Have you decided what you're going to say to Shane?"

Perching on a chair at the table next to her mother, Elle cradled her mug between her hands

and shook her head slowly. "No. I haven't even decided if I'm going to answer the phone," she admitted.

Though her mother's expression was sympathetic, her tone was firm when she admonished,
"Honey, you have to talk to him eventually. You
can't just pretend you never met him."

"I could try."

Her mom didn't smile. But then, it hadn't been
much of a joke. "I know you're annoyed with
him, but—"

"Annoyed with him?" Elle's fist bunched on
the table. "I'm furious! He deceived me from the
start! I let him hold my daughter, told him things
about our family under the mistaken impression
that he was simply a nice stranger who was…
well, who was attracted to me. Now I've found out
that it was all a lie. That he deliberately tracked
us down. And I still don't know exactly what he
wants from me. From us."

"Yes, I am aware that you hate falsehoods," her
mother murmured somberly. "And that you would
defend your child with your last breath. No one
who knows you doubts that."

"Don't try to tell me you weren't as stunned
by this as I was. Shane fooled you as much as he
did me about just accidentally wandering into the
shop and finding us at the festival."

Her mom didn't even try to fall back on her "psychic" act this time, for which Elle was deeply grateful. Instead, her mother merely nodded and said, "You're right, I had no idea. Yet, as far as I can tell, Shane never intended to lie to you. He was just waiting for the right time to give you all the facts."

Elle scowled. "The right time would have been the first day he walked into my shop. Before he insinuated himself into our lives."

Before they'd shared a kiss.

Even though she'd been the instigator of that kiss—especially because of that fact, perhaps—it ate at her that Shane had let her believe he was merely a good-looking visitor open to an innocuous dalliance. Now every time she had to deal with him, if she agreed to do so, they would both remember that she'd kissed him. Flirted with him. Her pride, just healing from the battering it had taken from her ex, stung with the memory.

Her mom, of course, didn't know about the kiss. Still, she validated Elle's resentment when she said, "He should have told you sooner. That was very wrong of him, and I hope he apologized properly."

Elle gazed down at her tea and shrugged. "He apologized. I wasn't impressed with his excuses."

"I don't blame you. You have every right to be furious. I'm angry with him, too. But—"

Elle looked up to ask sharply. "But what?"

Surely her softhearted mom wasn't going to suggest that Elle should simply get over what Shane had done.

But it wasn't Shane whose plight had caught her mother's sympathy. "The favor he asked you—to let his dying grandmother see Charlotte one more time. Are you considering it?"

Wincing, Elle gripped her mug again. "To be honest, I haven't thought about it much yet."

She'd been too caught up in her anger with Shane to give much consideration to the favor he'd had the nerve to ask. "I didn't give him a chance to elaborate, though he said he'd like to do so before he leaves."

"It sounds as though his grandmother is innocent in all of this. You said she doesn't even know Shane has found Charlotte. Maybe...well, maybe you should hear him out fully before you give your answer? And from what you've said, you should probably decide sooner rather than later. Not for Shane's sake, certainly, but for an old woman who has lost her grandson and would love to see his child."

Swallowing hard, Elle had to concede that her mother's point was well made. At least her mom wasn't trying to defend Shane's behavior, even though she knew her mom had been charmed by him. As had she.

"Fine," she murmured grudgingly. "I'll let him make his case. But I'm making no promises that I'll agree."

"That's fair. But then, you always are."

Elle wasn't so sure about that. When it came to her daughter, she wasn't certain she could be objective. But she had agreed to try—at least long enough to listen to what Shane had to say.

For the first time since she'd met him, she wasn't particularly looking forward to seeing Shane Scanlon again.

SHANE WASN'T SURE how he could have screwed this up any more than he had. Standing on the doorstep of Elle's house Sunday evening, he hesitated before knocking, not at all certain of his welcome.

After a long, restless night haunted by memories of the one kiss they'd exchanged, the slow dance they'd shared, the moment on the balcony when she'd made it clear she wanted to kiss him again, he'd spent several hours that morning trying to work in his suite at the resort and waiting for her to call. When she hadn't by midafternoon, he'd dialed her cell number and got her voice mail.

Had she been too busy at the shop to answer or had she deliberately chosen not to pick up? He still didn't know. He'd left a message telling her he hoped to hear from her again before he left the area that night. He'd almost given up hope when she'd finally called, just after she'd closed the shop for the day.

During that brief conversation, she'd agreed to let him explain himself to her and her mother, though she hadn't sounded particularly enthusiastic. She'd set a time for after dinner—after Charlotte's bedtime. It had been clear she was still as angry with him as she'd been when they parted last night. His apologies hadn't appeased her much. He'd tried to explain, but he'd made a mess of that, too.

He understood why she was so mad at him. They hadn't talked much about her divorce, but she'd told him just enough about her failed marriage that he knew it had left her with trust issues. She'd stated flat out that all she expected from her friends was honesty. She'd made it very clear that Charlotte was her number one priority—and that she was the one who'd make all decisions in that regard.

It had to have come as a shock to her, to say the least, to learn that a man she'd thought had come into her life by innocent coincidence had known who she was all along. A man she'd trusted enough to carry her daughter through the Halloween festival grounds, and to read picture books to Charlotte while Elle served customers. On top of all that, a man she'd liked well enough to share a memorable kiss. And from the very beginning

he'd concealed an investigator's file on her beneath the seat of his car.

Frankly, he wouldn't have blamed her if she'd
refused to ever see him again. Still, he hoped
she'd give him another chance.

Drawing a long, deep breath, he reached toward the doorbell, but once again the door opened
before he could ring.

"I just put Charlotte to bed," Elle said, moving
back to allow him to enter. "I don't want her to
know you're here. My mother's in the kitchen, but
she'll join us in the living room shortly."

As much as he'd have liked to see Charlotte, he
could understand why Elle had chosen not to let
him. Not tonight—not ever again if he couldn't
somehow smooth over his initial bad decisions.
She was the one in the right here, both legally
and morally—which only made him feel more
nervous about the upcoming conversation. "I appreciate you and your mother giving me a chance
to talk with you."

She looked at him without expression. "We'll
listen. I'm making no promises."

He pushed his hands in his pockets, not knowing what else to do with them. "I really am sorry
about everything, Elle."

"Yes, so you said."

Her tone made it clear the apology wasn't fully
accepted. Fair enough.

"You told your mother everything, I assume?"

"I did."

"Did she agree with your decision to invite me over tonight?"

She swept him with a cool look. "She convinced me we should give you a chance to make your case."

He barely managed not to grimace at the implication that he wouldn't be here now if it were totally up to Elle. "Your mother is a very generous woman."

"Yes, she is. With a trusting nature that has gotten her hurt a few times in the past."

Hearing the implied warning, Shane responded evenly, "I would never hurt either of you, Elle. And I would certainly never harm Charlotte. You have my word."

"Yes, well, I have no way of knowing if I can rely on that, do I?" With that, she turned and walked toward the living room, seemingly expecting him to follow.

Oh, yeah. She was still ticked off. Even though he was trying to be understanding about it, he felt his chin rise. "You can trust my word," he said stiffly to her back. "I never make promises I don't intend to keep."

She didn't look around but he thought he heard her give a skeptical huff.

He'd just perched on the edge of the chair Elle

waved him to when Janet entered with a tray carrying a ceramic teapot and three cups.

He rose to greet her. "Thank you for giving me a chance to explain, Mrs. O'Meara."

Ever the gracious hostess, she set the tray on the coffee table and picked up the teapot to pour. "Please sit. And you may still call me Janet, Shane. Which doesn't mean I approve of your behavior."

He accepted the tea—and the mild rebuke—with a chastened nod.

Handing another cup of aromatic herbal tea to Elle, Janet then poured a cup for herself and sat on the couch next to her daughter, both facing Shane. Shane didn't really want the tea, but the warm cup felt good between his hands and gave him something to do.

Elle held her own cup without tasting the tea as she frowned at Shane. "Okay, we're listening. Start from the beginning so my mom can hear what you told me earlier."

He drew a deep breath, then looked at Janet as he began. "My brother, Charlie, was two years older than me. He was a great guy and everyone loved him. Charlotte takes after him in both looks and that sunny, outgoing personality. Like her, he never met a stranger."

He went on to tell them about how Charlie had met Brittany when he was in basic training and she worked at a bar he'd frequented. Charlie had fallen hard for the pretty, flighty young woman despite cautions from friends and family.

"I don't know if it would have lasted," he added frankly. "Charlie was already starting to have doubts before he was deployed, but he told me he worried about how Brittany would take it if he broke up with her. He found out while he was in Afghanistan that she was pregnant. He called me, asked me to make sure she was cared for until he got back—but then he didn't come home."

Elle didn't look up from her drink in response to the story he'd already shared with her, but soft-hearted Janet gave a low murmur of distress.

"Anyway," he continued, "my family—my dad, my grandmother, my uncle, my cousin and her husband—we all tried as best we could to support Brittany through the remaining months of her pregnancy. We were all at the hospital the night Charlotte was born. A couple weeks later, I shipped out, but my dad told me he'd see that they'd have anything they needed while I was gone. I told Brittany we would always be there for her, that I would help her with whatever she needed as soon as I was back in the States. She seemed okay when I left—sad, of course, but attentive to the baby. She assured me she'd put Charlotte's needs first, that she wanted only the best for her child. I was worried, but I had no choice. I thought everything would be okay until I got back."

He swallowed hard before he added, "I'd been gone only a few days when I got a frantic call from my dad. Brittany had taken off with the baby and they had no idea where she'd gone. She left a polite note thanking the family for everything and telling us not to worry about her or Charlotte in the future. She said she wanted nothing from us and didn't want us to look for her. That was the last anyone heard from her. The family was heartbroken and worried, of course. I couldn't get home for another eight months, so they had to deal with it on their own. Dad's health took a bad turn, and he died just after I got home."

"Your poor grandmother." Janet's voice was husky with sympathy. "She must have been devastated by so many losses. So sad."

"We call her Dottie. And she has dealt with more than her share of grief," Shane acknowledged, "but my grandmother is a strong, resilient woman. Somehow she keeps her spirits high despite what she's been through. You'd both like her, I think."

When neither Elle nor Janet responded, Shane forged on. "After I got home, I was kept pretty busy for a few months dealing with the personal and business repercussions of my dad's death. By the time a private investigator located Brittany, the adoption had been finalized. She refused to talk with me at first, saying she wanted to put the past behind her, but a couple of months ago, she allowed me to visit her in New York, where she's living for now. After making me promise I wouldn't try to undermine her decision, she gave me your name, Elle. She said she understood that I needed to make sure Charlotte was safe and happy, but she didn't want me to interfere with your family."

"And yet…" Elle murmured pointedly.

He shot her a look but carried on doggedly. "I didn't have the investigator 'stalk' you, but I did ask him to confirm your identity with the information Brittany gave me. The photo you saw was the only one he took, just so I'd know who I'd be talking with. I could tell in the picture that Charlotte looked healthy and certainly happy, which was a huge relief to me. If I'm going to be totally honest with you—"

"As I expect you to be."

Okay, if that was what she wanted… "Yes, well, I was a little surprised that Brittany chose to give her daughter to a single woman. Apparently, she was quite taken with your application. She told me she believed you'd be the kind of single mother she wished she could have been. She could see how much having a child meant to you. She insisted she just knew you were the right one for her daughter—and she was pretty damned fierce about making me swear I'd respect that choice."

Elle set her cup aside with a thunk. "I'll always be grateful to Brittany. And I'll spend the rest of my life justifying her trust in me. You can be sure of that."

He wanted to be candid with her now. She deserved nothing less. "As I told you earlier, I'd have preferred that Brittany leave Charlotte with my family. Barring that, I think she made a good choice of adoptive mother. And grandmother."

"Was that why you didn't immediately tell us who you are?" Janet asked, looking as though she was trying not to let him see that the compliment had pleased her. "You wanted to watch us interact with Charlotte without us knowing we were being evaluated?"

"You were assessing my qualifications to be Charlotte's mother," Elle added in a mutter, not phrasing hers as a question. "Judging me."

"That's not it at all," he protested, almost feeling the waves of resentment pouring off her. "Just the opposite, actually. I wanted to give you both a chance to get to know me while I decided whether to tell you everything. I admit it probably wasn't the best plan—okay, it was a terrible plan, and I never meant to let it go on for so long. I hoped you'd see I'm a decent guy and no threat to your family. I wanted you to trust me."

Elle didn't roll her eyes. Exactly.

"You *can* trust me," he reiterated. "All I'm trying to do now is one last nice thing for my grandmother."

Keeping her gaze on Shane, Janet reached out to rest a hand on her daughter's knee. "You have to understand why Elle was so shaken by this, Shane. Frankly, I find it unsettling, myself. We've had our precious Charlotte all to ourselves for almost two years, and we never expected her biological family to appear. But—"

She sighed. "Well, I can't help putting myself in your grandmother's position. Knowing how deeply I love my granddaughter, I can only imagine how devastated your grandmother must have been to lose Charlie. Having his child taken from her must have felt like losing him all over again. The whole situation is heartbreaking."

Elle swiveled on the couch to face her mother, speaking urgently. "It isn't as if I took Charlotte away from them, Mom. It was a legal adoption, arranged by Charlotte's biological mother through a legitimate agency. I've done nothing wrong."

"Of course not! No one would accuse you of that, including Shane, I'm positive," Janet added with a pointed look at him. "He promised he has no intention of trying to take Charlotte away from you. As badly as he went about it, he just wanted to do something for his grandmother before she passes—possibly the only thing he believes he can do for her."

While Shane held his breath, Elle searched her mother's face. "So you think I should do this? Take Charlotte to North Carolina and introduce her to these people?"

"Think of it this way. Charlotte won't remember the visit in the future, but perhaps she'd like a photo of herself with her great-grandmother just to satisfy her own curiosity about where she came from. I'm sure Shane's family can provide pictures and stories about her father for you to stash away until she's old enough to start asking questions."

"We have plenty of photos," Shane dared to interject. "Some of Charlie's baby pictures look so much like Charlotte that it's startling."

Biting her lip, Elle glanced his way. He realized he'd put her in a position she couldn't get out of gracefully. He supposed she couldn't help but resent it. He'd probably feel the same way if the circumstances were reversed.

She twisted her hands in her lap so tightly he could see her knuckles whiten. "I'm sure Charlotte will have questions someday," she said in a low voice. "I always planned to be completely honest with her about the adoption, and to give her all the information I had. I'll admit it will be good to have more details about her family medical history, among other things."

"I'll provide all of that, of course…"

"But," she added, speaking over Shane as she turned to her mother again, "what if his relatives start demanding more than just one visit? What if they try to sue for scheduled visitations or try to interfere with my parenting?"

"Then you'd deal with it," Janet replied before Shane had a chance to reassure her those things wouldn't happen. He could certainly understand now why she'd be apprehensive. Damn, but he'd made a mess of this!

"You've never had any problem standing up for yourself," Janet added to Elle, "and you won't ever let anyone get between you and your daughter."

That certainty brought Elle's chin up. "No. I would never allow that. She *is* my daughter. I intend to make that very clear."

"Of course you will. And I'm sure it will all work out. I have a strong psychic feeling…"

"Don't start that, Mom," Elle warned firmly, though a barely perceptible smile played on her lips as she shook her head. Shane suspected Janet's cheeky claim had been deliberately used to lighten the mood. Unlike Shane, Janet obviously knew how to mollify her daughter.

Taking advantage of the moment, he asked,

"So, you'll bring Charlotte to meet my grandmother? If it makes you feel any better, Elle, I'll make very sure the family understands this is a onetime favor. I'd like to pay for a night in a nice hotel suite in Fayetteville when you come so you don't have to make the three-hour drive twice in one day. I don't know if you've ever visited the area, but there are some attractions that might interest Charlotte—parks and playgrounds, a children's museum, a couple of indoor play places. Maybe it could turn into a fun trip for her?"

"Oh, that does sound nice," Janet said with a smile, making it clear that she was somewhat more easily appeased than her daughter. "Charlotte would enjoy that."

"We aren't planning a family vacation, Mom. And I haven't said we'd do it yet."

Shane could only describe Elle's expression as cornered when she insisted to him, "You'll have to give me a little time to think about this. I know you want an answer soon, but I'm not prepared to make any decisions tonight."

At least she wasn't saying no. He'd have to find some consolation in that. "I'll give you as much time as I can. Dottie's doing pretty well now. Increasingly frail, but not at imminent risk."

She nodded, her expression darkening a bit at the reminder that time was of the essence. "I'll let you know when I've made up my mind."

"Thank you." It was all he could ask of her.

She stood. "I'll walk you out."

He had a sudden, ironic flashback to a time when he'd been called in to the principal's office in high school to be relentlessly grilled and chewed out for a stupid prank he'd pulled. His principal had ended the stern discussion by saying, "You may go now," in the same frosty tone Elle had just used.

As he had back then, he stood rather meekly. "Thank you again for giving me a chance to explain."

Janet looked at him with an expression he could only describe as regretful…with perhaps a touch of rueful sympathy. "Good night, Shane."

As he took his leave from her, he wished for a fleeting moment that she really was psychic. He'd ask her to reassure him that somehow he'd figure out a way to fix this mess he'd made and make it all turn out right. For his family. For Charlotte. For Elle and Janet.

As for himself…well, he couldn't worry about that until he'd taken care of all the others who were depending on him.

CHAPTER EIGHT

ELLE HAD THE outer door open before Shane could even reach it. She couldn't have been more obvious about her impatience for him to be gone from her home.

Now that all his cards were on the table, he'd made it clear he was leaving the control in her hands when it came to any future encounters, if any. He'd openly admitted that he'd been in the wrong. Would she ever forgive him for the jarring way she'd learned the truth?

He paused with one foot over the threshold, turning to look at her. She stood in the doorway as though guarding her family from him, which perturbed him even more…until their eyes met. For one unguarded moment, he saw the emotion that lay beneath her anger.

He hadn't realized until just then how badly he'd hurt her.

His momentary resentment faded. "I really am sorry," he said simply. "I know how much honesty means to you. While I never lied to you, I can't say I was completely honest, and for that I apologize."

She looked away, but not before he saw her brown eyes darken with tangled emotions he couldn't begin to define. She nodded, biting her lip. He remembered all too clearly just how soft those lips had felt against his. He regretted seeing the teeth marks there now, knowing he was the cause.

"For what it's worth," he said gruffly, "I wasn't pretending to have a good time with you. Or lying about finding you attractive. And I wasn't hanging around with you only to get closer to Charlotte."

Her eyes met his again then. Her chin rose.

"We won't talk about anything that happened between us before I learned the truth," she warned. "As far as I'm concerned, none of that was real. We started from scratch the minute I found out who you are and why you came here."

He felt himself frowning. He didn't like the implication that she could simply erase the conversations they'd shared from her memory, the smiles and laughs, the moments of real connection. The simmering attraction. The kiss she had initiated, damn it.

"You can tell yourself that there was nothing between us," he muttered roughly. "And I'll agree with you that it probably couldn't have gone anywhere. But we both know if we'd met under any other circumstances, without those complications, last night in my suite would have ended a whole lot differently."

Her cheeks flushed and her eyes sparked defiantly—but he was satisfied that they both knew he was right.

With that, he turned and headed for his car, saying over his shoulder, "I'll be waiting to hear from you."

He thought he heard her mutter something behind him, but wisely didn't ask her to repeat it.

He wasn't sure he'd enhanced Elle's opinion of him during the visit, he thought a few minutes later as he drove away. But at least she'd agreed to consider bringing Charlotte to Fayetteville. He was optimistic, if not fully convinced, that she'd agree in the end, if only because Janet seemed to understand why he wanted this so badly. He just hoped Elle didn't leave him hanging too long as payback.

He'd promised he would leave her alone after the visit. As he'd told her so indignantly, he kept his promises. If she asked him never to contact her or Charlotte again after she granted his favor, he would agree—no matter how badly it would hurt to walk away from his niece.

Of course, that meant he wouldn't see Elle again, either. Whatever might have been developing between them, whatever attraction had led to their kiss, all that had ended when she'd found that report beneath his passenger seat. At least on her part.

All for the best, he reminded himself. He wasn't sure where he'd thought that attraction would lead—hadn't been thinking at all, obviously—but it was probably just as well it had ended before it got too complicated. Sure, he was open to flirtations. To cordial flings with no expectations or demands. But under the circumstances, that would never have been possible with Elle, even if she could have forgiven him for what she saw as underhanded behavior on his part.

Too bad, he thought with a low exhale, the memory of that kiss lingering. Elle had been the first woman in a long time who'd tempted him to forget his other obligations.

SHE MADE HIM wait almost a week before she called. It had been all he could do to be patient and not call or text her to nudge for a quicker answer, but he'd managed to refrain because he suspected pushing her too hard would cause her to dig in. He was on another call in his Fayetteville office when he saw her number on his cell phone screen. He wrapped up the other call immediately to take hers.

"I'll do it," she said without bothering with

small talk. "I'll bring her for a short visit so your grandmother can see that she's thriving. We can come a week from Sunday."

Which would be the Sunday after Thanksgiving, he noted with a quick glance at his calendar. "Sure. Yeah, that'll work great. Thank you, Elle, this—"

"What I said before still stands," she cut in flatly. "I want it made clear that I'm Charlotte's mother. That her home and her family are here, in Shorty's Landing. If I decide this will be a one-time visit, I don't want you or anyone else harassing me about it in the future."

"You have my— We won't harass you," he substituted, suspecting his word would still be difficult for this wary woman to accept. "Would you like me to drive? I could pick you up at—"

"I'll bring my own car. I'll just need the address."

"I'll text it to you. And I'll reserve a suite for that night for you and Charlotte and your mother. With it being the end of the holiday weekend, I should be able to book you a nice suite for Sunday night."

"It probably would be easier on Charlotte and my mom not to spend six hours in a car on one day," Elle conceded grudgingly.

"Great, so—"

"But I'll pay for my own hotel room."

"No." On this point he intended to remain firm. "I'll reserve the suite. Two bedrooms so your mother will be comfortable. Elle, it's the least I can do, considering what you're doing for me. For my grandmother."

Perhaps she didn't want to waste time arguing with him over this when there were so many more important issues facing them. "Okay, fine. We'll visit your grandmother, spend the night at the hotel and then come back on Monday. After that, we'll consider it even between us. Deal?"

"Deal. I'll see you a week from Sunday," he said.

She disconnected without further delay. Shaking his head—and wondering why he didn't feel a little more satisfied—Shane set down his phone and focused on his work again. Or at least he tried, though he kept getting distracted by a memory of Elle O'Meara smiling up at him as she had swayed in his arms on a dance floor.

THERE WAS NOTHING at all about the house in front of her that should have filled Elle with such apprehension. It was a perfectly nice house—a white-frame two-story with a wraparound porch furnished with swings and planters. A big wreath embellished with fall leaves, chrysanthemum blooms and a rust-orange bow appropriate for Thanksgiving hung on the blue-painted door. The day was overcast, but a ray of early-afternoon sun broke through the clouds to glitter on the spotless, black-shuttered windows.

It was all very pleasant and welcoming. Yet Elle wanted nothing more than to throw her car into Reverse and make the drive back to Shorty's Landing without further hesitation.

Her mother reached across the console to pat her arm reassuringly. "It will be fine, honey. You're doing the right thing."

Moistening her dry lips, Elle unbuckled her seat belt. "I hope so."

She glanced back at the car seat in which Charlotte was dozing, her favorite stuffed kitten, the one she'd won at the festival last month, snuggled in her lap. To Elle's secret dismay, Charlotte had named the toy "Shane-cat." It rarely left her sight and when it did, she demanded her "Shane-cat" be located immediately. Charlotte had looked for Shane almost every day for the first week after he'd left, jumping up expectantly in her play corral when the door bells had jingled, asking, "Where Shane?" every few hours. Elle had been relieved when the child had stopped looking for him, but by then the toy cat was permanently named.

It was enough to make Elle grind her teeth now, especially knowing Charlotte's obsession with him would only be reinvigorated by this visit.

Who knew how long it would take for her to put him out of her mind after this? Though, considering that he was actually her uncle…

Elle could feel her jaw aching and realized she was on the verge of grinding her teeth again. She tried to relax her face, telling herself to stop over-thinking everything.

As for herself, she'd have appreciated not being reminded of Shane every day—though she could hardly blame her daughter. She was well aware she'd have thought of him, anyway. For some reason, she couldn't seem to stop herself. Every time a dark-haired man had strolled into her shop during the past weeks, her heart had skipped a couple of beats. And as much as she'd told herself it was only her anger keeping him at the front of her mind, she knew there was much more to her agitation than that.

Charlotte roused when Elle opened the back door to take her from the car. She rubbed her eyes, stretched, then reached out to Elle with the stuffed toy still gripped in one hand. Elle unfastened the buckles, then lifted the child into her arms. Charlotte looked adorable—as always, to her admittedly biased eyes—in a new outfit consisting of a bright rainbow-striped top and co-ordinating leggings. A rainbow-patterned bow held back her soft curls, though she had a habit of tugging accessories out of her hair and dropping them wherever she happened to be.

The child had been very good during the long drive broken up by two leisurely stretch breaks and a stop for lunch, but she was visibly pleased to be released from the restraints. She wrapped her arms around Elle's neck for a hug.

Smiling, Elle kissed her daughter's soft cheek. Her smile faded when Charlotte looked past her and squealed, "Shane!"

Swallowing hard, Elle turned. She didn't bother forcing a smile, but tried to keep her expression composed as she watched him step down off the porch and stroll toward them. Her pulse rate accelerated in response to seeing him. He was smiling at Charlotte, which brought out those sexy dimples, and he was wearing the leather jacket. It was totally unfair for a man who'd proven he couldn't be trusted as far as she could throw him to look so damned appealing!

"Hello, Charlotte," he said. "I see you brought your kitty to visit."

She was already reaching for him. "Shane!"

He started to take her, then hesitated, looking at Elle for permission. "Er—"

She sighed and handed over the eager child. "Go ahead. She wants to say hello."

Shane spun around with Charlotte in his arms, making her giggle and squirm happily. He cradled her on one hip as he said, "Thank you for coming, Elle. You, too, Janet. I hope the drive wasn't too bad."

Typically vibrant in a multicolored tunic worn with wide-legged pants and glittering jewelry, Elle's mother smiled. "We took our time and enjoyed the ride."

"That's great. Did you have a nice Thanksgiving?"

Elle wondered if he was deliberately stalling before taking them inside. Perhaps giving them a chance to prepare themselves for the encounter he must know they—or at least Elle—had consented to with deep reservations.

"Oh, yes, we had a lovely holiday," Janet said easily. "We had dinner in Charleston with my brother and his wife and their daughter and son-in-law. They're all crazy about Charlotte. My nephews are both in their teens now, so Charlotte was definitely the belle of the ball that day."

"I'm sure she enjoyed that." He glanced again at Elle. "My family is looking forward to meeting you all."

Janet smoothed her red hair with a clatter of bracelets the only hint of nervousness as she studied the house. "Is this where you grew up, Shane?"

"No, this is my uncle Raymond's house. He

moved Dottie in with him when her health took a downturn a few years ago."

"How kind of him."

After straightening her travel-rumpled wine-red top and dark charcoal pants, Elle locked her car and stashed the keys in her bag. "Okay. I'm ready."

With Charlotte perched happily on his hip, Shane gave her a wry smile. "It really won't be as bad as a root canal."

Elle's mother laughed. "She does have that look, doesn't she?"

"Neither of you is funny," Elle muttered.

Exchanging a look with Shane, her mom tried without success to stifle a smile. Elle didn't know why her mother wasn't taking this more seriously. They were about to meet Charlotte's blood relatives! People who could possibly assert they had as much claim to the child as the family who'd raised her for the past twenty months. How could her mother look so calm? Not to mention that she seemed to have at least partially forgiven Shane for stringing them along for so long. Elle was still struggling with that part.

"Do you want to walk, Charlotte?" Shane asked.

"Walk," she agreed. He set her down and she reached up to take his hand. She held up the stuffed cat to Elle. Elle took the toy and tucked it beneath her arm so she could lightly clasp Charlotte's other hand. Her gaze met Shane's for a moment across the child bouncing happily between them. She looked quickly away, just in case he could read her tangled emotions in her eyes.

"My family has promised to behave themselves today," he said. "You don't have to worry about anyone putting pressure on you."

"I appreciate that."

She'd noticed that Shane continually referred to his family as a collective, implying they were closely connected, united in their goals. Had Brittany felt left out of that unit, especially after the death of her baby's father, a man she hadn't been married to? Or rather overwhelmed by their attention? Or had she simply not wanted to be included in the clan at all?

The door opened again as they approached. A pretty brunette stood framed in the doorway with a happy-looking baby boy on her hip. Elle noted immediately that the woman bore a strong resemblance to Shane—and that her baby looked very much like Charlotte at the same age. The observation made her throat tighten even more, to the point that she was beginning to worry that she wouldn't be able to breathe if she couldn't find a way to relax.

The woman's gaze went straight to Charlotte and her eyes widened. Her lower lip quivered for a moment, and then she murmured to her cousin,

"She looks just as I imagined she would. Just like Charlie."

Shane nodded, then said, "Elle and Janet O'Meara, this is my cousin, Parker Scanlon Mendel, and her son, Aubrey."

He placed a hand lightly on Charlotte's head then. "Parker, meet Charlotte O'Meara. Elle's daughter."

Elle appreciated his firm tone as he made her position clear, keeping the promise he'd given her. She saw his cousin blink a couple of times before she gave them all a strained smile. "Hello, Charlotte. It's so nice to meet you, Elle. And Mrs. O'Meara. Thank you so much for coming. Please, come in."

Elle's mom surged forward first to ease the awkwardness with a cheery tone. "Please call me Janet. It's lovely to meet you, Parker. And what a beautiful little boy."

"Baby!" Charlotte squealed as they all moved into the welcoming foyer. Always fascinated by infants, she released Elle's hand to point up at the baby Parker held. "Mommy, look. Baby!"

Parker knelt down with her child so they could see each other. "This is Aubrey, Charlotte. Can you say Aubrey?"

"Aub'ey." Beaming, Charlotte patted the fascinated little boy's cheek. "Pretty baby Aub'ey."

Parker, Shane and Elle's mom all laughed.

Somehow Elle managed a smile, though she was still struck by the resemblance between the two children. Cousins.

As if he sensed her turmoil, Shane rested a hand lightly on her shoulder. "Ready to meet the others?" he asked, his expression sympathetic.

She took a deep breath and nodded, finding his touch surprisingly reassuring. "Yes, I'm ready."

Parker escorted them into an open, high-ceilinged living room arranged with cozy-looking furniture. Two men stood when they entered. Elle figured the distinguished-looking, silver-haired older man was Shane's uncle, Raymond, while the younger, scruffier-looking guy with longish brown hair and a charmingly crooked smile must be Parker's husband, Adrian.

A frail-looking woman with a halo of thin white curls sat in a wheelchair next to the gas fireplace. Wrapped in a white crocheted throw despite the warmth from the fire, she sat forward in the chair as she looked toward the newcomers. Her gaze went straight to Charlotte. Her hands gripped the armrests as if she'd have loved nothing more than to spring to her feet and rush toward them.

Shane escorted them across the room, where he placed a hand fondly on his grandmother's shoulder. He repeated the earlier introductions, emphasizing again that Elle was Charlotte's mother.

His grandmother smiled tremulously, addressing Elle first. "Thank you so much for coming. It was so kind of you to go out of your way to let us see Charlotte."

Despite her nerves, Elle couldn't be cool with this woman, who reminded her a bit of her own late grandmother. She gently took the fragile hand offered to her. "It's nice to meet you, Mrs. Scanlon."

"Please, call me Dottie. Everyone does. And this is your mother?"

Janet swept forward with her usual poise. "I'm Janet O'Meara. I'm delighted to meet you, Dottie. Your grandson is quite the charmer."

"He is," Dottie agreed, then chuckled softly, "but you should have met his brother. People always said Charlie could charm the stripes off a zebra."

Elle wondered if the woman had been as partial to Charlie during his lifetime as she seemed to be now. If so, it must have been tough for Shane to follow in his brother's footsteps. Had he become the family's go-to guy as a way of establishing his own value? This was only idle curiosity on her part, of course. It wasn't as though she needed to know more about Shane and his feelings now. Any personal developments between them had certainly come to an abrupt halt.

"Charlotte obviously inherited her father's charisma," Janet said with a smile. "Everyone loves her instantly."

Dottie looked back at Charlotte, who still hovered near Parker and the baby. Charlotte was showing Aubrey her stuffed cat, making him laugh as she bobbed it in front of him. "She's beautiful. She looks so much like him."

Dottie glanced back up at Elle then, her blue eyes glistening with tears. "She's named after Charlie, you know. Charlie and Shane."

Elle looked questioningly at Shane. "My middle name is Michael," he explained.

"Charlotte Michelle," she murmured. "I hadn't realized—"

As if she hadn't been unnerved enough by this visit. Now, to know that her daughter bore the feminine version of Shane's middle name...

She bit her lip.

"I'm glad you didn't change her name," Dottie added. "I know it was your right to do so, but it means a great deal to me that you didn't."

"She'd had that name for five months when she came to me," Elle explained quietly. "I didn't want to confuse her any more than she'd already been."

She didn't add that she'd considered changing the baby's middle name, but had ultimately decided to honor the woman who'd chosen her to be Charlotte's mother by changing the surname only. She'd figured Brittany had good reasons for selecting the first and middle names, though hearing those reasons now shook her once again.

Dottie wiped her eyes with a tissue clutched in one hand and looked longingly at Charlotte. Elle was grateful the family hadn't descended on the child to overwhelm her with attention. They were considerately letting her get used to the room and its occupants, allowing her to relax from the long drive by playing with Aubrey under Parker's supervision. Still, Elle knew Dottie was impatient to meet her great-granddaughter.

"Charlotte," she said, holding out her hand. "Come to Mommy, please."

Though reluctant to leave her new friend, Charlotte obeyed, looking curiously from Elle to Shane to the woman in the wheelchair as she approached. Elle knelt beside her. "Charlotte, this is Dottie. Can you say hello to Dottie?"

"Dottie," the child repeated obligingly, studying the wheelchair with interest.

Beaming, her great-grandmother clasped her hands together. "Yes, darling, I'm Dottie. It's so nice to meet you. I have a gift for you, if that's all right with your mother."

Elle nodded, having expected something like this. "Of course."

Dottie reached down beside her chair to pick up a brightly colored gift bag that she offered to Charlotte. Having celebrated her second birth-

day in early September, Charlotte knew exactly
what gift bags signified. She accepted it eagerly,
crouching to pull out the tissue paper and toss it.
She squealed in delight when she drew out the
gift—a brown-and-white wooden beagle with a
goofy grin and legs that "walked" when the toy
was pulled across the floor by the attached cord.
"Puppy!"

Because the toy clearly wasn't new, Elle wasn't
surprised when Dottie said quietly, "It belonged
to Charlie. It was one of his favorite toys at her
age. I thought she'd like to have it."

"I'm sure she'll treasure it. I'll keep it safe for
her." Swallowing a lump in her throat, Elle spoke
to her daughter, "Charlotte, can you say thank you
to Dottie for the puppy?"

"T'ank you, Dottie." The naturally affection-
ate child must have been drawn to the love in the
older woman's expression. She stepped up to give
her a hug and a smacking kiss on the cheek.

Patting Charlotte's back with tremulous hands,
her great-grandmother appeared too overcome
with emotion to speak. Elle felt her eyes prickle,
and she heard her sensitive mother sniffle beside her.

As if sensing a need to brighten the mood, Raymond Scanlon stepped forward to greet them.
"Perhaps you ladies would like to sit down? Have
you eaten?"

Elle's mom smiled up at the tall, handsome man. Elle estimated that Shane's uncle was within a year or so of her mother's age. "Thank you, Raymond," her mom said, "but we stopped an hour ago for a light lunch."

"Then perhaps you'd like a hot beverage and a dessert. Parker made one of her famous chocolate tortes. Adrian has been waiting impatiently for our company to arrive so he can cut into it." Raymond glanced at his son-in-law with a teasing chuckle.

Janet gestured with a jingle of her favored bangle bracelets. "That sounds delicious. We'd love some. We wouldn't want to make poor Adrian have to wait any longer, would we, Elle?"

Parker looked rather self-conscious when she said, "Shane told us you own a coffee shop, Elle, and that you're an amazing pastry chef. I'm hardly on your level, but I think I make a pretty good torte after a few years of practice."

"I'll attest to that," Adrian said eagerly, rubbing his flat stomach in emphasis. "I do most of the cooking in our family, as Parker will be the first to tell you, but her chocolate torte is amazing."

"Then we have to try it," Elle said with a smile, trying her best to play along with everyone else's efforts to keep the conversation lighthearted. "And coffee sounds wonderful after that long drive."

"Let's go to the dining room," Parker suggested, motioning toward the doorway. "There's no need to balance cups and plates in our laps when we can sit at the table and talk."

Raymond gripped the handles of his mother's wheelchair and guided her toward the door. Taking Charlotte's hand, Janet followed them, telling Charlotte they were going to have chocolate cake, which excited the child. Charlotte dragged the wooden dog behind her with her free hand, looking over her shoulder as she walked to make sure it was still there.

Elle found herself left behind for a moment with Shane. He touched her arm to detain her when she moved to join the others.

"Thank you," he said when she looked up. "I know I keep saying it, but I'm not sure I've made it clear enough how grateful I am."

"You don't have to keep thanking me." She gave a faint sigh and tucked back her hair. "Now that I've met your grandmother, I can understand why you wanted to make her happy before…"

She was unable to finish the sentence.

Shane nodded. His hand slid down her arm to brush her fingers. "I know you didn't want to come. But I hope you aren't sorry you did."

She cleared her throat. "Not so far."

He smiled, his gaze on her now-damp mouth. "I'll try to keep it that way."

"I'd appreciate that." She wasn't joking. His eyes were still on her lips. She felt them quiver, just a little, and she tightened them immediately, hoping he hadn't seen.

She lifted her chin and his eyes rose to meet hers. "You realize, of course, that I didn't know who you were when I kissed you that night after the concert. And that I'd had a couple of glasses of wine for the first time in quite a while."

What might have been a brief grimace narrowed his eyes for a moment. "I know."

"It won't happen again, of course. And we'll never refer to it again."

"That's probably for the best," he agreed, and she told herself it didn't bother her that he hadn't even hesitated.

She nodded and drew away from him. "Good."

"Elle?"

She hesitated in the doorway to look over her shoulder. "Yes?"

"Doesn't mean I won't think about it," he said with a crooked smile. "It was a good kiss."

Her left eyebrow rose. "It was a great kiss," she shot back before she could stop herself. "That's the only kind I give."

She turned with a flip of her hair and walked out of the room. She heard a low, choked laugh from Shane but she didn't look back. He was the one who'd let that kiss happen under false pretenses. She would darned well leave him with at least a little regret about what might have been.

She'd certainly had a few wistful thoughts of her own since that night.

CHAPTER NINE

THE TORTE WAS as good as advertised. Elle told Parker she would love to have the recipe for her shop, which seemed to please the younger woman.

Conversation flowed smoothly during the hour they spent around the table, which was also little surprise to Elle. Her mother was a master of sparkling dialogue, keeping the others laughing with her funny stories about Charlotte and their quirky small town. Both Elle and her mother had, of course, taken many photos of Charlotte from the day she'd joined their family and they passed their phones around to share some of the best ones. Dottie sent Shane to collect a photo album with pictures of Charlie at the same age, and after glancing through it, Elle had to admit the resemblance was striking.

"Oh, we need to show them the framed photo on my dresser," Dottie pronounced. "Shane, dear, run and get it for me, will you?"

"Yes, Dottie."

For the second time, Elle watched Shane leave the room on an errand for his grandmother, who seemed quite accustomed to giving him instructions. He was obviously crazy about Dottie—the fact that Elle, her mother and Charlotte were here was a testament to that devotion. He'd said his grandmother had helped raise him and his brother after they'd lost their mother. He probably thought of Dottie as much as a mother as a grandmother. He certainly didn't seem to mind jumping to wait on her when she asked.

He returned minutes later with the photograph, which he handed to Elle. Her fingers tightened around the gold filigree frame as she studied the picture. She'd already seen pictures of Shane as a child with his brother in the album she'd leafed through. Yet this photo affected her more than the others had, for some reason.

It was a professional portrait of their family. Shane's father stood in the background, wearing his dress blues and bearing a striking resemblance to his brother, Raymond. Shane's mother sat in a chair, pretty and smiling in a pink dress. Perhaps three years old, Charlie leaned against the arm of her chair. Shane couldn't have been more than a year old and sat in his mother's lap, grinning at the camera, his dark curls tousled, his dimples on full display.

Such a sweet photo of a happy-looking family. And yet only a couple years later, this lovely woman would be gone. And now Shane was the only one left. It made Elle's heart ache.

She didn't have to feel sorry for him, she reminded herself. He seemed to have a fulfilling, successful life, helping to run a growing company. The family he had left were obviously close. The sadness she'd occasionally seen in him had probably been because seeing Charlotte had reminded him so much of his brother, and maybe because he had wondered how to approach Elle with this request.

"It's a beautiful photograph," she said, handing the frame to her mother.

Dottie smiled wistfully. "Yes, it is. They would have loved Charlotte so much."

"Dottie," Shane murmured, as if in reminder of an earlier warning.

Rather pointedly ignoring him, Dottie tapped her empty plate. "I wouldn't mind another little piece of that torte, Parker. It's one of the best you've ever made."

"I'll get it, Dottie." Adrian leapt to his feet, because Parker was holding a now-drowsy Aubrey. "Mrs. O'Meara, Elle, would either of you care for anything else?"

Though most of the plates were empty, no one moved to leave the table while Adrian served Dottie more torte and topped off beverages for everyone else.

"Thank you, Adrian." Elle's mom patted his arm after he refilled her coffee. And then allowed her hand to linger there, her head tilting in a gesture Elle knew all too well. She glanced at Shane, whose barely stifled smile let her know that he, too, was prepared for what was about to come.

"Um, Mom—" Elle murmured, trying to ward off the awkwardness.

But her mother had already launched into her routine. "Oh, my goodness, Adrian, you have quite a strong aura. I know you're a musician, but you're also a poet, aren't you?"

"Well, I do write songs," Adrian replied with a slightly puzzled smile.

"I knew it! You were heavily influenced by the Beatles, weren't you?"

"The Beatles? Uh, no—"

"You come from a musical family. Is your father also a musician?"

"My father's an orthodontist. My mother sells insurance. Neither of them plays an instrument. They said they don't know where I came by it."

Not daunted by her lack of success, Janet gave it one last shot. "Some people have suggested that I'm a little psychic," she said, making Elle wonder just who those "people" would be. "Someone in your family has the gift, as well. Am I right, Adrian?"

Elle sighed while the others around the table

eyed her mother quizzically. "Give it a rest, Mom. This family doesn't know you well enough to indulge you in this."

"Actually," Adrian said with a grin, "my grandmother reads tarot cards."

"There! You see?" Ridiculously proud of herself, Janet sat straighter in her chair. "She *does* have the gift."

"I didn't say she was good at it," he added with a chuckle. "She lays the cards out, then reads from the little book that came packaged with the deck she bought at a novelty store. Her readings never make much sense, but she gets a kick out of playing with it."

"Something tells me Janet and your grandmother would get along very well," Shane murmured.

Janet laughed softly and winked at him. "I'm sure we would. Maybe I'll meet her sometime."

Elle wasn't sure how her mother would ever have occasion to meet Adrian's grandmother. She kept that thought to herself as she wiped a smear of chocolate from Charlotte's mouth and gave her permission to sit on the floor and play with her new pull toy.

She glanced at the framed photo now resting on the table, her eyes drawn again to Shane's father in the center. To redirect the conversation back to this family rather than her own, Elle said, "Shane told me you served in the army, too, Raymond."

He nodded. "Served twenty years before retiring to go into business with my brother. As a matter of fact, Parker was born in Germany when I was stationed over there," he added with a fond glance at his daughter.

Parker wrinkled her nose at him. "Someday I hope to go back and visit. I have no memory of Germany."

"My late husband and I were there many years ago," Janet mused with a nostalgic sigh. "Lovely countryside."

"It is," Raymond agreed, giving her a wry smile. "Unfortunately, my ex-wife didn't care for living there. She brought Parker back to the States when Parker was only a few months old, and we were divorced before I retired."

"Mom says she was just never cut out to be an army wife," Parker said with a slight shrug. "But I'd still like to see my birthplace someday."

Raymond cleared his throat rather noisily, causing his snoozing grandchild to squirm restlessly in his mother's arms. "Perhaps we could speak of something else now. Elle, tell us about your business. Shane said you own the shop?"

Though she still wasn't particularly eager to discuss her personal life, Elle had to admit the question was innocuous enough. "Yes, I do, with a partner. The shop is called The Perkery. We also serve soups, salads and sandwiches, but coffee and pastries are our mainstay."

Proclaiming himself a coffee buff, Adrian had several questions about the types of beans the shop served and the sources used for purchasing them. Dottie was more interested in the variety of pastries Elle prepared, admitting that baking had been one of her favorite hobbies "back in the day."

"I'm a little confused," Parker said, tilting her head toward Elle with a frown. "You said you're only open four days a week?"

"No," Elle replied patiently. "I said I run the shop four days a week. Wednesday through Saturday. My partner is there Sunday through Tuesday while Mom and I take those days off for other pursuits. It's a schedule we worked out before we even opened and so far, it's been good for us."

"Interesting," Parker murmured. "Where does Charlotte go while you're working? Do you have a nanny? Is she in day care?"

Was there an implied criticism there, or was Elle being too defensive, considering Shane had annoyed her once before with a similar question? Telling herself to just answer, she replied, "I leave early for work, before Charlotte is awake. Mom gets her up later, then brings her to the shop, where she stays with us until we close late afternoon."

"I love my morning time with Charlotte," her mother piped in. "She and I sing and play games while I get her dressed for the day. On nice afternoons when the shop isn't very busy, I take her to the park a couple blocks away where she loves to play on the climbing equipment and in the sandbox. Elle and Charlotte do other things on our days away from the shop, including swimming and gymnastics classes. We're so fortunate to have so much time together, aren't we, Elle?"

"Yes, Mom." Elle flicked her a glance to warn her not to oversell their commitment to Charlotte's well-being, though she wasn't sure her ultra-loyal mother got the message.

"But are you sure it's safe? For a baby to spend the day in a shop with hot stoves and foods and customers coming in and out, I mean."

This time it was Shane who responded, giving his cousin a rather stern look as he said, "Charlotte is perfectly safe at the shop, Parker. She's not wandering around unsupervised. She has a secure, fenced-off area behind the counter, away from the cooking equipment, where she has toys and a soft mat for napping. She's in full sight of her mom or grandmother or one of Elle's employees at all times."

"Thank you, Shane," Janet murmured.

"Just giving facts," he said with a shrug and a

glance at Elle. Their eyes held for a moment, and then she looked away.

"I'm sorry. That sounded insensitive of me, didn't it?" Parker shook her head. "My family tells me I have no tact. I wasn't questioning your parenting, Elle, just trying to learn what Charlotte's life is like."

Only slightly mollified, Elle nodded. She noted that Parker was looking from Shane to Elle and back as if she were trying to figure out if she was missing some subtext between them. But, again, perhaps Elle was just reading too much into this suddenly tense exchange. She wondered how soon she could escape this emotionally charged visit.

Raymond's phone beeped with a text. Under his mother's disapproving eye, he typed quickly with his thumbs. "I'll just finish this and then I'll put the phone away," he promised Dottie. "Shane, I'm forwarding this text to you to deal with later this afternoon, if you would. It's about the Lynch account."

Shane nodded without bothering to reach for his own phone as it buzzed in his pocket. "I'll look at it in a bit."

Adrian's phone rang shortly afterward—much to Dottie's increased disapproval—and he politely left the room to answer. He returned a few minutes later with a scowl. "That was the plumber," he said to Parker. "He says he's had problems on another job and it's going to be three more weeks before he can get to us."

"Three weeks?" Parker wailed. "He's already put us off for a month."

"Shane, is there anything you can do?" Raymond asked. "Would your contractor friend be able to pull any strings?"

"I'll call him tomorrow," Shane promised. "I think we can find someone to come sooner than that."

"Shane, dear, run and get my pocketbook, will you, please?" his grandmother requested. "I want to show Janet the pretty little wooden hand mirror Charlie made for my eightieth birthday. He was such a talented woodworker," she added with a sigh.

Elle watched as Shane left the room once again on an errand for his grandmother. Over the past ten minutes, every member of his family had turned to him with a request. From both her own observations and a few things he'd said, it was even clearer now that he'd been the dependable assistant for the family for years. She suspected that had been true even when his apparently favored older brother had been alive.

She wondered when, not if, he would begin to rebel against living for his family. Did any resentment simmer beneath that conciliatory facade? Would Shane someday walk away from all his responsibilities in search of his own happiness, the way her ex had? Especially after the grandmother he obviously adored was no longer here?

After showing Elle and her mother the small mirror in its pretty, turned-wood holder, and satisfied that they'd suitably admired her late grandson's talent, Dottie asked to have her chair rolled back to the fireplace. "Charlotte, come talk to Dottie, sweetheart," she added enticingly.

Shane took hold of the wheelchair handles to roll her to the other room. Charlotte jumped up. "I help," she announced as she squeezed in between him and the chair and reached up to grasp the handles.

"Thank you, Charlotte," Shane told her, contorting a bit to give her room as they pushed the chair together.

Adrian took his sleeping son from Parker, saying he would carry him into the other room to finish his nap. Elle's mom drifted away with Raymond, seeming engaged in conversation. Which left Elle alone with Parker.

Determined to keep her emotions under control and her thoughts hidden, she began to gather dishes from the table. "Let me help you clear these things away."

"Oh, that isn't necessary. You're our guest. It will just take me a few minutes to clean up in here."

"I don't mind."

Together they carried the dishes, utensils, cups and glasses into the kitchen to be rinsed and stacked in the dishwasher.

"Thanks, Elle." Wiping her hands on a towel, the younger woman cleared her throat. "Do you mind if I ask you one more question?"

Though she braced herself in response to Parker's somber expression, Elle replied, "What would you like to know?"

"Do you know Brittany? Is she a friend of yours?"

"Brittany?" This was one question Elle hadn't expected at all. "You mean Charlotte's birth mother? No, I've never met her."

Parker's shoulders seemed to sag with the answer. "Oh. I thought maybe—"

"Maybe what?"

Heaving a sigh, the younger woman tossed the towel aside. "I guess I'm still just trying to figure out why Brittany didn't want us to raise her daughter," she admitted. "I can't tell you how much it hurt when we heard she'd put Charlotte up for adoption without even considering us. Maybe it would be a little easier to understand if you were her friend, someone she trusted and cared about, rather than a…well…"

"Rather than a stranger," Elle finished evenly. She didn't care for the implication that it had been merely an accident that Charlotte had been entrusted to her. "When Brittany decided she couldn't raise her child herself, she contacted the adoption agency I'd already signed up with. She saw my application and introductory video and something in them spoke to her. The agency had done extensive background checks on me and approved me as a qualified adopter. There was nothing at all questionable about the proceedings, if that's what's worrying you."

Parker's expression held a mixture of lingering sadness and grave apology. "I wasn't implying that. I know it was all legal and aboveboard. Charlotte obviously loves you and your mom. I just wish I knew why Brittany kept pushing us away. Adrian and I had been married for a year when Charlotte was born, and we were already talking about having children. Brittany had to have known we'd have happily helped her or raised Charlotte ourselves if she'd allowed us to. It's nothing against you, Elle, I swear. I guess I'm still just trying to understand."

Elle didn't want to even consider the possibility that she'd been chosen in an act of defiance. The whole adoption process had been too sacred to her to spoil it with such a petty motivation. Elle refused to accept that Brittany might have been driven by anything other than trying to provide the most loving home available for her child.

"Whatever Brittany's reasons, I'm Charlotte's

mother," she said, closing the dishwasher with a click. "I'll make very sure Brittany would never have cause to regret her choice."

"I believe you," Parker said quietly. "Shane told us he couldn't imagine a better mother for Charlotte, outside the family."

It was a backhanded compliment—Parker hadn't been joking about her tactlessness—but still Elle couldn't help but be gratified by Shane's endorsement. More than she should have been, perhaps.

Parker cleared her throat, and something about her expression made Elle tense again. "Adrian and I just made a will to name a guardian for Aubrey, in case the worst happens. We chose Shane."

Unsure why Parker was telling her this, Elle nodded. "I'm sure he feels honored, though I imagine it's a scenario he'd prefer not to even think about."

"We should have taken care of this sooner, but we've just been so busy since Adrian was born. Have, um—have you made a will for Charlotte? In case anything happens to you, I mean, God forbid?"

It was all Elle could do not to snap her reply. This question was edging very close to the line of intrusiveness, if not just over. "I've made arrangements."

She'd had a will drawn up within a week of bringing Charlotte into her home and her heart.

She'd named her mother as guardian in case something happened to Elle while Janet was still able to care for a child. If that didn't work out, Elle's cousin on her mother's side, Melanie Brady, one of her favorite relatives, had agreed to take Charlotte into her family in Charleston. A few years older than Elle, Melanie was the mother of two well-behaved teenaged boys who were very fond of Charlotte. Melanie and her husband, Dan, would be excellent guardians if the unthinkable happened. Elle was doing everything within her power to ensure her child a secure future.

"So, you've named a guardian? In case—"

"Yes. I have."

Parker twisted her hands in front of her, almost babbling as she blurted, "Charlie, Shane and I were pretty much raised together, you know. While my dad was in the service, I spent more time with the boys and Dottie than I did with my own mother. They were like my big brothers and we were all very close. Charlotte and Aubrey are so near to the same age they could be friends as well as cousins. If Brittany had just given me the chance, I'd have raised them like siblings. Adrian and I adore children and we want a big family."

"Let me get this straight." Elle crossed her arms and studied Parker in challenge, not sure she understood where this seemed to be going. "You aren't seriously asking me to give you my daughter, are you?"

Parker's blue eyes widened, her mouth forming into a dismayed frown. "No! Of course not, though obviously we would take her in a heartbeat. I'm just saying that if you ever need us, for any reason, we'll always be here. For Charlotte and for you, of course."

"Thank you. That's very kind of you." And awkward as hell. Dropping her arms, Elle turned toward the doorway in an attempt to bring this increasingly uncomfortable conversation to an end. "I really should go check on her now."

"Just one more thing."

Elle looked over her shoulder with a sigh she couldn't quite suppress. "What now?"

Parker drew a deep breath as if bolstering her courage, but forged on doggedly. "I know we all promised Shane we wouldn't bug you, but I can't let today end without begging you to bring Charlotte back to see Dottie again before…well… Say you'll consider bringing her back, Elle. Please?"

"Parker!" Shane had appeared in the doorway just in time to overhear her last plea. He scowled at his cousin. "We talked about this. You promised me you wouldn't do this."

"I know," she murmured with a quivering lip. "And I'm sorry. But it's for Dottie, Shane. You saw how happy this visit made her."

His eyes darkened even more. "Don't do that. I gave Elle my word that no one in the family would ask for more from her than today. She already doubts my integrity, and now you've made me into a liar."

Elle could see he wasn't faking his irritation, and it was obvious Parker agreed. Her eyes widened and she gave a hard, nervous swallow. "Of course Shane can be trusted, Elle! He's the most honest, dependable guy I've ever known. If he says he'll do something, you can bank on it. I'm the one who broke the agreement, not him. Please don't punish Shane—or Dottie."

Shane heaved a sigh. "Elle, maybe you'd like to go join your mom and Charlotte while I talk with my cousin for a few minutes."

With a nod, Elle made her escape. Even though she was still rather annoyed with Parker, and a bit closer to understanding why Brittany hadn't cared for Charlie's bluntly graceless cousin, she could almost feel sorry for her at that moment.

RELIEVED TO HAVE gotten away from the kitchen, Elle stepped into the living room ready to take her leave from the Scanlon family and escape to the peacefully anonymous hotel. She paused in the doorway at the sight of her daughter snuggled sleepily onto the sofa next to Dottie, who was reading her a book in a soothing singsong.

The empty wheelchair was parked at the end of the sofa. Charlotte seemed content, while Dottie looked positively blissful.

Swallowing hard, Elle looked for the others. She didn't see Adrian, so she assumed he was in another room with the baby. Her mother and Raymond sat in a far corner of the room, their heads rather close together as they laughed over a shared joke. Her mom was holding Raymond's upturned right hand. With a faint sigh, Elle shook her head. Seriously? The palm-reading routine? Now? At least Raymond didn't appear to mind… Actually, he looked as though he was enjoying it.

Finishing the tale, Dottie closed the book. She gave Charlotte a hug and a kiss on the top of her curly head. Only then did she notice that Elle had come into the room, illustrating how intently she'd focused on the child. "Oh. We were just reading a story. It was one of Charlie's favorites. Shane and Parker liked it, too, of course," she added belatedly.

"Charlotte loves books." Remembering her mother had said Charlotte might appreciate a memento of this visit in the future, Elle lifted her phone and snapped a couple of pictures of Charlotte and Dottie snuggled on the couch with the book. The gesture seemed to please Dottie, who beamed brightly for the camera and said she'd like to have a copy of the photo to frame.

After promising to send the photo to Shane's phone for him to print, Elle glanced toward her mother. "We've had such a nice visit, but we really should be going now, Mom."

She watched as her mother closed Raymond's fingers and gave his hand a pat before releasing him to reply, "Of course, Elle. Whenever you're ready."

Dottie flinched visibly, her arm going around Charlotte as if to keep her on the sofa. But instead, she gave a forced smile and hugged the child one more time before saying quietly, "All right, sweetheart. Go to your mommy now."

Charlotte climbed down from the sofa and dashed across the room to Elle, holding up her arms to be lifted. Elle settled the child on her hip, trying not to let Dottie's obvious sadness affect her voice when she said, "It was very nice to meet you, Dottie. And you, too, Raymond."

Dottie wiped her eyes with a tissue. "We feel the same about you and your mother, Elle. It's…" She swallowed, then continued steadily, "It's comforting to know that Charlotte is part of such a loving family. You don't know how much it means to me to have spent this time with her today."

"As a grandmother, myself, I certainly understand," Elle's mom said firmly. She approached the couch to take the older woman's hand. "It was an honor to meet you, Dottie."

"I enjoyed it, too, Janet. I wish the visit could have lasted even longer," Dottie said with a deep sigh. "But I'm very grateful for the time we had, so I won't be greedy. Enjoy the rest of your stay in Fayetteville."

Janet looked at Elle, and Elle almost winced in response to her mom's expertly utilized "puppy dog eyes." Her mother didn't have to say a word for Elle to get the message.

She folded with a slight sigh. "You know, Dottie, Mom and I don't have to be back in the shop until Wednesday, so we have all day tomorrow free. We thought we'd do some sightseeing in the morning and then have lunch before getting on the road. Would you like us to make a quick stop by here to see you again before we leave town?"

Janet beamed in approval of her daughter's offer as she spoke up to add, "Maybe we can coax Charlotte into singing 'I'm a Little Teapot' for you tomorrow, Dottie. It's adorable when she's in the mood to perform."

Elle thought Dottie was going to float right off the couch and throw her arms around their necks. Had the older woman been able, she might have done just that, so happy did she look.

"Oh, my goodness, yes! That would be wonderful. Why don't you come for lunch, and then drive home from here afterward?" Dottie's faded eyes almost glowed in anticipation.

Elle could feel all the eyes in the room focused on her then. Shane and Parker stood in the doorway now, while Raymond hovered behind her mom. All of them waiting for her response to the older woman's impromptu invitation.

She glanced at Dottie's hopeful face again and felt something inside her melt. "We'd be happy to join you for lunch here, if it's not too much trouble."

Dottie clasped her thin hands in a happy clap. "Not at all. Shane will help me put it together, won't you, dear?"

"Of course, Dottie." To give him credit, he sounded more resigned than pressed.

"Thank you, dear. So, we'll see you all tomorrow, then?"

Nodding in resignation, Elle clutched Charlotte's hand and led her toward the door.

SHANE SAT IN a booth in a softly lit hotel bar, his attention torn between the entrance across the room and the candle burning brightly in a ruby glass holder on the table. Something about that flame was hypnotic…or maybe he was just tired. Down-to-the-toenails tired. Seemed like he'd done nothing but put out metaphorical fires for the past year-plus since he'd gotten out of the army.

Maybe things would settle down soon, he thought, reaching up to rub his eyes. The company would always keep him busy, but financially it was at least stable now, which it certainly hadn't been this time last year. Dottie…well, his grandmother's health wasn't improving, but she wasn't in immediate danger. He'd found Charlotte, so he could relax on that front. He'd fulfilled his promise to Charlie.

As for his inconveniently convoluted feelings about Elle…

"Shane?"

He looked up to see her standing beside his table. She'd changed clothes, he noted immediately. Rather than the maroon-and-dark-gray outfit she'd worn to meet his family earlier that day, she now had on a more casual black-and-white top with black leggings and flats. She looked much more comfortable and relaxed—at least, until he saw the tension around the corners of her eyes and mouth. Was the prospect of spending time with him stressful enough to do that to her now?

Remembering the easy smiles she'd exchanged with him before she'd learned the truth about him, he pushed back a wave of regret as he rose and motioned to the other side of the small booth. "Hi, Elle. Can you take a few minutes?"

"I suppose so." She slid onto the bench and looked at him across the table, the flickering candlelight reflecting in her somber brown eyes.

"Why did you ask to meet me, Shane? What did you want to talk with me about?"

He reached down to the bench beside him and picked up the cheery rainbow-colored bow he'd set there when he'd been seated. Sliding it across the table to Elle, he said, "I wanted to return this. I found it on the dining room floor after y'all left this afternoon."

Her left eyebrow rose in a look of skeptical surprise. "We could have gotten this tomorrow when we come for lunch. Or is that still on?"

"Of course it is." He gave a little shrug. "I'll admit the bow is an excuse. I wanted a chance to talk with you without the others around."

A server stopped by the table. "Good evening. What can I get you?"

During the ten minutes or so he'd waited for Elle to join him, Shane had delayed ordering anything for himself. Because he'd be driving home—and considering the way Elle perched on the edge of her bench, it wouldn't be much later—he ordered a glass of Riesling for himself and then motioned toward her. "Elle?"

She hesitated, and he thought she might decline to order. But then she glanced up at the server and requested a Chardonnay.

"I don't know about you," he said after the server moved away, "but I could've used something a lot stronger after today."

She pushed a hand through her hair with a rather rueful laugh. "I understand the feeling. But the wine sounds good, too."

"How's your suite? Is everyone comfortable?"

"Yes, it's lovely, thank you. Charlotte's already asleep and Mom's reading. It was nice not to have to make the long drive again today. Thank you for making the arrangements."

"Of course. How was the rest of your day? Nice, I hope?"

"We had a good time. I'd found an indoor bounce-house facility online that's not far from your uncle's house, so we took Charlotte there to burn off some energy before dinner. There was one area set aside just for toddlers and Charlotte had a great time playing with the other kids there."

"I'm sure she did."

She showed him a snapshot she'd taken with her phone of Charlotte sprawled headfirst and belly-down on an inflated purple slide, tumbled hair flying, a huge grin on her flushed face. Shane had to laugh in response to the sheer joy captured in the shot.

"Definitely looks like she had a great time," he said, sliding the phone back to Elle, who smiled and nodded.

For just a few moments he could almost imagine they were the friends they could have been had things been different. But then the server brought their drinks and Elle seemed to collect herself. Her companionable smile faded as she put the phone away. "You said you wanted to talk with me?"

Somewhat regretfully, he nodded. "First, I want to apologize to you."

She gave a sigh that sounded somewhat impatient. "You've done that enough already."

Shaking his head, he said, "This isn't about the way I found you or got to know you. That apology still stands. This time it's on behalf of my cousin. Parker shouldn't have confronted you in the kitchen the way she did. You were our guest today and it wasn't fair of her to corner you. She'd promised she wouldn't, but Parker lets her emotions get the better of her sometimes—okay, a lot of times—and she took advantage of what she saw as an opportunity to make her case. I let her know in no uncertain terms that she was out of line."

Elle gripped her wineglass tightly with both hands, as if she wasn't sure what else to do with them. "You aren't responsible for your cousin's behavior. Maybe she did cross the line, but I'm quite capable of holding my own, as I hope you've realized by now."

A wry chuckle escaped him. "Yeah. I'm well aware of that."

"So, other than nagging you to bring Charlotte for more visits," he said after tasting his decent wine, "did she say anything else I should know about?"

Elle looked down into her glass for a moment, then lifted her gaze back up to his. "No," she said, deciding his family had been through enough without her making any more trouble among them. "She said nothing else to concern you."

Shane studied her face for an uncomfortably long moment, then shrugged, obviously not convinced.

CHAPTER TEN

FIGURING HIS TACTLESS cousin hadn't been quite as restrained as Elle implied, Shane almost apologized again, but he bit back the useless words. He said instead, "This day had to be uncomfortable for you."

"To say the least." Rolling the wineglass between her fingers, she kept her eyes steady on his face. "I know you and your family want to make sure Charlotte's in a secure, loving home, and I hope we've reassured you about that. As for the future, I've made solid arrangements for Charlotte in case anything should happen to me, Shane. You don't have to worry about that."

He winced, immediately understanding what else Parker must have said to make Elle uncomfortable. "I wasn't worried," he assured her firmly. "It never even occurred to me that you weren't planning for Charlotte's future."

Looking only somewhat appeased, she nodded. "It was one of the first things I saw to. You've actually met my attorney. Walt Becker. He handled my divorce and the adoption, and he drew up my will."

Walt had mentioned that he'd known Elle for a few years, but Shane hadn't realized that was on a professional basis. He admired Walt's respect for her privacy in not mentioning she was his client. "Walt seems like a great guy. I'm sure he's a competent attorney."

"He is."

Shane wondered, of course, who Elle had named as guardian, but it wasn't his place to ask. He could only trust that she'd made a wise choice and hope it would never be an issue. He wanted to believe Elle would be around for a very long time to care for Charlotte herself. His life experiences had made him a realist, but he tried not to let his family tragedies turn him into a pessimist.

"Parker means well," he felt obliged to say. "She just doesn't have a lot of filters."

"I can tell your family is very close."

Elle's carefully worded response didn't directly address his comment, but he supposed it explained why she was hesitant to criticize his cousin. "We are," he acknowledged. "Always have been."

He couldn't help wondering now if he'd reopened old wounds in his family by arranging only a passing encounter with Charlie's daughter. He'd had the best intentions, but maybe he should have just left it alone. For his family's sake. For Charlotte's. And certainly for Elle's.

"I'm—" Realizing he'd been on the verge of another pointless apology, he stopped himself and shook his head before saying, "Anyway, I'll make sure Parker leaves you alone in the future."

"It isn't your responsibility. If she bothers me, I'll take care of it."

A chuckle escaped him before he could stop it. Didn't she understand yet that when it came to his family, everything was his responsibility? At least, in his own opinion, if not entirely in theirs.

Though she looked confused by his reaction, Elle didn't ask him to explain. Instead, she took another drink, then said, "I assume that lack of filters had something to do with Brittany's rejection of Parker?"

"Maybe," Shane conceded. "I think Brittany was jealous of Parker's close relationship with Charlie. And I'm sure she sensed that Parker had reservations about whether Brittany was the right match for Charlie. To be honest, I'm not sure Parker would have thought anyone good enough for Charlie. She idolized him."

"Apparently, everyone did," Elle murmured into her glass.

"Pretty much," he agreed matter-of-factly. "Charlie was…" He had to swallow a sudden hard lump. "Charlie was special," he finished after a moment.

Elle set down her glass and studied him with her head tilted curiously. "That had to be a hard act to follow for a younger brother."

That drew a frown from him, touching on emotions he'd never wanted to examine too closely. "Maybe a little. But it gave me something to live up to, as well."

"I wished sometimes that I had a brother or sister growing up. I've considered adopting a second child in a year or two so Charlotte will have a sibling," she confided. "I love children and adoption was always my plan after an infection in my teens made it unlikely that I could conceive."

He felt his throat tighten with that shared confidence. To be told so young that she wouldn't be able to bear children must have been a tough pill to swallow. He kept his sympathy to himself, figuring she wouldn't want to hear it just now.

"Despite anyone's reservations about my capabilities," she continued pointedly, "I believe I can provide a loving, stable home as a single parent. I thought my ex-husband and I would adopt children together, but it didn't work out that way. I wouldn't let his sudden change of heart prevent me from going through with my long-term plans. And I didn't want to put my dreams on hold on the off chance that I'd someday fall in love with someone who shared my desire."

He found that he didn't really want to think about that scenario. About Elle falling in love with anyone. He told himself firmly that was only because it wasn't currently relevant.

Elle seemed to have her future, and Charlotte's, pretty well planned out. He felt obligated for the sake of his niece—and maybe for other reasons he was trying to ignore—to do what he could to help.

He reached into the inside pocket of his leather jacket and drew out a thick envelope. "Elle, there are some papers in here I think you should give to your attorney."

Without taking it, she looked at the envelope with open suspicion. "What is that?"

"Several things. There's a family tree, of sorts, for Charlotte's information in the future, giving names of her paternal ancestors. I don't know much about Brittany's family background, only that they were estranged. Also, I made a list of any health issues I thought might be valuable for Charlotte's medical records."

Elle nodded, looking somewhat more relaxed. "That's very useful information, thank you."

He continued to hold out the envelope, his gaze level on hers. "There's also a copy of Charlotte's original birth certificate, naming Charles Raymond Scanlon as her father, and the paperwork to prove that Charlie was an army corpsman who was killed in action. I'm not sure how you'd go about securing survivor's benefits for his daughter, but since he died before the adoption, I would think she'd qualify for them. I'm no legal expert, of course, but Walt—or whichever attorney you choose—should be able to find out for you. For her."

He set the envelope on the table and slid it closer to her, next to the cheery bow. "It's up to you what to do with all of this, of course. I just wanted you to have it."

She nodded again, looking at the envelope without touching it. "All right."

"If you'd like, I'll talk to some—"

"No," she cut in quickly, her eyebrows drawing into a warning frown. "You've done enough. I'll handle it from here."

He gave in with a resigned sigh. He'd only wanted to help. "Okay, fine. You know how to reach me if you ever need me."

She set her almost-empty wineglass down. "I should go back up to the room now. Are you sure we should still come for lunch tomorrow? It's not too much for Dottie, is it?"

"Are you kidding? She's counting the minutes. And don't worry about the trouble. I've ordered food to be delivered to the house at exactly noon. It seemed the easiest plan."

"Will you be there?"

Was she hoping he would say no? "I promised Dottie I'd stop by, though I have a busy day of work lined up. I'm not sure I'll make it for lunch, but I'll do my best to be there before you leave."

"Okay," she said without changing her expression. "Then we'll see you tomorrow."

"Elle." He reached out to catch her hand when she started to pick up the bow and envelope he'd brought.

Her hand went very still in his and she stared at him across the table, the candlelight casting flickering shadows over the face he still found so appealing. "What?"

"Is there any chance you and I could somehow be friends again?"

He felt a slight tremor run through her small hand. "Were we friends?" she asked in a coolly impassive tone.

"We were getting there," he replied evenly. "I never pretended to be anyone other than I am— and you seemed to like me well enough until you found out I'm Charlotte's uncle."

"Until I found out you'd hidden that from me, you mean," she countered.

At least she hadn't accused him of lying to her. She knew he hadn't. Not in so many words, anyway.

"Okay. So…can we call a truce now?"

"We aren't at war, Shane," she said, letting weariness show through her carefully composed facade. "We both just want what's best for our families. But I won't make Charlotte the rope in a game of genetic tug-of-war."

"Neither will I," he assured her flatly, repelled by the image. "I promise you that."

"Then whether you and I could have been friends or…well… Anyway, it's moot now, isn't it? The only concern is what's best for Charlotte. And I'll be the one to make the final decisions on that."

He didn't immediately remove his hand from hers, nor did she try to pull away as she looked steadily across the table. Was she as aware of that point of contact as he? Did she feel his heart pulsing through his fingers, the way he felt hers? Was she remembering the kiss that still haunted him every time he looked at her soft lips?

Maybe he looked at those lips just a bit too long. She tugged her hand free, then stood, scooping up the bow and the envelope as she rose. "Good night, Shane. Thanks for the wine. We'll see you tomorrow."

He didn't offer to walk her out, since he doubted she'd accept. Rather, he couldn't resist saying, "Elle? I don't find it at all hard to believe that we could have been friends. Or…" he added meaningfully, leaving her to fill in the rest as he had when she'd stumbled over it.

She turned and walked away without responding, leaving him to finish his wine in a brooding silence.

A FORTYSOMETHING WOMAN Elle had never seen before opened the door when Elle, her mom and Charlotte arrived at the Scanlon home Monday morning. Tall and angular with bleached hair and a prominent chin, she introduced herself as Josie Oliver, Dottie's home health-care worker, and then ushered them inside.

Dressed in a red-and-white top with a teddy bear appliqué and bright red leggings, Charlotte bounced into the house with an eagerness that showed how much she'd enjoyed yesterday's visit. She was already calling out for "Aub'ey," though Elle had tried to warn her that Aubrey might not be here today.

But Aubrey was there, sitting in a plastic baby seat with brightly colored beads attached to the front. He watched in fascination as his mother hung shiny decorations on a tall artificial spruce tree that had been erected in the front window of the living room while Dottie sat in her chair giving Parker orders about the decorations. It looked as though the tree was almost finished, covered with so many ornaments that the branches almost sagged. Elle got the immediate impression that Dottie was being very particular.

Dottie looked away from the tree when they entered the room. Her face lit up. "Charlotte!"

Charlotte had already run to admire Aubrey, spinning the beads to make him laugh. She looked around at Dottie and pointed to the baby. "Aub'ey!"

"That's right, darling. That's your cousin Aubrey. And he's so happy to see you! We all are."

Only then did Dottie look up to greet Janet and Elle, who'd tensed at Dottie's emphasis on the word *cousin*. Still, Elle kept her tone gentle as she spoke to the older woman, who somehow looked even more frail than she had the day before. "The tree is beautiful."

Stepping down off a stepstool, Parker straightened the dance-themed graphic T-shirt she wore with jeans and sneakers. Her expression was carefully schooled when she spoke lightly in response to Elle's compliment. "We usually put the tree up the first weekend in December, but Dottie insisted we move it up a week so Charlotte could see it. Dad helped set it up this morning before he left for the office and I've been decorating it for the past hour and a half or so."

Dottie cocked her head, studying the tree with narrowed eyes. "Parker, move that shiny red ball—the one with the gold stripes—a little to the left. Hazel Porter gave me that ornament, you know. She bought it in Mexico."

Parker made a little face that explained why the job was taking so long, but she followed her grandmother's instructions. "How's this?"

"Better." Dottie glanced toward her guests. "I've been collecting ornaments for years. I know where each one came from. My late husband bought most of them for me, but friends and family have also given me special ones."

"It's lovely, Dottie," Elle's mother said warmly. "We'll have to put our tree up this week, won't we, Elle?"

"Maybe next weekend." Elle wasn't in the mood to think about Christmas just then. She had this visit to get through first.

Dottie's attention had already returned to Charlotte. "See my tree, sweetheart?" She motioned with a tremulous hand. "Isn't it pretty?"

"Pretty," Charlotte repeated. She gasped when Parker flipped a switch to turn on the multicolored tree lights. "Party dots!" Charlotte squealed in delight.

Elle and her mom shared a laughing look.

"Did she say party dots?" Parker asked, she and her grandmother both looking confused.

Elle chuckled. "She's been seeing trees going up in the businesses back home and for some reason, she's decided the little lights signify a party. So…party dots."

"Oh, that's so cute." Parker held out a sparkly silver ornament. "Would you like to hang this on the tree, Charlotte? I'm sure we can find the perfect place for it."

Charlotte looked at Elle, who nodded permission. Elle heard her mom snap a photograph with her phone as Parker helped Charlotte carefully hang the ornament from one of the few bare branches within her reach. Another picture for Charlotte's scrapbook of extended biological relatives. Another connection to a family that wasn't Elle's.

The doorbell rang. "Probably the food," Dottie said. "Josie will let them in."

Parker moved toward the doorway. "I'll give her a hand."

"Would you like some help?" Elle felt obliged to ask.

Parker smiled at her, obviously trying to be on her best behavior. "I've got it, thanks. You could keep an eye on Aubrey for me, though."

"Yes, of course." It was just as well, Elle thought, that she and Parker probably wouldn't see each other much, if at all, after today. Though she would try her best to be cordial, and suspected Parker was under stern orders from her cousin to do the same, she thought they'd have to work at being even casual friends. Between Parker's disappointment over Brittany's rejection and Elle's own defensiveness, there was just so much baggage between them.

Is there any chance you and I could somehow be friends again?

The echo of Shane's deep voice whispered in her head, as it had repeatedly during a restless night. She could almost feel her hand tingling where his had covered it, his vibrant heat seeping into her skin as he'd looked her in the eye and asked the question she still couldn't answer.

She very clearly remembered something else he'd said, as well. *I don't find it at all hard to believe that we could have been friends. Or...*

That "or..." had reverberated too many times through her mind, taunting her with what-might-have-been fantasies that had left her aching and frustrated with her rebellious imagination.

"Why don't I help Parker and Josie set up for lunch?" Providing a badly needed distraction, Elle's mom patted her arm as she walked past, as if relaying a message Elle couldn't quite interpret. "You can chat with Dottie and watch the children. We'll let you know when everything is ready."

Charlotte had already returned to sit on the floor beside Aubrey's baby seat, drawing giggles from him as she made silly faces and sang to him. Without taking her eyes from her great-grandchildren, Dottie motioned toward the couch. "Elle, dear, would you hand me that throw, please? It's a little chilly in here."

Though Elle thought the room was on the warm side, especially with the gas fire flickering in the fireplace next to Dottie, she obligingly fetched the white crocheted afghan draped over an arm of the couch. She wrapped it gently around the older woman's thin shoulders. "How's that?"

"Much better, thank you." Dottie smiled up at her then. "She's so beautiful. I've thought of her every day for the past two years. I prayed every night that she was well and happy and that I'd get to see her at least one more time before I join the ones I love on the other side. I can't thank you enough for bringing her, Elle."

Shaken by the intensity of the woman's emotions, Elle pushed back a strand of hair before saying, "It was mostly Shane's doing. He's the one who found us and talked me into coming. He's the one you should thank."

"Oh, I have."

Elle wondered if Dottie really understood the lengths her grandson had gone to just to make her happy. Though Elle might still harbor some resentment about the way Shane had gone about the whole thing, she did understand—especially now—why he'd felt the need to do so.

"Oh, by the way." Dottie motioned again, this time toward the coffee table. "Those two photographs on top of the books there? I want you to take them with you when you leave. For Charlotte. You can keep them safe for her. I hope someday she'll be grateful to you for doing so."

Elle looked down at the photos now in her hand. The one on top was a posed family portrait, the type often used for a Christmas card. She guessed that it had been taken about ten years ago. Her eyes went immediately to Shane, who looked young and carefree as he smiled at the camera from the far left of the photo. Though it was a bit difficult to draw her gaze away from his face, she looked at the others, identifying them one by one. Dottie, seated but still looking taller and stronger than the frail woman in the wheelchair now. An older man behind her Elle assumed to be Shane's grandfather. His sons and grandsons resembled him strongly. Raymond looked much as he had yesterday, if a little less gray, his arm around a dramatically made-up Parker who looked to still be in her teens.

Charlie stood between Shane and their dad. Even in this group shot, he appeared to be the focus of attention, his arms slung casually around his brother and father, just a little taller than anyone else in the photo, his lively blue eyes focused intensely on the camera in a way that made Elle fancy he could almost see her studying him. She could sense the energy and charisma exuding from him even in this flat, still surface.

And yet, her eyes kept returning to Shane.

"It's the whole family—except for Shane's mother, Emily, who died long before that was taken," Dottie said, though the clarification was hardly necessary. "I'll try to find a photo of Emily and Charlie to send to you later. Perhaps Charlotte will appreciate knowing what her biological family looked like. Maybe she'll see the resemblances she shares."

"I'm sure she will." With a little pang, Elle noted those similarities herself, and knew they would only be more obvious as her daughter grew and matured.

She looked then at the second photograph. Charlie stood in the center, against a spectacular backdrop of trees clothed in stunning autumn colors. He had one arm around a laughing Shane. With the other arm, he cradled a pretty, curvy young woman who snuggled against his side with a red-nailed hand placed possessively over his heart. Her hair was a golden blond and her eyes were large and a pale, almost lavender blue. Though there was little other resemblance to her daughter, the dimple in her chin looked exactly like Charlotte's.

"That's the only photo I have of Brittany," Dottie said, her tone more somber now. "I thought maybe Charlotte would want that one, too, despite…well…"

She left it at that, for which Elle was grateful.

Elle's attention was caught then by something else in the photo. Was Charlie wearing… Yes. He was. This was the same black leather jacket Shane wore so often now. Elle was sure of it.

She shook her head at this fresh reminder of how much this family still focused on one missing member. She suddenly recalled military funerals she'd seen on television—Air Force, she thought. During the ceremonies, several planes had executed the "missing man formation," in which one of the planes split off to disappear, leaving a noticeable gap. She sensed that this family had been flying their version of that formation for the past two years. It was part of the reason, perhaps, that Shane had been so obsessed with finding Charlotte.

Elle's mom appeared in the doorway then to announce that lunch was ready. "Are you hungry, Charlotte?" she asked.

"Hungry," Charlotte agreed, jumping to her feet. She pointed down to the baby who was gumming his fist and drooling around it. "Aub'ey hungry, too?"

"I'm sure he is. Elle, why don't you bring Dottie into the dining room? I told Parker I'd bring Aubrey."

"I help!" Charlotte dashed around to grip the wheelchair handles.

Dottie's laugh sounded a bit wheezy to Elle. "You're such a big girl, Charlotte."

Studying Dottie's face, Elle frowned. Was she looking a bit paler than she had only minutes before? "Dottie, are you okay?"

Dottie straightened in her chair. "Oh, I'm fine, thank you, dear. Maybe I'm hungry, too."

Parker was lighting candles on the table when they entered. Salads waited at five place settings and a couple of dishes that both looked and smelled deliciously Italian sat on the table to be served family style. Parker told them that Josie was taking advantage of this time to run some personal errands and would be back later in the afternoon to help Dottie with her meds and daily exercises.

With Charlotte's "help," Elle maneuvered Dottie's wheelchair into her space at the table. Beaming and cooing baby talk, Elle's mom carried Aubrey in. He gazed up at her in curious fascination, looking perfectly happy to be carried by this amusing stranger. But then he caught sight of his mother and reached out for her, whimpering.

Parker took him and sat at the table with the baby on her lap. "He's about ready to nurse and go down for his nap," she said, "but maybe he'll let Mommy eat first?" she added to her son, who giggled and made a grab for her earring.

Sitting on her knees in her chair, Charlotte ate the cherry tomatoes and cucumber slices from her salad, then dug eagerly into the pasta Elle scooped onto her plate. Charlotte wasn't at all picky when it came to pasta but this food was delicious.

"It's from a little Italian place just down the street," Parker explained. "One of Dottie's favorite takeout places, isn't it, Dottie?"

Her grandmother smiled faintly, though Elle noted that Dottie had barely touched her food. Dottie seemed almost unable to take her attention from Charlotte long enough to eat. Elle thought she looked rather sad; was the older woman already dreading saying goodbye again? Maybe it hadn't been so kind to agree to this extra time together after all.

Aubrey fussed again, squirming in his mother's lap. Dottie sighed and set down her fork. "You're going to have to feed that child, Parker. He's hungry."

Parker replied with exaggerated patience. "I know, Dottie. I was just going to give it five more minutes and then I'll feed him and tuck him in for his nap."

"I'm not sure he's going to wait. Five minutes

feels like a long time to a—" Dottie stopped talking with a sharp intake of breath.

"Dottie?" Elle paused with her fork halfway to her mouth. "What's wrong?"

Dottie met her eyes and Elle set the fork down on her plate with a clatter in response to the panic on the older woman's face. She charged around to kneel by the wheelchair. "What is it? Are you having trouble breathing? Are you in pain?"

Dottie nodded, her shaking hand pressed again her thin chest.

"Dottie?" Patting her increasingly fussy baby, Parker started to rise. "Dottie, can you answer? Are you choking?"

"Dottie hurt?" Charlotte asked, her eyes round with anxiety.

Elle had her phone already in hand. "I'm calling 9-1-1. Mom, would you take Charlotte into the other room to look at the Christmas tree and read a book or something? I'll stay with Dottie."

While Parker juggled her hungry child and hovered at Dottie's other side, Elle made the call for an ambulance. Reassured that one was on the way, she set down the phone and reached out to support Dottie, who was sagging in the wheelchair, her face colorless except for the blue tint around her mouth.

"Help is on the way, Dottie," Elle told her steadily, projecting a calm she was far from feeling. "Don't worry, we're going to take care of you, okay?"

Dottie nodded feebly and mouthed, "Call... Shane."

"I will," Elle promised. "Lean your head back and try to relax, Dottie. We'll look after everything."

Dottie started to comply, but then her eyes opened again and she scowled at Parker, raising her voice to a croak to be heard over the now-wailing Aubrey. "For heaven's sake, Parker...go feed that baby. Elle...Elle's got this."

Parker looked at Elle, who gave her a reassuring nod. "It's fine, Parker. I'll stay with her. I think she's already feeling a little better, aren't you, Dottie?"

Dottie's eyes were closing again as her brief spurt of spirited energy faded. Still she murmured, "Yes. Feed...Aubrey."

To Elle's almost overwhelming relief, the ambulance arrived quickly. She hadn't wanted to let go of Dottie long enough to use her phone for fear the woman would fall out of the chair, but as soon as two efficient EMTs came into the room, she called Shane.

"I'm sorry, I've been held up," he said when he answered, having seen her name on his screen. "I'll be there—"

"Shane, we're taking your grandmother to the

hospital. She's not feeling well. Parker is busy with the baby and Mom's watching Charlotte, so I'll ride with Dottie in the ambulance. You probably want to meet us there."

She heard the tension in Shane's voice when he asked, "What's wrong with her?"

"She's having shortness of breath and, I think, chest pains. The paramedics are putting her on a gurney now."

"I'm feeling better," Dottie muttered, twisting away from the oxygen one of the EMTs was trying to administer to her. "Tell Shane everyone's overreacting."

"Tell Dottie to behave herself and do what the EMTs think is best," Shane replied, overhearing.

After Elle had relayed the message and Dottie had subsided with a grumble, Shane asked, "Where's Josie?"

"Josie is running errands. I have to go now, Shane. I'll see you at the hospital."

"Elle—thank you. I'm glad you're there with her."

She swallowed hard, letting her fiercely controlled nerves break free for only a moment as she clutched the phone and let his deep voice wash through her. She wished he was here now. She found it deeply comforting that she would be seeing him soon—for Dottie's sake, of course, she told herself as she shoved the phone in her pocket and hurried after the gurney.

CHAPTER ELEVEN

ELLE WAS IN the emergency department waiting room when Shane and Raymond rushed in, both looking grimly worried. She was so relieved to see Shane, it was all she could do not to throw herself in his arms. It hadn't been her place to deal with Dottie's medical emergency, and she certainly hadn't felt qualified to do so. But no one else had been available, considering Parker's hands had been full with her hungry baby.

Shane must have seen in her face that she could use bolstering. He took both her hands in his, warming her cold fingers in his palms as he gazed down at her. "What have you heard?"

"Not much," she replied, clinging to his hands, feeling her nerves grow steadier with his strength. "She seemed to grow weaker on the way over, but she tried to give me a thumbs-up when they rolled her back."

"Do they think it's her heart?" Raymond asked, hovering close.

"I don't know. The EMTs weren't telling me anything, they just put her on oxygen and an IV and rushed her straight into the ambulance. I was told to wait here."

"I'll go tell them her family is here," Raymond said, moving toward the desk. "Maybe they'll tell me something more."

"Let's sit down, Elle." Still holding her hands, Shane drew her toward an empty vinyl bench. "You look like you need to get off your feet for a few minutes."

Drawing a deep breath, she sank onto the bench, pulling her hands from his to clasp them in her lap. "Sorry I fell apart when you came in. I guess this whole episode shook me more than I'd realized."

His eyebrows rose as he gave her a quizzical smile. "That was falling apart? If so, you must have nerves of steel."

"It didn't feel like it at the time," she said, though she appreciated the implied compliment.

"Charlotte and your mom are still at the house?"

"Yes. I got a text from Mom just before you came in. She said they're fine. Charlotte decided to take a nap while Aubrey did, so everything is fine there. Mom offered to babysit both kids so Parker could join us, though she wasn't sure Parker would be comfortable with that."

"I don't know why she wouldn't be. I'd absolutely trust your mother with the kids."

That, too, pleased her. "Thanks, Shane. She really is very capable, despite her playing around with the psychic thing."

"I know that." He spoke gently, but a bit absently, his attention turning toward the information desk where his uncle stood in serious conversation with a nurse. Elle knew Shane was worried about Dottie. Regardless of his conversations with Elle about preparing himself for the inevitable, he was far from ready to lose his lovably bossy grandmother.

Elle reached out impulsively to cover his hand on his knee with her own. Giving a bracing squeeze, she said, "She was awake, Shane. When they took her back. She was awake and alert."

He took her hand in both his own, seeming to draw comfort from the contact, as she had only minutes earlier. "Thanks for that. Maybe it's just a virus or something. A bad cold. She's prone to those."

"I'm sure it's something like that," she said, though of course they both knew she couldn't be confident.

Raymond rejoined them, glancing at their clasped hands before saying, "They're running tests. They said they'll come out to talk to us as soon as they know something. It could be a while."

Releasing Elle's hand, Shane motioned his uncle to a seat. "We might as well try to get comfortable. Can I get either of you anything? Coffee? A soda?"

Both declined.

Shane grimaced. "There's no need for you to hang around, Elle. I know you'd planned to be on the road home soon. Why don't I call you a cab to take you back to the house and I'll let you know later how things are going here."

She hesitated only a few moments before shaking her head. "I can't leave without knowing how Dottie's doing. Charlotte's still napping and Mom's got her e-reader loaded with several good books she hasn't yet had time to start, so there's no reason for me to rush back."

"You're sure?"

Elle pictured Dottie's pale face. "I'm sure."

Parker came through the waiting room door a few minutes later, spotted them and hurried to join them. "What have you heard?"

Her father tugged her down to the bench beside him, telling her what he'd already shared with Shane and Elle.

Parker glanced at Elle on the opposite bench, her gaze flickering to Shane beside her, then back. "Your mother is watching the kids," she said. "They're both sound asleep. I don't know about Charlotte, but Aubrey will be down for a good two hours yet."

"I wouldn't be surprised if Charlotte sleeps almost as long," Elle replied. "She was keyed up about being in a new place last night and didn't go to sleep until late. She was awake early this morning, ready to play and explore. I expected her to sleep through most of the drive home, but I'm sure she's more comfortable where she is now."

"It was nice of your mother to offer to watch them." Parker twisted the hem of her T-shirt nervously between her fingers. "She said she knew I needed to be here with Dottie."

"They'll be fine, Parker," Shane said. "Janet's been helping Elle take care of Charlotte for years now, and you've seen how well that's working out. Janet knows what she's doing."

Parker nodded, looking marginally reassured. "Adrian will pick him up after he gets off work, though maybe we'll be back by then. Dottie probably just needs some pills or something, don't you think? I mean, she was fine this morning. Bossing me around with her Christmas tree, making plans for the rest of her decorations. They'll probably just give her some medicine and send her back home, right?"

Raymond wrapped an arm around her. "That's a possibility, hon. Let's just wait and see, okay?"

She nestled into his shoulder, her expression making it clear she didn't want to think about the other possibilities. Sitting quietly beside Shane, Elle studied the father and daughter through her

lashes, remembering so many times when she'd
drawn comfort from her own dad in just that position.

Shane shifted restlessly beside her, drawing her
attention back to him. "I'm going to find some
coffee," he said. "I'll bring you a cup, too, Raymond. Parker, I know you're off caffeine these
days, but I'm sure there's bottled water in the machines. Elle? What can I get you?"

It was characteristic of the man she'd come to
know that he was determined to fetch drinks for
them. She suspected he felt helpless to do anything for his grandmother, so he would focus on
looking out for the family around him—and he
was including her in his care. With a faint sigh,
she stood when he did.

"Coffee sounds good," she said, more to go
along with the distraction than because she was
thirsty. "I'll help you carry them."

He gave her a nod of gratitude along with a
look that made her breath catch. "Thanks, Elle."

She turned quickly to move toward the vending
machines. She wondered if she was only imagining the feel of Parker's gaze following them as
Shane fell into step beside her.

ELLE HAD ALWAYS fancied that the rules of time
changed in hospital waiting rooms. She could almost feel the minutes tick by, drawing out the

tension as long as possible. People came and went around them—some looking ill or in pain, others visibly worried about loved ones. Some paced, some flipped through tattered magazines or stared at phones in their hands. A hush almost invariably fell over the room when the doors to the mysterious inner sanctum opened and a nurse or doctor came through to summon family members or call for the next patient, only for conversations to resume when the doors closed again.

Like the people around them, Elle, Shane, Raymond and Parker watched those doors while trying to distract themselves from their worries. Elle stayed in touch with her mother by text and exchanged a few business messages with Kristen, who assured her everything was running smoothly at the shop. Shane and Raymond talked in low voices, while Parker alternated between pacing and checking regularly on her son. After an agonizing hour, a young doctor approached them with an update.

Elle started to move away to give the family privacy, but Shane detained her with a hand on her knee, making it clear he wanted her to stay. Was he just being polite? Or seeking moral support? Whatever his reason, she felt the connection between them strengthen with the contact, and this time she was pretty sure she wasn't imagining it. For whatever reason, he wanted her there—and so she would stay. For now.

The doctor explained that Dottie was stable, but that a cardiologist had been called and more tests were being ordered.

"Are you saying my grandmother had a heart attack?" Parker asked bluntly, her cheeks pale.

"That seems to be the case," the doctor replied with typical medical prudence.

Elle felt Shane's fingers spasm reflexively on her knee, and she wondered if he even knew his hand was still there.

The doctor explained that the crisis had probably been caused by a blood clot, and that the cardiologist would let them know what treatment, if any, would be administered from this point. Elle heard the words *catheterization* and *stent*, both of which took her back to her own father's losing battle with heart disease. Her dad had been young, just shy of sixty, when a massive attack had taken him. How much harder would it be for Dottie, with her age and health issues, to fight this battle?

"Is she strong enough to survive these procedures?" Shane asked quietly.

After assuring them that such procedures were performed successfully on senior citizens every day, the doctor took a step back, promising to keep them informed.

Parker moved away then to call her husband with an update, while Raymond went off in search of the men's room. Shane looked at Elle when they were alone. It seemed to occur to him then that his hand was still on her knee, though she had been all too aware of the warmth seeping through her jeans. She imagined she could feel the temperature drop when he drew back.

"Seriously, Elle, you don't have to stay," he said gruffly. "I can arrange a cab for you. I'm sure you'd rather be with your mom and Charlotte."

"Charlotte's still sleeping, the last I heard. And Mom's perfectly content babysitting two napping babies. She'll have a great time with them when they wake up."

"Still—"

"Shane." She twisted on the bench to look at him steadily. "Do you *want* me to leave?"

He hesitated only a beat before he sighed and pushed a hand through his hair. "No," he admitted, his eyes fixed on her face.

Her deep reactions to his words and his expression were complicated, to say the least. Still, she kept her face impassive as she said simply, "Then I'll stay."

"I know you'd planned to be on the road home by now."

"Charlotte will sleep in the car if we don't get away until late. Neither Mom nor I would be comfortable leaving while you're all still waiting to hear if Dottie's going to be okay. For now, Mom can help with babysitting and I—well, I'm here for whatever you need."

"Thank you, Elle."

He continued to gaze at her as he spoke, and she found herself unable to look away. She was aware of the bustle and noise surrounding them, but the heart-wrenching expression in Shane's beautiful sapphire eyes was all she could focus on. She wanted desperately to reassure him, to tell him that his beloved grandmother would be okay, but that was a promise she couldn't make.

She settled back into her seat, out of ideas for how to help other than simply to be there for him. Maybe that was enough.

IT WAS LATE afternoon before Shane could be somewhat reassured that Dottie was out of immediate danger. With her age and frailty, the procedure had not been a simple or risk-free choice, but the efficient cardiologist had assured the family that Dottie was a fighter. She was stable and awake, and after a night or two in the hospital for close observation, she would most likely be discharged to resume her home health care.

Only then did Shane allow himself to draw a deep breath for the first time since Elle had called him to tell him his grandmother was being loaded into an ambulance. He was so grateful to Elle for having been there for Dottie, for riding to the hospital with her to give Parker a chance to settle her baby and, most of all, for staying with him—with all of them—providing a calming and reassuring presence.

He'd given her several opportunities to leave, all of which she had politely declined. He was well aware that having lunch with his grandmother had been a generous impulse on Elle's part—and he hadn't missed the strongly hinting look her mother had given her beforehand. Yet she'd stayed to offer any assistance she could when Dottie took ill. She'd fetched coffees and waters here at the hospital, gently urged Raymond to eat a sandwich and encouraged nursing-mother Parker to stay hydrated. She'd quietly located tissues when Parker dissolved into tears as Dottie was wheeled to the operating room. Shane wasn't sure they'd have managed nearly as well without Elle, though she waved off any attempts to thank her.

Dottie had to lie still for several hours after the procedure. Two visitors at a time were allowed back to see her. Because Parker needed to leave to take care of her baby, she and Raymond went first. Once again Elle stayed behind with Shane.

"It's sounding very promising," she said to him when the others had been escorted back.

"Yeah." He allowed himself a slight smile. "Dottie's tough. She's not ready to check out yet."

"No. She has too many orders still to give," Elle replied with a chuckle.

His smile deepened. "You've gotten to know her pretty well in a short time."

"Maybe she reminds me of what my own mom will be like in another thirty years. If you add in a caftan and a novelty-shop crystal ball, of course."

For the first time in hours, he laughed. And he could thank Elle for that, too.

Shane was touched again by the kindness both Elle and Janet were showing his family. They had expected to be back in their home by now, having said their goodbyes—permanently?—to the Scanlon clan.

With the immediate crisis averted, Parker left then to go take care of her child. After seeing her off, Shane turned to his uncle. "How is Dottie?"

Raymond rested a hand on Shane's shoulder. "She's irritated that we're hanging around here all day when there were more important things to tend to. She wanted Parker to decorate the mantel this afternoon."

Shane felt a little more tension seep out of him. "Okay, that sounds about right, coming from her."

"She wants to see you next, but the nurse asked you to wait about an hour to go back, if you would. They're taking vitals and running a couple more tests and they want her to rest a bit."

Shane glanced at his watch with a nod. "I was planning to hang around for a few more hours, anyway, just to make sure she's okay for the night. Raymond, you head home. Have something to eat, get some rest. And would you give Elle a ride—"

"Mother wants to see Elle, too. She insisted on it. She got a little agitated before I promised I'd relay the request."

Taken aback by his uncle's interruption, Shane said, "Did she?"

Raymond turned to Elle. "Shane can give her a message if you'd rather leave with me now, Elle. Mom will understand that you can't stay all evening. She's still rattled from all the commotion and the pain meds they've given her."

Though she, too, appeared startled, Elle shook her head. "I'll stay if she wants to see me. I can call for a ride afterward. You should go home to rest, Raymond."

Shane was beginning to think Elle didn't want to leave. Was she still worried about Dottie? Or was she staying for his sake? He should probably try again to reassure her he was fine here on his own—but he didn't want her to go, either.

A few minutes later they saw Raymond off with promises to call immediately if anything changed. Shane left his phone number with the woman behind the information desk, saying he would be in the hospital cafeteria in case he was needed for any reason.

"I could really use a bite to eat," he admitted to Elle, almost feeling his stomach gnawing at him now that the initial fear for his grandmother had abated somewhat.

"I'm a little hungry, too," she agreed. "Even hospital cafeteria food sounds good."

He motioned toward the elevators. "Actually, the cafeteria here is pretty decent. Especially when you haven't eaten all day."

"All day?" She glanced up at him with a lifted eyebrow. "Didn't you have breakfast?"

"Only three cups of coffee," he confessed. "I was running late for a meeting and figured I'd make up for it with the Italian food I'd ordered for lunch with Dottie."

She shook her head in reprimand. "I tried to get you to eat something this afternoon."

"I know. I wasn't hungry then. I am now."

Unlike the surgery waiting room, the cafeteria was far from somber and quiet. Between the chatter of diners and workers and the clanking of plates and cutlery, Shane had to lean forward over the table to make himself heard when he spoke after they'd been seated with their trays of food. "How's your veggie pizza?"

Elle looked up from her plate with a smile that

wrinkled her nose in a way he found captivating. "Well—it's not nearly as good as the lovely Italian meal you ordered for us for lunch. But it's not bad."

"Did you get any of that meal at lunch?" he asked as he tried to focus on his food instead of her charms. A juicy burger and a pile of crisp-fried onion rings waited for his attention. He'd been too hungry to worry about eating healthy tonight.

"I only had a couple of bites. Enough to know it was delicious."

"Sorry you didn't get to enjoy more of it."

"So was I," she assured him.

They ate without speaking for a few minutes. Shane's food was good, but he had trouble focusing. His attention kept wandering across the table. He couldn't seem to stop looking at Elle. She looked tired, understandably, he thought with regret, but still striking enough that he noticed a few second glances from men who passed by their table.

She glanced up to find him looking at her, not the first time their eyes had met. "What?"

He pushed away his nearly cleaned plate. "I guess I just keep asking myself why you're still here."

Elle wiped her fingers on a napkin and took a sip of her water before replying. "Your grandmother asked to see me. It would have been rude to leave without stopping in."

"Not just that. You've been here all day. Something tells me it wasn't just because you like hanging out in hospitals."

"Hardly." She made a face and tossed the napkin on her plate. "I suppose I was so shaken by what happened that I needed to do something to try to help. Even if that was just to keep you company in the waiting room. I know how much she means to you all, and how scared you were for her. I like her, too. Being available in case any of you needed me seemed like the least I could do."

He didn't want to hear her downplay her contributions. Instead, he smiled and said, "So maybe we're still friends, after all?"

For a moment, he thought perhaps he'd pushed his luck. But then she sighed and spread her hands in a gesture of resignation. "Okay, fine. I guess we're friendly enough."

It wasn't exactly what he'd said, but her put-upon expression made him grin nonetheless. And he was deeply satisfied to see a smile teasing the corners of her lips. On impulse, he reached across the table and caught her hand, giving it a squeeze before he released her. "We should probably go back to the waiting room now. We'll be able to get in to see Dottie soon."

DOTTIE LAY ON her back in a hospital bed hooked to monitors and IV bags, looking so tiny and frail against the pillows that Elle felt her throat tighten. She felt Shane falter a bit when he entered the room beside her, and she suspected he had been just as deeply affected. Still, he kept a smile on his face as he crossed the room to plant a kiss on her forehead while Elle hung back.

"Hey, Grandma. What's with all the drama today?"

"Just everyone overreacting," Dottie shot back, her voice weak but spirited as she looked up at her grandson. "And don't call me Grandma."

He chuckled and kissed her again before straightening. "How are you feeling?"

"Like crap."

The blunt response made Shane laugh and Elle smile. She knew Shane must be relieved to hear Dottie's spunky spirit reasserting itself.

"Raymond said you asked to see Elle. Here she is."

Shane shifted so Elle could slide in next to him beside the bed. He stayed close, so that their arms brushed when she stopped just short of the IV pump to smile down at the older woman. "Hello, Dottie."

Dottie's thin hand fluttered as if she were trying to reach out. Elle caught it in her own, holding it gently. "Elle. Thank you. Thank you for everything."

"You're welcome. But all I did was call for an ambulance. Parker would have done the same, or your home health-care worker, if I hadn't been there."

"But you were there," Dottie insisted. "I'm not going to lie, I was anxious when they loaded me into that ambulance. I appreciated having you ride with me."

"Of course."

"And then Raymond said you stayed to help them with whatever they needed and to keep Shane company when he and Parker were in with me. Thank you for that, too, dear."

Elle was starting to feel embarrassed by all this gratitude. She really had done very little. "I just wanted to make sure you were going to be okay, Dottie. Not that I ever had any doubt," she added, imitating Shane's teasing tone. "I've gotten the impression you don't give up easily."

"Never have." Dottie gave a rather wheezy laugh, rubbed irritably at the oxygen cannula in her nostrils, then sighed as her eyelids started to close. "I hate hospitals."

"You need to rest," Shane said. "Get some sleep. I'm going to make sure Elle gets back safely to her family and then I'll stay here with you."

"No." Dottie opened her eyes again with a

scowl. "No need for you to stay tonight. The doctor said I'm doing fine and I'll have nurses in and out all night. I don't want a bunch of people hovering over me while I'm trying to sleep. You take Elle back to Charlotte and Janet and then you get some rest, too. Tell Raymond he can come back early tomorrow. I'm going to want my toothbrush and my hairbrush and something I can wrap around me when I get up so my whole backside's not hanging out of this silly gown."

"I'll tell him, Dottie."

"And tell him to stop by somewhere and get me a good blueberry muffin or a cinnamon raisin bagel. You know that hospital breakfast is not going to be fit to eat."

Elle saw Shane bite his lip before he said solemnly, "I'll give him the message."

Dottie shifted on her pillow again, then perked up one more time. "Elle."

A little wary after hearing all the orders barked at Shane, she responded, "Yes, Dottie?"

"I guess you'll be taking Charlotte home before I get out of this place."

Softening her voice, Elle nodded and said, "I'm afraid so. You'll probably be here a couple of days and I have to be back at my shop on Wednesday. I would bring her to say goodbye, but children aren't allowed in this wing."

It was a sign of how tired and vulnerable Dottie felt that she allowed her lip to quiver briefly. She firmed it immediately and nodded. "Thank you again for bringing her. If maybe you think to send me a photo every once in a while, I'd be grateful."

Elle supposed there would be no harm in that, though she didn't want to commit to too much while emotions were running so high. Though she was reluctant to break a frail old woman's heart, she wanted to take her time to think about any ramifications of further involvement with the Scanlons, both for her daughter and for herself, before any final decisions were made.

"I'll send photos by text occasionally, if you like."

Dottie's smile made her glad she'd agreed to that much. "Thank you, dear. You really are doing a wonderful job with her. She's...she's a joy. I like your mother very much, too. Charlotte is a lucky little girl to have you both. And again, it was very kind of you to let us see her this one time. It made me feel so close to our Charlie again..."

Her voice trailed off as if her throat had tightened too much to go on.

Feeling a lump forming in her own, Elle blurted precipitately, "I know you regret not having gotten the chance to say goodbye to Charlotte today. Maybe...maybe we could drive back up for an afternoon at Christmastime. Maybe the day after Christmas?"

That was still a month away, but she wanted to believe Dottie would still be around to welcome them. She was all too aware there were no guarantees when it came to that. And it had suddenly occurred to her that Charlotte hadn't had a chance to say goodbye, either, even if she was too young to know exactly what that meant.

If anticipation served as medicine, she thought she'd just administered a healthy dose to Charlotte's great-grandmother. Dottie's face lit up with a renewed energy, even a bit of color was seeping into her face. "I would like that very much, if you can arrange it. I can't think of a nicer Christmas present for myself. And I know the rest of the family feels the same way, don't we, Shane?"

Shane was looking at Elle again, and she felt her cheeks warm in response to his expression. All she'd promised was one more visit, if it worked out. She didn't want them to make that big a deal of it.

A nurse came into the room with a thermometer and a pill tray. "I have some pills for you, Mrs. Scanlon," he said with the same enthusiasm he might have used to announce he'd brought ice cream.

"Poison, more like it," Dottie muttered without opening her eyes.

Shane laughed and patted her cheek. "Behave yourself. Get some rest, okay? I'll check on you later."

"Good night, Dottie," Elle added. "Rest well."

She thought the older woman wasn't going to reply to either of them. They were almost out the door when Elle heard Dottie murmur, "Christmas."

With a tired sigh, she walked down the long hallway at Shane's side, aware that her life had just gotten even more complicated. He placed a hand at the small of her back to escort her into the elevator, an almost absent gesture that probably meant nothing—but still made her pulse race. A *lot* more complicated, she thought.

CHAPTER TWELVE

ELLE AND SHANE didn't say much during the drive home. She wondered wearily what on earth had possessed her to invite herself for another visit next month. She must have had a moment of insanity brought on by an overload of compassion. As if the holidays weren't busy and stressful enough without adding six-plus hours in a car and another afternoon filled with Dottie's Charlie obsession, Parker's quirks and Shane's—well, Shane.

He seemed lost in his thoughts, too, his eyes fixed on the road ahead, hands tight on the wheel as he drove toward his uncle's house. He hadn't yet acknowledged her announcement that she would be back at Christmas. She thought he'd looked approving, but he hadn't said.

The clock on the dashboard told her it was after seven. Charlotte should have been in bed by now. Her mom had let her know that Charlotte had slept for quite a while that afternoon and was still in good spirits. Still, Elle felt a little guilty for being gone so long, even though her mother wouldn't have expected her to do anything else under the circumstances. The decision now was whether to make a nighttime drive with Charlotte asleep in her car seat, or stay another night and head home tomorrow morning.

They had enough clothes for another day. Her mom was compulsive about always having at least one spare outfit, a habit Elle had fallen into. She didn't mind driving at night, usually—she enjoyed it with less traffic and soft music playing in the darkened car—but she was rather tired tonight and she suspected her mother was, too. She decided to wait and see what her mom wanted to do.

Shane parked in front of the house and turned off the motor, but he didn't immediately get out. She glanced his way to find him half turned away from her, rubbing his eyes with one hand. Something about his posture made her reach out to him, laying her hand on his thigh. "Shane? Are you okay?"

He straightened and nodded, dropping his arm. "It's just… Damn, she looked fragile."

His husky tone went straight to her heart. "I know," she said, giving his leg a bracing squeeze. "But she made it through today, Shane. She'll make it through tonight."

With a little sigh, he shifted to look at her. He raised his hand and cupped her face before she realized what he was going to do. His thumb traced her lower lip. His gaze followed that movement as he murmured, "I keep thanking you. I know you're tired of hearing it, but...thank you, Elle. Telling Dottie you'd bring Charlotte back after Christmas—well, I could almost see her perking up, as if you'd just given her something more to live for."

"I sort of blurted it out," she confessed, her lips moving against the light brush of his thumb. Just that whisper of a touch was enough to liquefy her resolve. "I hadn't planned on coming back so soon. If—well..."

"If at all," he finished for her.

"Yes."

He smiled, and though it was too dark in the car for her to see his dimples, she knew they had appeared. "I can't say I'm surprised Dottie worked her magic on you."

"Like I said, she's a lot like my mother. Both of them have a way of getting what they want and making it appear that it was the other person's idea all along."

He chuckled. "Dottie certainly does that."

He sounded more heartened now. More himself. Maybe he'd just needed a moment to relax before facing the others. A little teasing in a quiet car, away from the controlled chaos of the hospital and the anxious family waiting to be reassured.

Maybe he'd just needed an encouraging touch from a friend. Maybe that would be enough…

Or maybe not, she thought as his mouth lowered to hers.

Unlike the first kiss they'd shared, this one wasn't playful. Wasn't flirtatious or uncomplicated. Much more had happened between them since that night, which seemed so long ago now. Hurt and anger, grudging respect, acknowledgment of their devotion to their families. But underlying everything from the very beginning there had been this. Attraction. Chemistry. Whatever label she applied, this feeling was potent. And it was mutual.

His mouth moved hungrily over hers. The hand that had rested lightly against her cheek slipped behind her head to tangle in her hair, holding her in place though she'd made no move to draw away. Her fingers curled into his shirt, feeling his heart racing against them. His lips were hot. Hard and soft all at the same time. If she had ever in her life been kissed quite like this, she couldn't remember now.

She didn't know which of them returned to reality first. Maybe it was simultaneous. They broke off the kiss with a gasp that could have come from either of them, though Elle suspected it was her.

"Okay, that—" She paused to draw a steadying breath. "That can't happen."

"Agreed," he said after a moment. "Probably not the best idea."

"To say the least," she said, reaching up to straighten her hair. "I mean, I understand. It's been a long day. An emotional roller coaster. We were both so worried about Dottie, and so relieved that she's going to be okay. It makes sense that we got carried away."

He let her finish her rambling without interruption. And then he shrugged. "Or maybe I just wanted to kiss you again," he said and opened his door to climb out.

She blinked a few times, then shook her head with a grudging laugh and reached for her own door.

"MOMMY!" CHARLOTTE SQUEALED in pleasure when Elle walked into the living room. Wearing purple pajamas covered in playful kittens—her favorite pair—she dashed across the room and threw herself into Elle's arms, babbling a mile a minute. The only words Elle could make out were *baby Aub'ey* and *blocks* and *Gammy*, but it sounded as though Charlotte had had a good day.

Elle buried her face in her daughter's soft curls, inhaling the scent of shampoo and Charlotte, savoring the big hug she received in return. And then the child noted the second person who'd come into the room. "Shane!" she shrieked almost directly into Elle's ear.

Wincing a little, Elle reluctantly released her daughter and watched as she threw herself at Shane with more frantic babbling. Though it was obvious he didn't understand a word of it, he grinned and swung her off her feet to make her giggle.

Having waited her turn, Elle's mother moved forward with a searching look. "Dottie's still doing well?"

Giving her mom a quick hug, Elle confirmed, "Yes, she was doing amazingly well when we saw her. Pale and still shaky, of course, but talking clearly. The procedure was only minimally invasive, so the recovery time will be much shorter than if she'd had to have surgery."

"Raymond told me all about it. Poor Dottie, she must have been so frightened."

Elle glanced at the glittering Christmas tree Parker had decorated that morning for Dottie to enjoy. She hoped Dottie would be home soon to appreciate it.

"Parker's gone home?" she asked, looking around to where Shane and Raymond stood talking on the other side of the room. Charlotte was still perched on Shane's hip, swinging her feet and winding her fingers in Shane's hair. Apparently her daughter shared her appreciation for his thick waves.

"Yes," her mom said, reclaiming Elle's attention. "Parker and Adrian left right after dinner to put the baby to bed. She asked to be called immediately if there's any news. Are you sure someone shouldn't be with Dottie? They have a sleep chair or a cot in the room for family, don't they? Should I go?"

"That's very kind of you, Janet," Raymond said, overhearing, "but my mother would have to be in critical condition before she'd allow anyone to stay with her. I think mostly she doesn't like the idea of being that much trouble, even if we assure her we don't mind."

"She's quite a handful, isn't she?" Janet said with a laugh.

Raymond chuckled. "You could say that again."

Elle noted that her mother and Shane's uncle had become quite friendly in the past couple of days. Not that she should be surprised. Her mom always made friends easily. Still, it was one more tie they were developing to this family. To Charlotte's other family.

She cleared her throat, glancing to where Shane was still playing with her daughter, giving her a horsey ride on his shoulders now. "About tonight..."

Her mother broke in to suggest tentatively, "Raymond has invited us to stay here tonight. There are twin beds in one of the two guest rooms, so you and Charlotte could take that one and I'd take the other. We could check on Dottie in the morning and then get a fresh start home."

Elle blinked. "Um—"

Her mom touched her arm. "We can head home now if you'd rather, but you must be tired. I know too well how exhausting it is to sit in a hospital waiting room. Or we could go to a hotel, if you'd be more comfortable."

Elle gave it a moment's thought, then smiled wearily. "I am tired, Mom. It will probably be better if we rest before making the drive. Raymond, it's very kind of you to offer your house."

"It's a pleasure having you," he assured her, then glanced toward Charlotte. "You're welcome anytime."

All this oh-so-polite formality was setting Elle's teeth on edge. She realized suddenly that she was actually standing there blandly chatting and watching Shane playing with her daughter, and all the while she was trying to act as if he hadn't just kissed her senseless. As if she wouldn't lie awake half the night reliving that kiss and repeatedly reminding herself that getting further involved with him would be courting disaster. He was Charlotte's uncle, for pity's sake! Could it get any more complicated?

"Shane, have you eaten? We had some food left over from dinner."

"Thanks, Janet, but I had a burger and onion rings at the hospital."

Elle's mother tsked before asking, "Well, how about dessert? I made apple cobbler."

He gave a little groan. "Cobbler?"

She smiled. "With a scoop of ice cream, of course."

"Well, maybe just a small serving."

Never happier than when she was taking care of someone, Janet beamed. "I'll warm it up for you. Maybe a nice cup of tea with it? I'm sure you've already had too much coffee today. Raymond, would you like tea?"

"I'm going to put Charlotte to bed now." Elle reached out to take her daughter from Shane, who handed her over, holding Elle's gaze for a moment above the child's head.

"There will be an extra serving of cobbler for you when she's asleep," her mom told her.

"Thanks, Mom, but I'm really not hungry."

"I hungry," Charlotte said. "Cobb'er?"

"You've already had your cobbler," her grandmother chided indulgently. "Give Gammy a kiss and go with Mommy, sweetheart."

Charlotte pouted. "Want cobb'er with Shane."

It was rare for Charlotte to misbehave, but she was still a two-year-old with the corresponding rebellion on occasion. Elle really hoped this wasn't going to be one of those times. "Mommy's going to read you a story, Charlotte," she said enticingly. "What book would you like to read? The kitten book? The one about the ducklings?"

"Duck book!"

"Okay, we'll read the duck book." Relieved, Elle turned with Charlotte in her arms. "Kiss Gammy and say night-night."

"Night-night, Gammy." Charlotte gave a smacking kiss to her grandmother, then insisted on kissing Shane and "Unc Way." Clutching her stuffed cat in hand, she allowed herself to be carried off for a bedtime story and snuggles before being tucked into bed.

One more night, Elle promised herself. Tomorrow night she would tuck Charlotte into her own bed, under a blanket Elle's mother had made for her.

Yes, these people were Charlotte's biological relatives, but Elle and her mom were Charlotte's family. Mr. Hot-Lips-and-Sexy-Dimples had already disrupted her household enough. Tomorrow she would try her best to get things back as best she could to the way her life had been before he'd swept into it.

THE HOUSE WAS quiet when she wandered back downstairs a while later, after finally getting Charlotte settled down to sleep. It was still a little too soon for Elle to go to bed, though she planned to make an early night of it. She had no interest in the cobbler her mother had mentioned, but she was thirsty. A glass of cold water sounded good.

No one was in the living room when she walked through, and the dining room was also empty. Following sounds, she moved into the kitchen, where she found her mother humming as she washed dessert plates and teacups and set them in a rack to dry. Her mom greeted her with a smile. "Would you like some cobbler? Tea?"

"Just water, thanks. Where is everyone else?"

Her mom filled a glass with water from a pitcher in the refrigerator, showing that she'd become rather familiar with the kitchen during this long day. "Raymond's in his study dealing with a few things that piled up while he was at the hospital this afternoon. Shane left about fifteen minutes ago. I think he wanted to make sure Dottie was settled in for the night before he went home."

"I see."

As she sat down at the kitchen table with her water, Elle told herself she was relieved that she probably wouldn't see Shane again until the Christmas visit. And speaking of which...

"I think you should know, Mom, I sort of invited us back to see Dottie at Christmas. The day after, probably, since that would be one of the few free days we have during the holiday."

"I know, dear." Her mother beamed at her.

"Shane told us. That was very sweet of you. He said it cheered Dottie right up, which I'm sure she needed."

Elle responded with a groan. "It wasn't something I planned. I just blurted it out when Dottie was thanking me for bringing Charlotte to visit this time. She was just lying there looking so sick and fragile and still being so damned grateful and noble about it all... Well, next thing I knew we're coming for Christmas."

With a wry smile, her mom slid into another chair, holding a glass of water for herself. "I swear, I think Miss Dottie has secret hypnotic powers."

Laughing, Elle nodded. "I think you could be right. Judging by the way she runs this family, even as tiny and delicate as she seems, that could explain it."

Her mother's smile faded. "I admire her, Elle. She's held this family together through some extraordinarily difficult times. Raymond told me a bit about how she supported her sons when one was widowed and the other divorced, how she helped raise her grandchildren, what a rock she was for them all after Charlie's death, even though she was devastated by it. If they want to spoil her a bit during the time she has left, I say more power to them."

"I agree, of course. I just—" Elle sighed, trying

to find the words to describe some of the complicated feelings she was dealing with. "I'm nervous about how the Scanlons seem to be slipping more and more into our lives. Into Charlotte's life. I don't want her to be confused."

"Why would she be confused by having more people to love her? Some adoptees spend years looking for their biological families, even if they're very happy with their adoptive families. Charlotte won't have to wonder who her people were or why she was put up for adoption. We already know her paternal family are good, decent people. Perhaps someday we'll learn more about Brittany's family, but there's no rush. Brittany provided the medical records she'll need in the future, and that's what's most important at this point."

As usual, her outwardly unconventional mother had offered sound, practical insights. And Elle acknowledged the validity of each point she'd made. And yet...

"What is it, Elle?" her mom asked gently, reading her face too well.

Elle released a heavy sigh. "I guess I'm just feeling petty and selfish," she admitted. "I'm a little jealous of the biological ties she'll always have with these people. And I don't want to have to share her."

"Oh, sweetheart." Her mom reached across the

table to pat her hand. "You are neither petty nor selfish. You're human. These past few weeks have been understandably difficult for you. Having Shane and his family show up so unexpectedly must have made you feel as though your own special relationship with your daughter had been placed at risk. I felt the same way at first—and I'm still aware that there will be life-changing decisions ahead for you. But whatever comes, you can be confident that you are a very good person and a wonderful mother. I couldn't possibly be prouder of you."

Swallowing hard, Elle felt emotion flood through her. Her mother understood. It helped just to hear her own fears stated so concisely, so matter-of-factly. "Thanks, Mom. I love you, too."

"I know you do. And Charlotte adores us both. That's not going to change because she suddenly has new relatives to visit. Why would it? We're awesome."

Elle had to laugh even as she blinked back grateful tears. "Yes. Yes, we are."

After giving Elle's hand a squeeze, her mom drew back with a self-satisfied smile. "There. Don't you feel better?"

Picking up her water glass, Elle nodded. "I do, thanks."

"Anytime, darling. Now, tell me about you and Shane."

Elle choked on her water. After coughing a few times, she cleared her throat and asked, "Uh, what about me and Shane?"

Her mom looked at her quizzically. "Are you okay?"

"Yeah. Just swallowed wrong. So…?"

With a shrug, her mom said, "I simply meant it looked as though you were getting along better tonight. Raymond said you were very kind to all of them this afternoon. Does that mean you've forgiven Shane for taking so long to tell us who he really is?"

"For deceiving us, you mean," Elle corrected with a grumble. Then sighed. "But yeah, I guess I have, at least in part. I've been telling myself he was as much under Dottie's spell as the rest of us."

"He really does seem like a fine man, with a good heart. I'm glad you're friends again."

The unconscious echo of Shane's words made Elle moisten her lips that felt suddenly dry despite the water she was sipping. "Yes, well. It's not the same as it was before, but there's no reason we can't be cordial."

Once again, her mom's eyes were a bit too knowing. "You were falling for him before, weren't you? Maybe a little? There was a spark in your eyes around him before…you know."

Resisting an admittedly cowardly urge to firmly

deny any such thing, Elle shrugged. "When I thought he was just a nice guy I'd met by coincidence, I saw no reason not to go out with him. I thought it might be time to get out socially again. I thought Shane and I could have a few dinners, see a movie or enjoy another concert, maybe, whenever he passed through town. Obviously, that's all off the table now."

"Does it have to be?"

Shaking her head in disbelief, Elle said, "Of course it does! I'm certainly not going to date Charlotte's uncle, even if I could trust him after the way he introduced himself. Can you imagine how complicated that would be?"

"You're assuming the worst, of course."

"I've been through the worst," Elle answered grimly, glaring down at her bare left hand.

"I think I've mentioned before that Shane isn't Glenn."

"Still, the point is moot now." Elle stood abruptly and carried her glass to the sink to wash. "I'm turning in early tonight, Mom. Maybe you should, too. We have a long day ahead of us tomorrow and Charlotte will probably be awake at the crack of dawn."

Though she didn't look entirely satisfied, her mother didn't try to prolong the conversation Elle had somehow found both comforting and unsettling.

As they prepared to leave the next morning, Elle's mom announced that she wanted to stop by the hospital on their way. "I'll just run up and check on Dottie," she said. "I'd really like to see her once more before we leave town."

Wondering if her mother secretly feared this might be her last chance to see the older woman, Elle agreed, saying she would walk with Charlotte in the atrium and gift shop during the short visit.

Raymond set their bags in the trunk of Elle's car and closed the lid with a snap. He brushed off his hands as he smiled down at his guests. "I think that's everything."

Janet rested a hand on his arm. "Thank you for your hospitality, Raymond."

"It was my pleasure. I was glad to have company in the house last night," he admitted.

"Tell Parker and Adrian and sweet little Aubrey that I said goodbye, will you? And that I'll see them when we come back at Christmas."

"We'll all look forward to that."

Raymond turned then to Elle, who'd been watching the rather cozy exchange with a tiny frown that she smoothed instantly. Her mother was naturally warm and outgoing, she reminded herself. It didn't mean a thing that she and Raymond Scanlon had become buddies. They were close to the same age, both had only daughters, each had one grandchild. Made sense they'd have bonded over those things.

"Have a safe drive home, Elle," he said to her, his tone still friendly but a bit more formal with her. "Thank you again for all you did yesterday."

"Of course. Charlotte, say goodbye to Uncle Raymond." The nickname had been assigned by her mother while Elle was at the hospital yesterday and now it was how Charlotte thought of Raymond. Elle had decided not to try to change that. After all, what else would the child call him?

"Bye-bye, Unc Way."

Raymond picked her up to plant a smacking kiss on her cheek. "'Bye, Kitten. We'll see you again soon, okay?"

The slight edge of huskiness in his deep voice made Elle swallow hard before she reached out for her daughter's hand. "Okay, kiddo. Into your car seat."

She supposed it was inevitable that she would see Shane at the hospital. She and Charlotte had just made a second leisurely lap around the atrium when he walked in. Her rebellious heart gave its usual excited leap when she spotted him, a reaction she now half expected even if her brain didn't approve. At least she was relatively confident she kept those traitorous flutters at bay when she greeted him.

Charlotte, of course, made no attempt to downplay her joy at seeing Shane. She all but climbed his leg in her eagerness to be swung up into his arms and he laughed as he complied, giving her a snuggle that brought out the giggles. Only then did his eyes meet Elle's. She saw in their sapphire depths the same conflicted emotions she was trying to hide, and she doubted she was doing any better a job of it.

She'd once speculated that Shane wasn't entirely skilled at hiding his feelings. She recalled thinking that was a good thing. But as her gaze locked with his and undeniable memories of hungry kisses passed between them, she wasn't so sure of that now.

"I saw your mother upstairs," he said, his tone carefully schooled. "She said you're about to head out."

Elle nodded. "She wanted to see Dottie first. How is your grandmother?"

"Dottie," Charlotte repeated, looking around as if in search of her great-grandmother.

"Dottie's doing well, considering," Shane said, smiling at Charlotte but speaking to Elle. "She's very sore today and still weak. Looks like a strong wind could blow her right out of the bed. But she's got all the nurses on the ward hopping to cater to her—and somehow they're enjoying it."

Elle laughed. "That does sound encouraging."

"She'll be fine." At least, this time, his tone added.

Her smile turned bittersweet. "I'm not going up today," she said. "She doesn't need a lot of visitors and Charlotte can't go, anyway. I told Mom to give her my best. Please do the same for me."

"I will. And you'll see her in five weeks."

She would be seeing him again in five weeks, too, she thought. Would her fascination with him have faded by then? Would she have gotten beyond the simmering physical awareness, the pang of regret?

She could only hope so.

Her mother joined them then, looking searchingly from Elle to Shane. Not being genuinely psychic, her mom couldn't know everything that had gone on between them, Elle reminded herself. But then again, her mother had always been a bit too perceptive for comfort.

"We should go, Mom. I'd like to get home before noon."

"All right, dear. Shane, let us know how Dottie's doing, will you? She'll be in our thoughts."

"I will, Janet." He leaned down to brush a light kiss over her cheek, making her smile rosily.

And then he kissed Charlotte and handed her back to Elle. "Drive carefully," he said, looking for a moment at her mouth.

Feeling her lips tingle as if he'd actually

touched them, she muttered. "I will. Bye, Shane. Let's go, Mom."

"Bye-bye, Shane." Charlotte waved enthusiastically over Elle's shoulder as she was carried out of the hospital. Elle couldn't resist glancing back one last time. Shane stood where she'd left him, watching them. He was still standing there when she walked out, her heart heavy with too many emotions.

CHAPTER THIRTEEN

THE THURSDAY AFTER the trip to Fayetteville was quite hectic in the shop, but Elle didn't complain even when a clumsy customer dropped two full cups of coffee on the floor, shattering the cups and splashing the hot beverage everywhere. The customer happened to be dressed like a clown, having stopped in after performing at an assembly at a nearby school. Fortunately no one was injured, so Elle was able to clear away the clutter quickly and with a grin when the good-natured clown did a rueful mime routine of hiding his painted face in shame.

Even with ungainly clowns making messes, Elle would so much rather be busy than to have spare time on her hands. When she was busy, she had no chance to brood about…well, about anything.

Her mother hadn't come in today, staying at home with Charlotte, who'd woken up with a case of the sniffles. Instead, Elle was assisted that day by Amber and DeShawn. Despite the brisk business, they worked smoothly and efficiently together. Elle was in a good mood when she locked the door at closing time, knowing today's sales totals would be healthy and that there was every reason to expect business would remain good through the rest of the Christmas shopping season.

Before she headed home, she had a rather lengthy phone conversation with Kristen in lieu of their usual weekly in-person meeting. Kristen had requested the phone update this time. It was all very civil and professional, as most of their conversations were these days. Yet something had most definitely changed between her and Kristen. There was a…well, an invisible wall was the best description she could find for it, and Elle didn't know why. Kristen had repeatedly said she wasn't angry with Elle and had no issues with her. She just needed some space to get her head together after the breakup, she always added.

Elle was beginning to believe the breakup had been more than a heartbreak for Kristen. It seemed almost as though it had changed her friend's whole perspective on life. Kristen had never seemed the restless type. She'd never indicated she craved anything more career-wise than making a success of their little coffee shop. She'd agreed with Elle that they should consider opening a couple more shops in the area once they were on solid financial footing. She'd insisted that singing on weekends and staying active in community causes she was passionate about were enough to fulfill her in other areas.

Elle had the distinct impression that her friend was beginning to think she wanted more. Or at least, something different. And that suspicion concerned Elle for many reasons—admittedly, some rather selfish.

The scent of sautéed onions and seasonings filled her home when she walked in at five thirty that evening. Her stomach rumbled in response. Her mom had said she was making Elle's favorite stuffed peppers for dinner tonight, so Elle estimated they would be going in the oven soon. She headed straight for the kitchen to see if there was anything she could help with.

As she reached the kitchen doorway, she heard her mother chattering and thought she must be talking to Charlotte. Instead, her mom was holding her phone to her ear with one hand and stirring a pot on the stove with the other. While Janet talked and laughed, she kept one eye on the high chair nearby where Charlotte picked at a divided toddler plate of chicken nuggets, peas and applesauce, usually one of her favorite meals. Elle noted that Charlotte's eyes were droopy, the tip of her nose was red and her cheeks were more flushed than usual.

"Hi, sweetie," she murmured, leaning over to

place a kiss on the child's head. "Poor baby, are you still feeling bad?"

"We'll talk later," her mom said into the phone, then set it aside to greet Elle. "She's been feeling better this afternoon. She even played for quite a while with her construction set, but she started getting listless again just before her dinner. I think she's tired."

Placing her hand against Charlotte's face, Elle assured herself that the skin wasn't too warm, just slightly damp. "Don't you want any of your applesauce, Charlotte? You love applesauce."

Gripping her spoon in her first, Charlotte took an unenthusiastic bite of the puree, smearing part of it across her face but getting a least some of it in her mouth.

"If she's not better tomorrow, maybe she should go see her pediatrician," Elle murmured. "It's probably just a cold, but it might be best to have her looked at."

Of course, Charlotte was just as likely to wake up in the morning feeling perfectly fine. That seemed to be the course of these toddler bugs.

Her mom agreed, then turned her attention back to the meal she was making, saying it would be ready to go in the oven in about twenty minutes. She assured Elle she had everything under control, which meant Elle had the next hour and a half or so to devote to Charlotte before having dinner with her mom. She pulled a chair closer to the high chair to try to get a bit more food into the child.

She tucked her daughter into bed at seven, after bath time, story time and lots of snuggle time. Though she made a token protest about going to bed, Charlotte was asleep almost immediately, her stuffed kitten clutched to her chest as she lay on her back in her bed, her breathing still congested, but deep and steady.

Elle stood for several minutes in the room she had decorated so painstakingly for her child, with inviting furnishings and cheery framed prints. An overstuffed bookcase sat in a reading corner outfitted with a polka-dot beanbag chair, a small wooden table and a chintz-covered love seat designed for snuggling together with a shared book. The room was illuminated now only by a nightlight shaped like a glowing rocket ship. The light had been a gift from Kristen, who'd said every child needed to be encouraged to develop an interest in science and technology, a philosophy with which Elle agreed. And which brought her thoughts back again to her concerns about Kristen.

She acknowledged with a sigh that she wanted her friend to be happy, even if that meant Kristen's leaving Shorty's Landing. Elle felt so blessed herself, so fulfilled as a mother, daughter and business owner, but she couldn't discount the possibility that this wasn't the life Kristen wanted.

Somehow or another, she had to let her friend know that if she needed to spread her wings, Elle would always be there to encourage her. Elle would figure out how to tackle the newest challenge and make it work out for herself. She always had.

She kissed her fingers and pressed them against her daughter's soft cheek, then turned and walked quietly out of the room to join her mother for dinner.

Elle was getting ready for bed that night when her phone buzzed. She picked it up, then swallowed hard when she saw the name on the screen. So much for sliding peacefully into sleep…

Refusing to be a coward, she pressed the accept button. "Hello, Shane."

His rich voice rumbled in her ear, causing a predictable, if still exasperating, reaction along her nerve endings. "Hi, Elle."

"How's Dottie?"

"She's doing amazingly well. It's like she came out of the hospital with renewed energy. She's kept us all hopping with decorating and errands since. I might have mentioned to her today that I do have other responsibilities."

Elle laughed softly. "And her answer to that?"

"She patted my cheek and told me I've always been very good at multitasking."

"You definitely have your hands full there," she commiserated.

"As you do there," he replied, typically uncomplaining. "I heard Charlotte was sick today. Is she better?"

"I think she's feeling a little bet— Wait. How did you know she was sick?"

"Your mom told Raymond, who passed it along to me. He decided not to mention it to Dottie because he didn't want her to worry. It isn't serious, right?"

Elle remembered her mother chatting on the phone while making dinner, a call she'd disconnected when Elle walked in. Judging by her mom's warm and familiar tone, Elle had assumed it was a call with one of her good friends. Had that been Raymond? And if so, just how many times had her mother talked with him during the past two days since they'd returned home?

Not that she minded, of course, she told herself hastily. Her mother was certainly free to make friends with anyone she wanted. Elle didn't really feel like her mom was passing secrets to the other side. That would be foolish and irrational.

"Charlotte has a cold," she said impassively. "Just a cold. She'll be fine, but thank you for asking."

"She didn't get it visiting the hospital, did she? I mean, all those germs…"

"For heaven's sake, Shane, she was in the gift shop and the atrium, not in the wards."

Pushing down her automatic defensiveness, she drew a breath. "Mom took Charlotte to a play group yesterday morning. One of the moms brought her twins, who were both fighting colds. She said she knew she should have kept them home, but they were so looking forward to seeing their friends. Half the kids who were there have had the sniffles since. Kids are pretty much adorable little germ bags," she added lightly.

Shane seemed to sense that he'd said something insensitive, though she wasn't sure he knew exactly what it was. "I hope she feels better tomorrow," he said carefully.

"Yes, so do I. If she doesn't, I'll take her to the doctor."

"I wasn't questioning your parenting, Elle."

She bit her lip, regretting the tension that had crept into the call—and was probably her fault. She wanted to blame her sensitivity on her busy day, her concern about Kristen and her natural worry about her sick child—but she was aware it was Shane who brought out that response from her. Perhaps because she'd spent so much time thinking of him during the past four days.

"I'm a little tired tonight," she said by way of apology. "Long day."

"Are things okay at work?"

"We've been very busy."

"That's good, isn't it?"

"Of course." To soften the mood, she told him about the coffee-juggling clown. Shane's deep laugh was her reward.

In return, he shared an amusing story about a frantic senior neighbor who'd called him that morning for assistance with a wild bird that had flown into her living room through an open balcony door. He painted a funny picture of himself holding a broom and herding the bird through the woman's apartment toward the same door that it inexplicably wanted to avoid then.

Even as she laughed, Elle thought it was only one more example of how often Shane was called on for help. By family, clients, even neighbors, apparently. She wanted him to understand that he didn't have to look out for his niece, as well. She was fully capable of handling that on her own.

"I'll let you get some rest," he said. "I just wanted to say hello and check on Charlotte. Let me know if there's anything you need."

In keeping with the promise she'd just made to herself, she answered briskly, "Thanks for calling, Shane, but we don't need anything. Good night."

There was a notable pause before he replied, "Good night, Elle."

She checked on Charlotte one more time before turning in, gratified to feel her daughter's face no warmer than usual when she slept. She thought Charlotte's breathing sounded a little clearer now, too, making her much more optimistic that there would be no need for an urgent care visit in the morning.

After such a busy day, she should have slept soundly when she nestled into her pillows soon afterward. She was certainly tired. Yet the echo of Shane's deep laugh in her ear and the memory of his lips against hers haunted her restless dreams, making it clear that she was a long way from being immune to him, despite her best efforts to convince herself otherwise.

DECEMBER BLEW INTO Shorty's Landing with gusty ocean breezes and pleasantly moderate temperatures. Despite the rarity of snow in coastal Carolina, inflatable snowmen and dangling plastic snowflakes were popping up all over town. A week and a day after her phone conversation with Shane, after closing for business on Friday, Elle and Kristen spent a couple hours decorating The Perkery for the season. They had assistance from a fully recovered Charlotte, whose job was to take unbreakable decorations out of a storage box and hand them to her mother, a task she took very seriously.

Because space was at a premium, Elle and Kristen had decided not to put up a full-size tree, opting instead to set up a display with a two-foot decorated tree on a shelf, surrounded by coffee and tea gift suggestions. Other seasonal items were grouped on the counter and on tables as centerpieces. After putting away the storage containers, Elle stood with Charlotte on her hip surveying their efforts. "What do you think, Charlotte? Pretty?"

"Pretty," Charlotte said with a forceful nod of her head. "Pretty party dots."

Laughing, Elle kissed her daughter's cheek. "Yes, they are."

Kristen had left a few minutes earlier, so Elle and Charlotte were alone in the shop. It was already mostly dark out, almost time for Charlotte to have her dinner and bath before bedtime. Everything was ready in the kitchen for the morning, and there was nothing left to do here. "Ready to go home, sweetie?"

"Home."

They sang "Jingle Bells" in the car, Charlotte chiming in from the back. Charlotte didn't really know the words, other than "Jing' Bells," but she sang along loudly, anyway, stringing together cheery nonsense syllables. Elle was in a very good mood when she parked in her garage and took Charlotte out of the car. She looked forward to a quiet evening with her family.

They entered the house through the kitchen

door. Mouthwatering scents came from the oven. Lasagna? Elle licked her lips in anticipation.

Charlotte sniffed appreciatively. "Hungry, Mommy!"

"Okay, let's find Gammy and ask when dinner will be ready."

Charlotte dashed ahead of her toward the living room, calling out, "Gammy! Gammy!"

Smiling indulgently, Elle hung her car keys on the decorative hook by the door, then set her purse and a tote bag on the bench beneath it. Only then did she follow her daughter, figuring they would find Elle's mom in the living room.

Before Elle had stepped out of the kitchen, she heard her excitable daughter shriek again. "Shane! Unc' Way!"

Elle stumbled. Surely not…

Two men rose to their feet as she entered the living room where her mother held court. Charlotte had thrown herself at Shane, demanding to be spun, as was his habit now when he lifted her up. He laughed and held her high, skillfully avoiding her happily kicking feet.

Standing motionless with surprise in the doorway, Elle only half heard Charlotte urging Shane to look at her Christmas tree. Staring at her studiously innocent-looking mother, Elle waited for an explanation.

"Come in and welcome our guests, Elle. We've been having a lovely visit."

Pasting on a smile, Elle smoothed the rumpled red T-shirt she'd worn with jeans and sneakers for decorating the shop. "This is a nice surprise," she said, and hoped they didn't see what it cost her to make that sound true.

Because Shane was still occupied with Charlotte, Raymond greeted her first. "Janet just informed us that she didn't let you know we were stopping by this evening," he said, casting an indulgently chiding look at her mom. "Granted, it all happened on short notice, but I thought she'd give you a call."

"I thought it would be a nice surprise." The look her mom gave her let Elle know that she expected to be scolded later. And, oh, was she right.

"It's very nice to see you, of course," Elle said, looking at Raymond rather than Shane until she had her shaken emotions under control. "What brings you to town?"

Again, Raymond responded. "We're doing an insurance and liability audit for a business in Bluffton. It was a referral from Trevor Farrell. Most of the audit will be done online and through reports, but the company owner likes preliminary face-to-face meetings, so we had hastily arranged meetings with him and his staff today. When I mentioned to Janet during a phone call this morning that we'd be passing not far from Shorty's Landing, she urged us to make a detour to join you for dinner. I assumed," he repeated with another look at Janet, "that she'd tell you about the invitation."

"I would certainly have seconded the invitation," Elle told him. And she would have, of course. Though it would have been nice to have had the option, she added silently. "How is Dottie?"

"She's doing well, thank you for asking. Parker and her family are staying at the house with her this weekend while they're having some remodeling work done in their kitchen, so I have a little time off."

Setting Charlotte on her feet, Shane spoke to Elle then. "I'm sure you're tired after work, so we won't stay long. I booked a room at Wind Shadow Resort tonight so Raymond could see the place and meet Trevor. We're heading back to Fayetteville tomorrow."

He sounded almost apologetic. Had she appeared ungracious in her surprise? "Please, sit down. I see Mom's served drinks—is there anything else I can get you before we eat?"

"Hungry," Charlotte announced, tugging at Shane's pants leg as if expecting him to do something about it.

Her grandmother laughed. "Dinner's almost ready, Charlotte. Give me ten minutes and I'll have everything on the table. Why don't you show Shane your favorite ornament on the tree? Your Santa kitty?"

As Charlotte all but dragged Shane to the tree to see the plastic cat-in-a-Santa-hat ornament she'd personally hung on a low branch, Elle volunteered to help her mother finish the meal preparations.

"Oh, that's not necessary," her mother said, waving a hand with a clatter of bracelets. "I have it—"

"I'll help you." Elle took her mother's arm and led her out of the room. Only when they were alone in the kitchen did she release her mom and plant her fists on her hips. "What the heck, Mom? Why didn't you tell me they were coming for dinner?"

"Like I said—"

"You thought it would be a nice surprise." Elle shook her head in exasperation. "Not buying it."

"Okay, fine." Her mother shoved her hands into mitts and opened the oven door, releasing waves of tantalizing aromas. "I sort of invited them on impulse and then I spent the rest of the day worrying that I'd overstepped. I guess I was just putting off the lecture."

Oh, great. Now Elle felt guilty, even though she'd done nothing wrong. Her mother had a knack for that. "You have every right to invite guests for dinner," she conceded. "This is your home, too, after all. I just think you owe me a heads-up, that's all."

After all, her mom had claimed to understand that Elle didn't like being taken by surprise—especially where her daughter and the Scanlon family were concerned. Elle had every right to be annoyed. She was getting increasingly tired of being blindsided, and of having decisions taken out of her hands—even by her mother, whose antics she could usually indulge.

"You're absolutely right." Her mom's crestfallen expression acknowledged the misstep. "I'm sorry. I promise I'll warn you next time. If there is a next time, of course," she added hastily.

Elle jerked open the fridge door, finding salads already plated. "What can I do to help?"

"You could set the table." Her mom gave her a searching look before adding, "We'll talk about this more later, okay?"

They would perhaps discuss again the ill-planned surprise, but certain topics would be off-limits, Elle vowed silently. She couldn't talk about her complicated feelings for Shane even with her mother, with whom she could normally talk about anything. And she still hadn't asked her mother exactly how often those calls with Raymond were taking place.

CONSIDERING SHANE'S WORDS EARLIER, Elle half expected him and his uncle to eat quickly and then be on their way. Instead, they lingered over the meal, neither seeming to be in a hurry to depart. Charlotte had been allowed to stay up later than usual for the visit, and she made the most of the attention. Elle did her part to keep the conversation easy and amusing, and she could tell that Shane was trying, as well. They swapped stories and jokes, talked about business and family, touched on current events and upcoming holiday activities.

"This just might be the best lasagna I've ever eaten, Janet," Raymond told her with a wink. "I see where Elle got her talent for cooking."

Though it wasn't really a joke, Janet still giggled in response. She actually *giggled*, Elle thought with a smothered sigh. How much more complicated was this situation going to get?

After such a busy day, Charlotte was starting to droop by the time she'd finished her dinner. Elle decided to skip the bath tonight and go straight to story time. Her mom could bathe Charlotte before bringing her to the shop in the morning. Excusing herself while the others had dessert and coffee, she carried the tired child to brush her teeth and change into pajamas.

She and Charlotte had just settled into the cozy love seat in Charlotte's bedroom when Elle heard a noise from the doorway. She looked up from the book to find Shane standing there, peering into the dimly lit room.

"Shane!" Charlotte started to sit up, but Elle held her down with a gentle hand.

"Were you looking for me?" she asked him.

He held up a stuffed animal—Charlotte's stuffed black cat. "Your mom insisted I should bring this to you. She said Charlotte can't sleep without it."

While it was true that Charlotte often slept with the cat, she was just as happy with the yellow teddy bear currently snuggled into her side. Elle kept the comment to herself, though she made a mental note to remind her mother yet again to stop trying to interfere. She had no doubt her mom had motives for sending Shane with the toy.

"Thank you," she said as he crossed the room to hand the cat to Charlotte. She added wryly, "Mom could have brought it herself rather than sending you. I did say that my mother and your grandmother have a great deal in common, right?"

He chuckled. "You did. And they do."

Charlotte scooted as close as possible to Elle and patted the sofa at her other side. "Story time, Shane."

"Oh, I—"

Charlotte patted again, turning big eyes up to him. "Story time."

Elle could almost see him melt. "Um—" He looked at her.

She nodded somewhat ruefully. "You're welcome to join us for a story if you like. But I can appease her if you need to leave."

"I can take a few minutes for a story," he said, perching carefully on the other side of the small love seat, to Charlotte's delight. "Raymond's having a second piece of your mother's pie."

Elle looked down at the book again. "They're getting pretty friendly, aren't they?"

"Seem to be." From his tone, Shane wasn't much more enthusiastic about the development than she was.

"Story, Mommy."

Thinking that Charlotte, too, had a bit in common with her great-grandmother, Elle started reading. Though a little self-conscious with Shane there, she used the silly voices Charlotte loved, making her daughter giggle sleepily. She even heard Shane chuckle a couple of times. She was struck by the cozy intimacy of the scene, the three of them all snuggled on the little sofa. The strong feeling that flooded through her felt very much like yearning. She had to focus fiercely on the simple story just to read it correctly.

After finishing, she closed the book and looked down at her daughter. Charlotte was already nearly asleep. Smiling faintly, Elle set the book aside and stood to tuck the child into her crib with a soft kiss on the forehead. Shane paused for a moment to look down at the child. He reached down to brush the backs of his knuckles over a soft cheek, then turned and moved toward the door.

He was waiting in the hallway when Elle stepped out after turning off the lamp to leave Charlotte's room illuminated only by the rocket night-light.

"She really loves books, doesn't she?" he asked, keeping his voice low.

"Yes. We've been doing this since she came to us. I want her to have an appreciation for reading. Mom and I are both avid readers."

"So's my family. Dottie says the more she loses the ability to get around, the more she finds escape in her books."

"You'll have to tell me what she likes. Charlotte can give her a book for Christmas."

"She'd love that."

Because they were speaking so quietly, they stood close together. A bit too close, Elle realized suddenly. She took a step back, but that only brought her up against the wall.

"Look, Elle." Shane shifted with her, perhaps so she could hear what he was about to say. "I didn't know your mom was going to spring us on you. To be honest, I didn't know about this myself until we left Bluffton. Raymond informed me we'd been invited to stop by for dinner and he'd accepted. He said it would be rude of us not to go. I'm sorry you were caught off guard."

"I asked Mom to let me know next time just so I'd have a chance to prepare, but she can certainly ask anyone she likes for dinner. This is as much her home as it is mine."

"Still, I know this is getting complicated. All I asked for was one visit, and it's morphed into a lot more."

She couldn't argue with that. Couldn't think of a response at all, actually. Perhaps that had something to do with his proximity.

His hand rose slowly to brush her hair back from her cheek. He let his hand rest there, fingers cradling her jaw, his eyes boring down into hers. "Speaking of complicated…"

"We talked about this. We can't…"

His head lowered. "Definitely shouldn't…"

"Damn it, Shane," she groaned on a sigh.

One lone dimple appeared with his wryly tilted smile. "Damn it, Elle," he echoed and covered her mouth with his.

She clutched his shirt, not sure whether she was trying to push him away or pull him closer. Her head tilted back, even as she told herself to resist.

Each time they kissed, the taste and feel of

him became more familiar, more unique. More significant. She was beginning to wonder in despair if any future kisses would ever measure up.

After what felt like a very long time—yet not nearly long enough—he released her lips, only to rest his forehead against hers.

"So, that happened again," he murmured.

She almost laughed, though the way her pulse raced and her entire body ached was hardly funny. Her voice was slightly hoarse and tinged with wistfulness when she said, "I wish I understood why."

He exhaled quietly, his breath warm on her face. "Maybe because I can't stop thinking about you? Or because every time I'm near you I can't stop wanting to touch you? And maybe because you don't seem to want to stop any more than I do."

Both pride and innate honesty kept her from denying the truth. She stood without moving for several long moments, their heads still touching as she—as they both—struggled with the implications and potential consequences of this attraction they were struggling so hard to resist. She had no doubt Shane was as aware of the pitfalls as she, though perhaps he wasn't as afraid? Did that make her more of a coward—or simply more realistic?

"I think about you, too," she admitted. "And

you're right. I kissed you for the first time because I was attracted to you and that hasn't changed, even when I was angry with you. It would have been so much easier if you really had just been a random customer. I'm not saying anything serious would have developed, but the stakes would have been so much lower."

"I get that." He lifted his head, took a step back—as if out of temptation's reach—and glanced toward Charlotte's dark, quiet bedroom. "Whatever happens between us, we can agree that Charlotte comes first. I've told you before that I would never do anything to hurt her—or you. That hasn't changed. I just think we need to stop pretending that there isn't something between us. Time for you to stop acting like you don't know that I've wanted you from the first time I laid eyes on you, even when I didn't think there was a chance in hell anything would come of it."

The rough admission made a hard quiver run through her. A silent acknowledgment that he wasn't the only one who wanted.

"Shane?" Elle's mom appeared at the end of the hallway, peering questioningly at them. "Your uncle is asking for you. He has a business text he needs to discuss with you."

With one last meaningful look at Elle, Shane turned, pushing a hand through his hair. "Of course he does. I'm coming. And thanks again for dinner, Janet. It was delicious."

"You're very welcome, Shane. I hope we can do it again sometime soon."

"So do I," he said, not looking back as he left to join his uncle.

Resisting an urge to massage her aching temples, Elle followed, though she would have liked to hide in her room until the men were safely away.

"You're very quiet tonight. Something on your mind?"

Looking up from his drink in the resort bar where he and his uncle had stopped for a nightcap before turning in, Shane shrugged. "Just tired, I guess. Long day."

"There've been a lot of those lately."

Shane lifted his glass to his lips, murmuring, "You can say that again."

Raymond rolled his tumbler between his hands, studying Shane from across the table. "Elle wasn't too happy that Janet surprised her with us at dinner, was she?"

Swirling the amber liquid in his own glass, Shane shrugged. "Elle doesn't care much for surprises. Her mother should have known that. I apologized for both of us, by the way."

Raymond's left eyebrow rose slightly. "Not sure

what you were apologizing for. We were invited to dinner by her mother. We didn't know Janet hadn't informed Elle."

"Still."

"Janet means well, Shane. She's just impulsive. Maybe a bit too accustomed to being indulged in her whims by her family and friends. But she's got a good heart. A kind and forgiving heart."

It was Shane's turn to lift an eyebrow as he searched his uncle's face. "Is there something you want to tell me?"

"Only that she and I have become good friends. I like her very much, and I enjoy talking to her. She makes me laugh."

Shane couldn't help wondering if it was more than that; he couldn't remember the last time his uncle had spent so much time chatting on the phone with a woman. He decided to let it go. No need to borrow trouble when he had plenty of his own to deal with.

"So, what about you and Elle?"

Shane managed not to choke on the sip he'd just taken, though the alcohol burned its way down his tightened throat. He set his glass on the table with exaggerated care. "What about us?"

"Come on, Shane, you think I haven't noticed how taken you are with her? I've never seen you look at anyone else quite the way you look at Elle when you think no one is watching."

Shifting uncomfortably in his seat at the thought of being watched, Shane grimaced with the realization that this must be only a fraction of the dismay Elle must have felt at seeing that photo. He thought maybe she understood a little better by now why he'd felt the need to locate Charlotte—but would she ever truly forgive him for deceiving her? Having come to his own understandings in the past few weeks, he had to admit he wouldn't blame her if she still resented the way he'd disrupted her life—but he wanted to believe that her reluctant admission that she was still attracted to him meant that some progress had been made.

Though he hadn't admitted his convoluted feelings for Elle to anyone, hadn't even examined them too deeply himself, he wondered if it would be helpful to share even a little with his uncle. "Elle is…special," he said, choosing the word deliberately. "I admire her very much."

"More than admire, I think," Raymond responded simply. "I think you've fallen for her."

With memories of kisses and echoes of sighs playing at the back of his mind, Shane cleared his throat. "Like I said, she's special."

"I agree. I admire her, too, for what she's accomplished, for her devotion to Charlotte and Janet. But you know she has good reason to be cautious, Shane. A single mom has much to con-

sider when it comes to getting romantically involved with anyone. She's been hurt before,
and that would be bad enough if she were disappointed again—but this time, she also has to
consider all the consequences for Charlotte. That
has to be daunting."

Shane's fingers tightened around his glass.
"She has to know that I would never hurt either
of them."

"Not deliberately. But she also has to be sure
that your feelings are solid. That you haven't been
unduly influenced by...well, by the emotional turmoil you've both been in since you met."

Shane frowned. "Unduly influenced?" he repeated. "What does that even mean?"

"Maybe Elle wonders—and justifiably so, you
have to admit—if your feelings about her are tied
up with the fact that she's your niece's mother. If
you're interested in her because you feel responsible in some way for Charlie's daughter—not to
mention to the rest of our family."

Shaking his head to reject the very suggestion,
Shane protested, "I'm not trying to use Elle to
stay close to Charlotte, Raymond. I would never
do that."

"Not consciously, perhaps," his uncle murmured.

"Not for any reason," Shane said flatly. "If anything, my attraction to Elle only complicates the

situation with Charlotte. You think I'm not aware of that?"

"I'm just saying that I know how much you've taken since we lost Charlie and your dad. I've seen you trying to do everything in your power, whether consciously or instinctively, to fill the holes. To soothe our pain, to ease our worries, to be the rock we needed. Maybe we don't tell you enough how much we appreciate everything you do for us, Shane—but never doubt that we're aware of it."

Shane couldn't help but be touched by his uncle's praise, even as he tried to decide just how much of it was warranted. Had he really been trying to step in for his dad and his older brother? Did Raymond really wonder if he was trying to do the same in Charlotte's life, influencing his growing feelings for Elle?

Was there even a ghost of a chance that Raymond was right?

"You need to be very sure of your intentions before you go much further with this," Raymond said quietly. "For once, take the time to make sure you're doing what you want, following your own heart. I'd hate to see any of you hurt. Not Elle, not Charlotte—and certainly not you."

Tossing back the last of his drink, Shane pushed the glass aside and stood. "I'll think about what you said, Raymond. And thanks for your concern.

But now I think we both need to get some sleep. Like I said, it's been a long day."

He was gratified that his uncle agreed immediately and without further conversation. He'd left Shane with enough to think about as it was.

CHAPTER FOURTEEN

AT LEAST ELLE wasn't caught by surprise when Shane and Raymond walked into The Perkery the next afternoon. Even though Shane hadn't specifically said they'd be in, she'd been waiting for him to bring his uncle by to see the shop. She'd even put aside a couple of chocolate-filled doughnuts—just in case.

Shane grinned when she set a plated doughnut in front of him just as he reached the counter. His dimples flashed, and his wind-tossed hair tumbled onto his forehead above his glittering blue eyes. He was wearing the jacket again. She didn't even try this time to convince herself she wasn't drawn to him like Charlotte's favorite fictional yellow bear to a pot of honey. But what she was going to do about that, if anything…well, that remained to be seen.

"Have you had a nice day?" she asked him, setting a coffee cup beside the plate.

"I have," he agreed. "Raymond and I walked nearly every inch of the resort and had a nice lunch with Trevor and a few members of his management team. Trevor seemed impressed with my uncle's encyclopedic knowledge of insurance regulations. He didn't know Raymond reads insurance updates like some people read the morning paper."

Elle glanced across the room to where her mother had joined Raymond at a table for coffee and pastries. Charlotte sat on Raymond's knee, shamelessly cadging bites. Other customers in the shop occasionally looked that way with appreciative smiles. Elle figured that anyone who didn't know her mother would assume they were looking at a couple with their grandchild. Especially since Charlotte bore a family resemblance to Raymond.

With a wistful sigh, she surrendered any last resistance to accepting that these people were now a permanent part of her child's life. And her own.

She glanced back at Shane, who was studying her face. "What about you? Do you read insurance regulations for fun?"

"Hardly. I read them because I have to, but it's not exactly my favorite part of the job."

"What is your favorite part?" she asked, genuinely curious.

To his credit, he didn't stumble over his response. "I like the customer service aspect, setting our clients' minds at ease about whether they're adequately covered, saving them money on their premiums and deductibles, reducing their liabilities. It feels good to know we've helped them."

Of course that was his favorite part, she mused as she moved to take an order from a backpack-laden college student while Shane joined his uncle and her mom and Charlotte. Service to others seemed to be Shane's primary purpose, at least in his mind. As always, that observation roused both respect and disquiet in her.

She served bowls of butternut squash soup and vegetarian chili to two hungry students seeking Wi-Fi and a relatively quiet corner in which to study for winter finals. With no one else needing her attention then, she stepped into the kitchen to make sure DeShawn had everything under control. When she came back out, the table where her family had been sitting was empty and Shane stood at the counter again, apparently waiting for her as he sipped his coffee.

"Where are the others?" she asked, depositing a fresh basket of cookies and motioning toward the vacated table.

"Janet asked me to tell you that she and Raymond are taking Charlotte for a walk and to visit a couple of shops along the street. She said you should text her if you need help and she'll hurry right back."

Glancing around the shop, Elle saw that the customers sitting at tables looked content. She had always considered her mom's job at the shop to be as much caring for and entertaining Charlotte as serving customers, so she certainly didn't object to the outing. "We're fine here for now. I'm sure Charlotte will return with a new toy or book."

If true, she hoped for the latter. There was always room for more books. Toys, not so much, and Christmas was only a few weeks away.

Shane chuckled. "I wouldn't be surprised. Raymond's already bought a couple little gifts for Aubrey on this trip."

He set down his coffee cup and leaned an arm against the counter so he could speak to her in a low voice. "So, here's the thing. I think your mom and Raymond want to have dinner again this evening, whether out at a restaurant or back at your place, if she clears it with you first. They were just starting to hint about it when they left, but I wanted to give you a heads-up."

She felt her eyebrows rise. "Don't you and Raymond have to get back to Fayetteville? Is he planning to be on the road at midnight?"

With a rather bemused sigh, Shane shook his head. "Raymond has decided he'd like to spend another night at the resort. He says he hasn't had a weekend off work in more than two years and since Parker and Adrian are staying with Dottie, there's no need for him to rush home. I don't disagree, but it would have been nice of him to let me know his intentions sooner."

On that point she could absolutely agree.

"Anyway, he said if I want to head on back to Fayetteville today, he can rent a car and follow tomorrow. In other words, he's not budging tonight."

"I see. Well, you're both welcome to dinner, of course. Um…are you staying, too?"

Shane shrugged. "I figure I might as well."

He reached across the counter to run a finger lightly across her hand. Just a touch, nothing out of place in her shop, but still enough to make her shiver a bit.

"And maybe I'm in no more of a hurry to leave than Raymond is," he said.

The doorbells jingled and Elle moved into place to greet the incoming customers and take their orders. Shane carried his coffee to a table, settling into a chair where he could see out the window, though she was all too aware that his eyes were on her more than the view. Just as hers went to him whenever she wasn't busy with anything else.

Her mom and Raymond returned with Charlotte not long before the shop closed for the day. As Elle had expected, Charlotte had a new book in one hand and a lollipop in the other. Because the child all but glowed with fresh air and fun, Elle could hardly disapprove.

330 THE WAY TO A SOLDIER'S HEART

Amiable Bo Meadows ambled through the door for his weekly purchase of leftover pastries, predictably the final customer of this Saturday afternoon. Because Elle was holding Charlotte, Janet bagged Bo's selections and fielded his impudent flirting this time. Afterward, she followed him to the door, then locked up behind him.

Glancing at her watch, Elle saw that it was straight-up four o'clock. The day had gone by quickly.

"I suppose Shane told you he and Raymond are staying another night at the resort."

Elle nodded in response to her mother's comment, noting the slightly challenging tone. "I just told Shane they're welcome to join us for dinner, of course." She included Raymond in the comment, seeing that he was watching her for a reaction.

"Actually—"

Never knowing what would follow when her mother began a statement that way, Elle tensed.

"I found out today that Raymond has never seen the movie *Ghost*," her mom said brightly. "Can you believe it? I told him he absolutely must watch it with me after dinner this evening. So, I thought maybe Charlotte could eat with us and then I'll put her to bed and you and Shane can go do something more fun than having pot roast with us and watching an old movie I'm sure you've both seen. Maybe you could go to that new Japanese place across town? Maybe see a new film in the theater next door?"

Elle couldn't believe her mom was actually giving her an innocent look and all but orchestrating a date. She didn't even seem to be trying for subtlety. Just what was going on with her mother these days, anyway?

Elle opened her mouth to say that she, for one, would be perfectly happy to eat the pot roast her mother had put in the slow cooker that morning and then to watch an "old movie" she liked well enough, even though it always got her mom started on that psychic whim again. Before she could speak, Shane cut in smoothly, "That sounds like a plan. What do you say, Elle? Sushi and superheroes? Katsu and comedy?"

Her mother giggled. "Very clever, Shane."

Elle managed a tight smile. Should she allow herself to be manipulated into this outing, or insist on staying home and subject herself to her mother's mournful looks all evening?

"Okay, sure," she said. "But I have some things to do here before I can leave. Another hour, perhaps."

"Do you need me to stay and help, dear?"

"No, thanks, Mom. It would be better if you take Charlotte home and feed her dinner. I'll clean up here and get everything ready for Kristen in the morning and then I'll come home to change."

"I could stay," Shane offered, then gave a little smile. "As you may recall, I'm pretty handy to have around. I can push a broom with the best of them."

"Oh, that's so nice of—"

"No, thank you, Shane." Elle spoke firmly over her mother. "I have things under control. I'll see you at the house."

"Have you heard from Kristen?" her mom asked with a slight frown. "She will be here tomorrow, right?"

"I haven't heard from her, but of course she'll be here."

As if sensing trouble, Shane lifted his head, narrowing his eyes on Elle's face. "Problem?"

She waved a hand dismissively. "No. It's fine."

Charlotte, who'd been resting against Elle's shoulder after her outing, raised her head. "Hungry, Mommy."

"Okay, baby, Gammy's going to take you home to eat. I'll be there in a little while, before you go to bed."

Though she whined a bit, Charlotte went with her grandmother out through the kitchen, mollified by being accompanied by Shane and "Unc' Way." Shane looked back over his shoulder as he left, his gaze holding hers for only a moment. In his expression, she detected a mixture of rueful amusement and anticipation. She wondered what he read in hers.

CANDLELIGHT LOOKED GOOD on Elle. Shane studied her over the top of his wineglass as he sipped an excellent Merlot. But then, sunlight looked good on her, too. And artificial light. Hell, she looked good in any light.

Setting down the glass, he glanced around at the elegantly quiet restaurant. Rather than the popular sushi place, they'd somehow ended up at Torchlight, the most upscale dining option at Wind Shadow Resort. To give Raymond a way back to the resort after his evening with Janet, Elle had volunteered to drive for dinner with Shane. Shane had gotten the impression that she was reluctant to choose a place in little Shorty's Landing, where she knew so many of the locals.

Was she worried about the potential gossip if they were seen together? The possible speculation about their relationship, especially if word got out about his connection to her daughter? He supposed he didn't blame her for that. He would be leaving the area tomorrow morning, while she would be staying and running her business here. When he'd suggested Torchlight, in which most of the other diners would be from out of town, she'd agreed—but only after a significant hesitation. She had to know as well as he did that dining here could lead them into his suite afterward, for conversation or...

"The food here really is amazing," she commented, breaking into his thoughts. "I'll have to send my compliments to the chef before we leave."

Clearing his throat, Shane cut into his butter-tender filet mignon. "Yeah, everything I've had here has been great. Though I'd still give you the edge on pastries," he added with a little wink.

She laughed, looking as though she was just now beginning to relax a bit. "Thanks, but I'm not sure my coffee-and-doughnut-shop fare stacks up to what a classically trained chef can do."

"Does for me." With that unequivocal endorsement, he took a bite of his steak.

Still smiling, Elle turned her attention again to her own meal.

She really had been sort of railroaded into this date, he mused, remembering the determined look on her mother's face as she'd cheerily made plans for Elle and Shane's evening without consulting them. He was aware that he'd taken advantage of the opportunity, jumping in before Elle had a chance to demur. Sure, she could have still declined, and she'd known it as well as he, but he was glad she hadn't.

"I'm almost afraid to ask this..."

He looked up with a lifted eyebrow in response to her murmur, tensing slightly in preparation for what might follow. "You can ask me anything you like."

Pushing a strand of hair away from her face, she gave him a puzzled look. "What the hell is going on with my mom and your uncle?"

Startled into a dry chuckle, he shook his head. "When I asked Raymond, all he said was that Janet makes him laugh, and he's been needing that. Hard for me to argue with that. Raymond's had a rough time since my dad got sick, trying to deal with the business primarily on his own until I got out of the army, taking care of Dottie, worrying too much about Parker. I guess it's good for him to have a friend who helps him let go of some of the stress."

"And how do you let go of the stress, Shane? Just when are you not working or taking care of the family?"

Again, she'd caught him off guard with a blunt question. This one was harder to answer. He shrugged and cut into what remained of his steak as he muttered. "I have friends."

"I'm sure you do. When's the last time you hung out with them?"

Throwing her a look that felt a little beleaguered, he shrugged. "I've been busy."

"Right." She picked up her wine and took a sip, making her thoughts clear.

He turned the tables deftly back on her. "What about you? When's the last time you spent a night out with those friends I met back in October?"

Her mouth twisted into a rueful, self-deprecating half smile that made his body harden with a desire to taste it. "That would be on that night in October. What can I say? I've been busy."

He couldn't resist reaching across the small table to run a finger along the back of her hand that was still loosely holding her wineglass. "Pot, meet kettle."

She laughed softly, but her smile faded rather quickly. He saw her throat work as she swallowed. "The difference is—I chose this life. I knew when I opened the shop and adopted a child that I was making major commitments, a lifelong commitment where Charlotte is concerned. I wasn't pressed into service for either of them because I felt obligated."

Frowning now, he drew back his hand. "That's not why I—" He cleared his throat, then tried again, "I made my choice, too." He'd tried not to sound defensive—but he knew he wasn't entirely successful.

"You did," she murmured. "For as long as you can keep going with it."

Realization slammed into him. "Surely you aren't comparing me to your ex."

Her eyelashes flickered, making him wonder if he'd spoken more loudly than he'd intended. He looked around quickly but no one seemed to have noticed, so maybe it was only the intensity of his tone that had concerned her. "I'm only pointing out that it's hard not to burn yourself out with stress if your dreams are pulling you somewhere else."

"That sounds like a fortune cookie message," he grumbled. "And I'm not going to abandon my family or my company to go off and 'find myself,' if that's what you're hinting."

She didn't look particularly convinced by his tone. She merely took another sip of her wine and then turned back to her dinner. Telling himself this wasn't the time or place for this conversation, he finished his steak.

They stepped out into the fairy-light-bedazzled resort grounds after dinner, and Shane was flooded with the sights and sounds of the place—the immaculate landscaping, the sparkling Christmas trimmings, the glint of black velvet ocean, the voices and music and rustling of leaves and distant splashing of waves. He could certainly see why this place had such loyal guests, just as he could see that Trevor had poured his heart and soul into building it. Which made him think of

Elle's implication that his own heart wasn't invested in the risk management business.

Was she right? *Would* he someday wish he'd made another choice, maybe have found other business solutions for his uncle and followed a different path for himself?

That wasn't something he particularly wanted to think about. He glanced down at Elle beside him, his attention lingering on the way the lights glittered in her honey hair and dark caramel eyes. She'd worn flats this time with her body-flattering cardigan, top and slacks. "Would you like to walk on the beach? Have drinks in the bar maybe?"

She looked at him without expression for several long moments, and he honestly had no idea what she was thinking. "We do need to talk," she said finally. "And I'd rather do so in private. Mom and Raymond have probably just started the movie. We can talk in your suite."

Though he wondered if anything good had ever followed the words *we need to talk*, he nodded and motioned toward the path for her to precede him.

SHANE'S SUITE THIS time wasn't quite as large as the last, but it was still beautifully appointed. Elle noted that there was only one bedroom and a smallish sitting room. "Are you sleeping on the sofa?" she asked.

"No. Raymond has a separate suite one floor

up. There were no two-bedroom suites available this weekend, and not many one-bedrooms. Trevor's Christmas attractions really pull in the weekend guests."

She nodded and paced to the balcony slider, noting that the view wasn't quite as impressive as last time, either, but still beautiful. There was probably no suite on the property that wasn't plush.

But she hadn't come up to admire the accommodations. She turned away from the window to look at Shane, who stood in the center of the room, watching her.

"There's a coffeemaker," he said, motioning toward a credenza. "Or wine in the cooler. Can I get you anything?"

"No, I'm good, thanks."

"Would you at least like to sit down?"

Instead, she stepped a little closer to him, drawing a deep, bracing breath.

"My life is pretty crazy right now," she said. "With my partner having issues and my daughter's biological family showing up out of the blue and my mom…well, my mom acting even more unpredictably than usual, it's got me rattled. I'm not sure how clearly I'm thinking."

"I get that," he said. "What can I do to help?"

She shook her head with a gusty sigh. Of course his first impulse would be to try to take on her problems along with everyone else's. "I'm not asking for your help, Shane."

He pushed a hand through his hair. "So what do you need?"

It was so apparent to her that he hardly knew how to act around someone who wasn't asking for his assistance. She found that rather sad.

She took a step closer to him. "I could use the same thing I think you need."

His arm fell to his side as he studied her intently. "And what is that?"

"A couple hours of escape." She reached out to walk her hands up his chest, easing them beneath the arms of the ubiquitous leather jacket to slide it off his shoulders. "No strings. No promises. No future expectations or obligations. And above all, no awkwardness or unpleasantness when we cross paths in the future."

Tossing the jacket onto the sofa, he drew her closer, initial surprise replaced now by anticipation. "Your mother isn't the only one in your family who's unpredictable," he murmured, his hands on her hips as she looped her arms around his neck.

Her heart pounded in her throat, but still she managed what she hoped was a sultry smile. "Maybe we prefer it that way."

His mouth hovered an inch over hers. "I'm finding that I have a strong preference for it, myself."

Even as she closed the distance between them to capture those tantalizing lips with her own, she told herself this was imprudent. Borderline reckless. But she'd made the decision and she was owning it. She figured the only way she was ever going to stop obsessing about Shane, the only way to get him out of her system was to satisfy her rampant curiosity. Not to mention that it had just been too damned long since she'd allowed herself to indulge certain very healthy and natural needs.

The kiss was epic. With her decision to stop fighting him—to stop fighting herself—she'd given them both permission to express the hunger that had been building between them since that very first day. He dragged her against him and she all but climbed him to get even closer, diving into him with an eagerness that had been restrained for far too long.

He felt so good, tasted so good. His hands were strong, skilled. Thorough. His shirt was left on the floor beside the couch. Hers fell somewhere on the way to the bedroom. Shoes were scattered through the suite, and his belt lay over the foot of the bed. She kicked off her pants, tossed her bra aside as he tumbled her onto the turned-down bed.

The only light in the bedroom was from a small, dimmed lamp on the nightstand, but it was enough to let her see the lines and planes of his solid torso, the sprinkling of hair angling to a deep V, the line of tan and scattered scars that testified to an active outdoor life. Her attention wavered between her exploration of him and the sensations he evoked in her with his fingers, his lips, his furnace-hot body.

He nuzzled her throat, nipped gently at her earlobes, cupped her breasts in his hands before lowering his mouth to explore them more thoroughly. She arched upward, every square inch of her responding. Aching. Yearning for more.

Growing impatient, she pushed against his shoulders, rolling him onto his back, sliding down his body to do some exploring of her own. She took her time about it and she could feel him almost vibrating with the attempt to keep his control. She enjoyed that power over him, even as he slid a hand between her legs and had her melting around him.

He disappeared for a moment into the bathroom, then quickly returned with a foil packet gripped in one hand. Rejoining her on the bed, he kissed her deeply, leaving only a sliver of space between their mouths when he muttered, "I've wanted this since the first moment you looked up and smiled at me."

"And I've wanted it since you strutted into my shop," she admitted, tangling her hands in his tousled, wavy hair. There could be nothing between them at this moment but honesty. She'd worry about the future later.

He nipped gently at her kiss-dampened lower lip. "I don't strut."

"Oh, you most definitely strut," she murmured, tugging him down to her. "And it annoys the hell out of me that it looks so damn good on you."

She swallowed his rumble of laughter, then wrapped her legs around his hips and welcomed him into her with a soft cry of gratification echoed by his deeper groan. He took his time, carrying her right to the edge of climax again and again before finally losing his rigid control. She was swept away with him then, shuddering, trembling, gasping. Flying.

Sated.

ELLE WAS STILL trying to remember how to breathe when Shane's phone beeped with a text, bringing her back down to earth with a crash.

Lying half on top of her, his face buried in her throat, Shane mumbled a curse, his own breathing ragged. "Ignore it."

The phone beeped again. She nudged his damp shoulder. "You know you have to check."

With a rough exhale, he fumbled for his phone, finally locating it on the floor beside the bed. He squinted at the screen, then tossed the phone aside with a mutter.

"Everything okay?"

"Yeah. Just one of my army friends asking if I'll help him move next weekend."

"Of course it was." Why wasn't she surprised?

Propped on one elbow, he smoothed her tousled hair from her face, letting her comment pass. "So…"

"So." She sighed and gazed up at him. "That happened."

"Regrets?"

"None."

Shane blinked a couple of times. Her immediate and unequivocal reply was apparently not what he'd expected. She meant it, though. She wasn't the type to waste a lot of time on regrets.

"But," she said before he could speak, "that doesn't necessarily mean it will ever happen again. Remember what I said earlier about the no expectations thing."

"So this was just 'wham-bam-thank-you-Sam'?"

She laughed in response to both his words and his wry expression, but she noted his eyes didn't quite reflect his smile.

"This," she said, reaching up to trace one of those irresistible dimples, "was very, very nice. But now I have to go."

He didn't try to detain her, though he did give her a lingering, savoring kiss that drew a sigh of regret from her when it ended. She knew that much had changed during the past hour...and yet some things were still very much the same. Once she stepped out of this room, she had to put aside selfish desires and remind herself of the responsibilities waiting for her.

She gathered her clothes from their various landing spots around the suite and carried them into the bathroom, emerging a few minutes later relatively back in order. She'd been careful not to look too closely into the mirror while she was in there; there'd be time enough later to stare at her reflection and wonder if she'd lost her mind. But no regrets, she promised herself.

Shane had donned his jeans and shirt again, though the shirt was unbuttoned and his feet were still bare. He'd apparently straightened his hair with his hand, leaving it appealingly tumbled. Her mouth went dry, and her fingers twitched with a renewed urge to reach out to him, but she held herself back and managed what she hoped was a breezy smile.

"We'll talk later about scheduling Charlotte's Christmas visit with Dottie," she said, picking up her purse as they moved through the sitting room toward the door. "I'm sure the visit will be very pleasant."

"Now that we've gotten this out of our system, you mean." His voice was a little too bland.

She shot him a look, trying to decipher his expression. "Um—"

"That's the way you're looking at it now, right?" His eyes challenging her to disagree with him, he took a step closer. "Just a one-off? A temporary aberration?"

"Well—"

He cupped her face between his palms. "Just so you know, I don't think you're out of my system now, at all. As a matter of fact, it could be just the opposite. I'll back off if you ask me to. I'll be a friend, a civil acquaintance, whatever makes you comfortable. But I won't stop wanting you, and I'll never look at tonight as a one-night stand. It was a hell of a lot more than that to me."

Everything inside her reacted to his intense tone, his piercingly direct gaze. She knew without doubt that however affable and disinterested she and Shane acted in the future, he had just shattered any foolish illusion she'd had that this night together hadn't changed everything.

"I…um… Good night," she said, reaching behind her to jerk open the door. With that clever and oh-so-coherent response, she made her escape— an awkward, far cry from the breezy, sophisticated exit she'd planned.

CHAPTER FIFTEEN

SHANE CALLED THE next evening after he knew Charlotte should be in bed. Just, he said, to let Elle know that he and Raymond had gotten back to Fayetteville and that Dottie was doing well, and still greatly looking forward to their visit. Sitting against the pillows of her bed where she'd been reading before turning in, Elle was a bit reserved at first, but soon found herself laughing when he told her a funny story about something Dottie had done earlier.

In return, she told him about her day shopping with Charlotte for new clothes because she was growing so rapidly. Charlotte, she informed him wryly, had decided she wanted to buy black clothes—like "Bamber."

"Ah. A little Goth toddler, is she?"

Elle chuckled. "A little Goth wannabe, apparently."

"So? Can I expect to see her dressed like a tiny Wednesday Addams at Christmas?"

She laughed again. "No, though I did find a couple of cute little outfits that had black mixed with other colors like red and blue. She decided she liked both sets well enough to consider them close enough."

"Got a mind of her own at an early age, doesn't she?"

"Oh, yes."

"I've been told that Charlie announced when he was about five that he wasn't wearing any more shirts with collars. After several, um, negotiations with Dottie, he grudgingly agreed to wearing them only to church on Sundays. I'm not sure he broke that pattern until he went into the army."

Elle must have been getting used to hearing her daughter compared to Charlie now. She didn't even tense this time. They chatted for a few more minutes, and then Shane told her good-night in a deep murmur that left her feeling warm when the call ended. They hadn't talked about last night, though she suspected memories of their lovemaking had been as much on his mind today as it had been on hers.

Needless to say, she hadn't confided in her mother. She'd come home to find her mom and Raymond in the kitchen, drinking herbal tea and deep in discussion about the movie they'd just watched. Declining an invitation to join them with the excuse that she was tired after a long day, Elle had checked on her sleeping daughter, then turned in. She'd expected to toss and turn all night, but she'd slept surprisingly well, waking up rested, refreshed and deliciously heavy-limbed.

Maybe her mom had her suspicions about what had gone on between Elle and Shane last night, but she hadn't asked. Nor did Elle ask any questions about her mom and Raymond. Even though they lived in the same house—maybe even especially because they did—it was important that they maintain some boundaries.

Shane called again Tuesday night. For some reason, Elle had more than half expected him to. They talked for about thirty minutes, swapping stories about work, family, a couple of the day's news headlines. He didn't even make an excuse for calling this time. And when he ended the call, he said, "I'll talk to you tomorrow."

She didn't protest. And she was smiling again when she snuggled into her pillow in preparation for her very early start the next morning.

The December days seemed to whizz past in a blur of work and holiday preparations. Elle felt almost as if she sprinted from the time her alarm buzzed before dawn until those precious moments every evening when Charlotte had her bath and story time before bed. And every other night, the last voice she heard before sliding into a weary sleep was Shane's.

She wasn't sure how it had happened, but she simply expected those conversations now, and he was equally matter-of-fact about them, offering no reason for calling except to hear her voice, to share their lives. He made several business trips during those two weeks, but he called all the same, and he told her about his travels and meetings. He always asked about Charlotte, of course, and he seemed to relish every story about her—but Elle was beginning to believe he called because he simply wanted to talk with her, not just to keep tabs on his niece. Risky thinking, that, but she was having trouble keeping her barriers up.

For one evening, they had been lovers. But now they were becoming friends, as well—which was even more of a risk for heartache if it all went south.

Elle had one call from Fayetteville that wasn't as stress-free during the second week of December. She felt her shoulders tense instinctively when Parker Mendel identified herself. "Hello, Parker. Is everything okay there? Is Dottie okay?"

She couldn't imagine any other reason why Shane's cousin would be calling her.

"Dottie's fine, thank you," Parker assured her immediately. "Everyone's great here."

"I'm glad to hear that. What can I do for you?"

"Well, I'm trying to finish up my Christmas shopping this week. And I wanted to ask if it's okay with you if I buy a gift for Charlotte."

Elle hesitated. She appreciated Parker asking

permission, of course, but it did rather put her on the spot. "Of course it's okay, though certainly not necessary."

Elle made a quick mental note to buy a small gift from Charlotte to Aubrey, though she certainly wasn't ready to start any traditions. She'd suggested this one visit only because the last one had been cut short so abruptly for Dottie and Charlotte, she reminded herself.

"Oh, lovely! I was hoping you'd agree," Parker enthused. "So, next question. Does Charlotte already have a tablet of her own?"

"A tablet?" Elle frowned. "You mean a computer tablet?"

"Yes. I thought maybe she'd like one of those mini-tablets in a childproof case. They have the cutest pink-and-purple shatterproof case that I think she'd like. You can load the tablet with educational videos and toddler learning games and there are several videos that promote interest in music and dance and…"

"Thank you, Parker," Elle cut in firmly. "It's a very kind thought, but I'd rather you choose something else."

"Oh. She already has one, then?"

"No. But that's far too expensive. Besides, she's only two. I'm still limiting her screen time. It's probably better not to have that sort of temptation around."

While Elle wasn't one to criticize other parental choices, she wanted her child to be allowed to savor the fleeting, simple pleasures of childhood— going to the park, splashing in puddles, constructing imaginary skyscrapers out of twigs and pebbles and Popsicle sticks. She wanted Charlotte to experience the feel and smell and visual appeal of a book, the sounds she could produce with a metal pot and a wooden spoon, the fascination of crawling bugs and teeming tide pools and drops of dew on unfurling new leaves.

Of course Charlotte would learn about computers and other modern technology. They did watch the occasional educational video or even a silly toddler-friendly cartoon. Elle was hardly a Luddite. But Parker had asked her opinion about the gift choice and Elle would stand firm.

"If you'd like to get her an educational gift, how about a construction set or puzzles or art supplies?" she suggested instead. "Mom and I aren't getting her a lot of gifts, but we've found her a toy cash register and a little plastic cupcake assembly set so she can play coffee shop. Charlotte loves using her imagination. Perhaps you'd like to get her a dance-related dress-up gift—a tutu or a wind-up musical toy she can dance along to?"

"Oh, that would be fun," Parker said, and Elle was relieved the other woman immediately conceded Elle's authority on behalf of Charlotte's gifts.

"I'm sure Charlotte would look absolutely adorable in a tutu."

"Well, I think she looks adorable in everything. But as her mother, I suppose I'm not very objective." Had that been a bit too emphatic? She winced a little, chiding herself for a defensiveness that seemed unjustified considering that the whole reason for Parker's call had been to defer to Elle's wishes about the Christmas present. "I really have to get back to work now, Parker. Thank you for calling."

She held the phone to her aching forehead for a moment after disconnecting. This entanglement with the Scanlon family was getting much too convoluted. There were so very many things that could go wrong. She worried, of course, about being hurt herself—but more than that, she was furiously determined to protect her relationship with Charlotte. She would make that very clear to all of them, and if that caused problems between her and Shane—well, wasn't that something she'd prepared for, anyway?

Satisfied that she'd made her point with Parker, she tried to put the call out of her mind. She didn't mention it to Shane when he called that evening, nor did he. She wondered if Parker had even told him about it.

The concern still nagged at the back of her mind that she couldn't say with certainty which side Shane would endorse if a line was ever drawn between her and the Scanlon family.

As for Elle's remaining source of concern…she was still having a hard time figuring out what was going on with Kristen. Their relationship hadn't gotten back to the close, warm connection they'd once shared, but neither had it drifted further off course. Some days Kristen seemed almost like her old self, and other days she was moody and sad again. Elle knew the holidays were going to be particularly difficult for Kristen after the breakup, but surely everything would be better once the festivities were behind them and they were back to normal business.

And then, on a Saturday afternoon one week before Christmas, Elle looked up from sweeping the floor after closing the shop to find Kristen standing in the kitchen doorway, her face streaked with tears and misery. And she knew her life was about to take another difficult detour.

ELLE LOOKED TIRED. It was the first thing Shane noticed when she opened the door to him Sunday afternoon, though she tried to hide it with a warm smile. Yet the hint of purplish shadows beneath her dark amber eyes and the faint lines of stress around her mouth in no way diminished her attraction for him. He drank in the sight of her, mentally counting every hour since he'd last seen her. Touched her.

Throwing caution to the wind and not caring who saw, he leaned over to kiss her. He was gratified when she didn't pull back, but returned the kiss in a way that let him know he wasn't the only one aware of how many days had passed.

He'd called an hour ago to ask if it was okay to visit, though he hadn't told her why. She probably thought he was passing through on business again. She would be wrong. He was here only for her.

She ushered him into the living room. Hearing no sounds from elsewhere in the house, he asked, "Where are your mom and Charlotte?"

"Charlotte's taking a nap and Mom's seeing a movie with friends. Can I get you anything to drink? Are you hungry?"

"No, thanks, to both. How are you, Elle?"

She tucked her hair behind one ear. Her gaze darted away from his as she said too brightly, "I'm fine, thanks. You didn't mention when we talked last night that you were coming through Shorty's Landing today."

"That's because I didn't know when we talked."

Her eyebrows rose. "Oh? Did something come up at Wind Shadow or one of your other accounts?"

"No." He took her hands and drew her to the couch. Sitting half turned to face her, their knees touching and fingers still linked, he said, "I know what's going on, Elle. I've come to help you."

She blinked. "What are you—"

"I could tell last night that something was bothering you." The stress had been clear in her voice when he'd called, though she'd brushed off his questioning, telling him she was just tired. "Janet told Raymond what happened with Kristen, and he told me. He assumed I already knew."

Her face darkened, though he wasn't sure whether it was because of the reminder of her troubles or because he'd heard about them from others. Maybe both.

When she didn't immediately speak, he continued. "Your mom told Raymond that Kristen wants to sell her portion of The Perkery as soon as possible, and that you're afraid that means you'll have to close. She said you've been very upset. I wish you'd felt comfortable sharing that with me."

Her eyelids lowered, hiding her expression. "I wasn't ready to talk about it," she admitted in a low voice. "I needed some time to process it."

"I get that," he conceded, though it still hurt. "Anyway, I just want you to know you don't have to worry anymore. Raymond and I talked about it, and we want to help. We've decided to invest in your business by buying out Kristen's share. We agreed completely about this."

Elle went still beside him. He could almost feel

her hands going cold in his. Surprise? Definitely. Happy surprise? He searched her face, wondering warily why she didn't look more pleased.

"Did you now?" she asked, her tone chilly and oh-so-polite. She drew her hands from his and folded them tightly in her lap.

"Look, I'm not saying we would interfere in your business," he assured her hastily. He could certainly understand her hesitation, considering she'd been senior partner in the enterprise since it had opened. "We'd stay strictly out of that aspect. You'd have to hire an assistant, I suppose, to take over Kristen's days. We'd be happy to look over your liability and workers' comp policies to see if you could be saving there. You could even buy us out over time, if you like. This could just be a temporary measure to help you stay afloat."

She sprang to her feet and everything in her posture let him know that she was not at all pleased. Just the opposite, in fact. For some reason, she looked thoroughly incensed.

"As generous as your offer is," she said, somehow making *generous* sound like a curse word, "I have to decline."

He rose more slowly, never taking his eyes from her flushed face. "I don't understand why you're angry about this. I'm only trying to help."

Pushing back her hair, she eyed him coolly. "I should thank you, I suppose, but I don't need your help. I have it all under control. Now, if that's all you wanted to discuss, I think we can consider this meeting concluded."

She'd made it perfectly clear that she *wasn't* thanking him. And that she was dismissing him from her home—from her life? What the hell?

"Elle. I don't understand," he said again.

Her eyes glittered now, both with anger and with unshed tears that tore at him even as he struggled to grasp the reason for them. "Just answer this, Shane. Have you and your uncle been looking for a company to invest in? Have you been just waiting and hoping an opportunity would come along for you to be silent partners in a coffee shop?"

"No, of course not. This—"

"And didn't you tell me your company was struggling when you stepped into your father's shoes? That the new accounts you've acquired are only now helping you get back on solid ground?"

"Yes, but we don't expect to lose money with your shop," he assured her, wondering if that was part of her distress. Was she concerned about him taking a loss he couldn't absorb? That was thoughtful of her, but not necessary. "We've decided we can take the risk for the sake of family. It's what we Scanlons do."

It was what he did, he added to himself. He fixed problems. Why couldn't she appreciate that?

"Yes, well, there's just one flaw with that logic," she replied flatly. "I am not your family. I'm not a Scanlon. You can let yourself out."

With that, she turned and walked out of the room. He heard a door close quietly, but pointedly, somewhere down the hall.

His first instinct was to chase after her. To insist that she tell him exactly what he'd done to make her so angry. To help him understand how he'd hurt her this time—because he had little doubt that, inconceivable as it might be to him, he'd done just that. He put a hand to the back of his neck, squeezing against the pain that knowledge caused him.

For most of his life, he'd taken care of others. It had been his role in the family, among his friends, in his military service and in his career. But how could he fix this situation with Elle if he didn't know what he had broken?

And if she was so insistent that she didn't need his help, just what did he have to offer her?

"YOU REALLY ARE going to wear a path, Elle. If you keep having these squabbles with Shane, we should probably invest in granite floors."

Elle knew her mom was trying to make her smile, but she was still too angry—and too hurt—to be appeased that evening. "He just walked in here and announced that he was buying half of my business. He didn't even ask, just flat out made the statement and then sat back and waited for my gratitude. My gratitude!"

"Imagine. Gratitude. For what he drove three hours to offer."

Elle shot her mother a suspicious look. "He doesn't think I can manage my own business!"

"Although he did tell you he would stay out of your way and let you run it as you wanted. That was probably just to gain your trust so he could take over, huh?"

"Stop it, Mom." Elle slammed a hand down on the kitchen counter, then winced as she hoped the clatter hadn't disturbed her sleeping daughter. Not to mention that it had left her hand stinging like crazy. Still not as painful as the ache in her chest, of course. "Don't you see? He and his family have already manipulated their way into my daughter's life. And now he's trying to buy even more influence over our family."

"Or maybe he's trying to buy his way into your heart," her mother murmured. "Still foolish, of course. But something one would expect from a man who has spent his whole life trying to live up to his larger-than-life and now sainted older brother by trying to be everything to everyone he cares about."

Elle bit her lip, then drew an unsteady breath before saying, "And when he gets tired of trying to be everything to everyone? When it all becomes too much for him? When he finally admits that he never wanted to run his family's business, much less my coffee shop?"

Her mother's steady gaze turned soft, warmly understanding. "He's not Glenn, Elle."

Chewing her lip again, Elle thought about those words her mother had said to her a few times before. No, Shane wasn't Glenn. Glenn had never taken on even a portion of the responsibility Shane had been dealing with for years. Yet still Glenn had buckled at the thought of adding a child to his responsibilities. How long could Shane hold up under so much more pressure? And what had made him think she would consent to becoming another of his burdens?

She'd gotten along very well without Glenn. She could continue to do so without Shane. If there was one thing she'd proved during the past two years, it was that she was a strong, capable woman who could take care of herself and her family. She wasn't looking for rescue. If she were to have a partner in her personal life, that relationship would have to be kept entirely separate from business. She would want someone who relied on her as much as she depended on him.

Had she overreacted to Shane's gesture? Had he truly only been trying to help, without any ulterior motives? Was she letting her previous failed relationship color her feelings for Shane? Not that she thought they were close to anything like a relationship, she assured herself hastily.

Maybe rather than fear, she was operating this time with a healthy sense of self-protection. Considering all the other complications with Shane, her fiasco with Glenn could look like a walk in the park in comparison if everything fell apart this time.

"YOU'D HAVE THOUGHT I'd told her I wanted to burn her shop to the ground. She went ballistic. For no reason at all." Shane paced the motel room in a burst of frustrated energy as he spoke into his phone. "She practically threw me out of her house. And all I was trying to do was help."

"It must have been something about the way you offered, Shane," his uncle replied calmly. "What exactly did you say?"

"I was totally respectful. I told her you and I would buy out her partner's share of the business and then stand back out of her way unless she needs us for anything else. I even offered to look over her insurance expenses to try to save her money."

"Did you now?"

Raymond's unintentional echo of Elle, complete with the dry, uninflected tone, made Shane scowl. "Okay, fine. Since you seem to have it all figured out, what did I do wrong?"

"Shane...when you made this generous offer to Elle, did you *tell* her your plan, or did you ask her first if she even wanted our help?"

"I—" Shane frowned. "Why wouldn't she want our help? You said Janet told you that Elle was very upset by her partner's decision. I thought she'd be pleased that we had a solution."

"Or maybe, since you barged in on her and made your sweeping announcement without any explanation or any input from her, she's wondering if you have ulterior motives. You forget, Shane, she hasn't had a lifetime of simply expecting you to solve her problems the way our family has. How could she know what you were thinking if you didn't bother to tell her?"

Shane winced. He could almost hear Elle's words. *I am not your family. I'm not a Scanlon.*

"Be honest with me, Raymond," he said after a pause. "Have I gotten arrogant? Have I fallen into the habit of thinking I have all the answers? That I know what's best for everyone?"

His uncle's silence was a gentle reply.

"Damn it."

"To be fair, Shane, you didn't exactly choose this role. It was pretty much thrust upon you. Charlie was our entertainer and you were our go-to guy. Still are. You think I don't see how we run you ragged? Like I said before, maybe it's time for you to stop worrying about everyone else for a change and start thinking about what's best for you. Elle can take care of herself—and Charlotte, of course."

"I've no doubt of that." Shane's tone was bleak. If there was one conclusion he'd reached since he'd walked into Elle's shop that first time, it was that his niece would always be loved and protected by Elle—Charlotte's true mother. And that would be true even without his or his family's influence.

"You'll figure it out, Shane. You always do. Now try to get some rest. As those wise pundits always say—tomorrow is another day."

Shane tossed his phone on one of the two beds in the generic room in the same no-frills motel where he'd stayed on his first visit to Shorty's Landing. Damn, that seemed like a lifetime ago. He hadn't known his niece then. Hadn't met Elle. Hadn't fallen head over heels for her like some smitten schoolboy.

"Damn it," he said again, his voice echoing in the depressingly quiet room.

Though he'd planned to spend the day and a few hours tomorrow with Elle and Charlotte when he'd left home this morning—foolishly thinking that she would be happy about his offer—he'd almost headed back to Fayetteville after their contentious clash earlier. He'd stayed because he'd still had a slim hope that she would give him another chance to explain himself.

A quiet tap on his door brought his head up, had him spinning in that direction. He told himself it was very unlikely that it was Elle. Not when she'd been so angry when she'd walked out on him in her own living room. Maybe a maid? Someone at the wrong room?

He looked out the peephole. Felt his whole body tense. And then opened the door.

Elle tucked her hair behind her ear, looking at him with that familiar mixture of uncertainty and challenge. "Well? Are you going to ask me in?"

Without a word, he moved out of her way.

ELLE NOTED IMMEDIATELY that Shane looked more stressed than she'd ever seen him before. Deep lines were carved around the corners of his mouth, and his roguish dimples were nowhere in sight. His hair looked as though he'd dragged his hand through it a few dozen times, and his clothes were wrinkled from a day of driving. Maybe a few hours of pacing and brooding on the rumpled bed behind him. Apparently she wasn't the only one who wore a path in the floor when perturbed.

"How did you know where to find me?" he asked.

She made a rueful face. "Your uncle told my mother where you were staying."

His mouth twisted a little. "Of course."

She drew a deep breath and started speaking at the same time he did. "Shane—"

"Elle, I—"

"Let me go first," she said when he paused. He nodded and motioned for her to proceed.

"I'm sorry I didn't give you much of a chance to talk earlier," she said, speaking slowly so she wouldn't end up babbling. "I overreacted, and I apologize for that."

He nodded solemnly. "Now it's my turn. I way overstepped my bounds when I made it sound as though you had no choice but to accept our partnership offer. It wasn't what I meant, but I can see now how it must have felt. I should have asked if there was anything you needed, and not assumed I knew what was best for you."

She glanced at his phone, which lay on the bed as if he'd tossed it there after a call. Had he been subjected to the same sort of lecture from his uncle that she'd gotten from her mother? The thought of him meekly submitting to a scolding went quite a ways toward assuaging her pride— which still stung from his noble rush to her rescue earlier, as if she were some cartoon princess waiting for her prince.

She pushed her hands down the sides of her jeans, lifting her chin to meet his gaze squarely. "Okay, so we've both apologized. Where do we go from here?"

He sighed and ran a hand through his hair. "Maybe we could sit down?"

She perched on the very edge of the bed that looked as though he hadn't been slouched on it. He sat on the other, facing her, the beds so close their knees almost touched.

"Do you want to talk about the offer my uncle and I made?" he asked. "It's still on the table—but only if you're interested. Only on your terms."

She made a massive effort to respond more rationally this time, though her answer hadn't changed. "Thank you, Shane. It's a very kind gesture, but I still have to decline."

"Look, if you're worried that we can't absorb the cost and the risk of the investment, you don't have to be. We understand risk, remember? How to minimize it, how to approach it, how to deal with it, if necessary. But as it happens, we think your business would be a profitable investment. I've been impressed with the loyal customer base you've built."

Shaking her head slowly, she realized that he still didn't have a clue. "It has nothing to do with

368   THE WAY TO A SOLDIER'S HEART

risk or potential profits or anything like that, Shane."

His puzzled expression confirmed her deduction. "Then why? What are you going to do?"

"I'll find new financing if I can. Or if necessary, I'll sell the shop and start over with a smaller establishment I can run myself, until I can build up business again."

He looked utterly baffled. "You'd really rather do that than accept our help?"

"Yes," she answered simply.

"Why?"

"Because I won't mix my business with your family."

The way he pulled back his head let her know her wording had been less than tactful. Had she hurt his feelings?

"Like I said," she assured him, "I know you mean well. But surely you can understand that this involvement between us is complicated enough. Charlotte will always connect us. I won't try to keep her from getting got know her Scanlon relatives as she grows up, but I want her to understand that my side is just as much her family even if they aren't genetically related."

"Of course."

Though Elle wasn't sure Parker would agree, she appreciated Shane's unequivocal tone.

"You and I don't need yet another entanglement," she said. "Something else to potentially cause problems or hard feelings between our families. I take care of myself, my child and my career. I won't give away control."

"I wasn't trying to take control, Elle."

"I didn't say you were. I'm just making my boundaries clear. I've known for several years exactly what I want from my life. Being a mother was always a priority for me. Owning my own business was a very close second. Whatever challenges I face, I won't be deterred. My ex wasn't emotionally invested in owning a coffee and pastry shop, and it turns out not to be Kristen's lifelong ambition, either. It certainly isn't yours. With the exception of my mother, I've learned that the only one I can truly depend on to nurture my dreams without ever giving up is me."

She saw him swallow hard before he asked quietly, "So you're saying there's no room in your life for anyone else? No place for me?"

Her stomach tightened in response to the direct challenge, but she kept her gaze steady. "No, I didn't say that. Frankly, it's taken me a while to get to a place where I'm open to a new relationship. I think I'm there now. Or at least, mostly there. But I need to protect myself from being blindsided again by someone who can't keep chasing someone else's dreams indefinitely. No matter how well intentioned."

He took several long moments to digest her words before saying, "You keep implying that I don't know what I want. That I've sacrificed my dreams to take care of my family and our business. And maybe I'll agree with you that it started like that. I'm a problem solver. A caregiver. It's what I do. And if I'm to be totally honest, maybe there were times when I thought that was all I had to give."

She shook her head in dismay, but he pressed on before she could speak.

"Maybe I've wondered in the past if people loved me primarily because I took care of them. I've even told you, I think, that the last woman I tried a relationship with broke up with me because she said I didn't have enough of myself left for her. Maybe I thought that to be with you, I needed to figure out a way to give even more. I decided it was up to me to make sure you and Charlotte had everything you wanted or needed. As I do for everyone I care most about."

Her heart tripped a couple of beats at hearing herself included in that group. Still…

"So, what's your dream, Shane? Do you wish you'd gone to medical school? Because there's still plenty of time…"

"No." He leaned forward a bit more as he interrupted, shifting so their knees were touching now. "Medical school was an old fantasy I obviously didn't want badly enough to pursue. I got that out of my system as a medic. I'm damned proud of my military service and I wouldn't take it back—just as I know Charlie was honored to serve, despite the risks. Being an army medic was satisfying, but that's not my dream."

He shrugged. "I told myself at first that I was only working with my uncle because he needed me, but the truth is, I like my job. I'm good at it. I like the freedom I have in it, the travel and the interaction with a wide variety of people. I like having my family close by, being there for them when they need me, knowing they'd do the same for me. It's a good life."

She twisted her fingers in front of her. "You're really so sure you won't grow bored with that routine and need to find something new?"

Like Glenn and Kristen, she almost added, but she told herself it wasn't fair to keep comparing him to others.

"I'm as certain about that as you are that you won't walk away from the life you've made for yourself and Charlotte," he answered evenly.

She looked down at her hands. "About Charlotte…"

He sighed. "And now you're wondering about my ulterior motives again."

That brought her gaze back up. "The mind-reading thing doesn't work from my mother, Shane. It doesn't suit you, either."

A slight smile toyed with his lips, but his eyes were serious. "I love my niece, Elle. I'm overjoyed that we've reconnected with her, that you've agreed to let us keep seeing her. But I would never use you to get closer to her. For one thing, as you've repeatedly pointed out, getting involved with you is more of a complication than a convenience, which is why I tried my damnedest to keep my distance. But, as *I've* said repeatedly, I wanted you the moment I first saw you. I want you even more now."

He reached out to take her hands in his. "Loving you is a risk I'm willing to take, if you're willing to take a chance on me in return."

Her fingers laced with his. She tilted her head, eyeing him gravely, keeping her voice calm despite the way her heart was racing. "You know, I think I've finally figured out what it is you need, Shane. What to give the man who's always giving."

A light shone in his eyes now. Hope, perhaps. Desire, definitely. Both emotions that echoed strongly inside her.

"What do I need?"

"You need someone who'll hold you accountable. Somehow who'll make sure you're taking as much as you give. Someone who'll demand nothing more from you than honesty. Someone who loves you for no other reason than that you deserve it."

He leaned even closer, narrowing the distance between them. She saw just a flash of dimples as he murmured, "That sounds exactly like what I need. And if it's honesty you want, then read my lips…"

He smothered her giddy laugh in his kiss.

A gentle tug brought her across the slim gap between the beds, tumbling her on top of him as he dropped backward. Laughter melted into sighs and moans as clothes peeled away. Tentativeness was replaced by demand and acquiescence on both parts. Both gave. Both received. And their responses were completely, nakedly honest. Elle wouldn't have asked for anything more from him.

EPILOGUE

SPRING CAME TO Shorty's Landing and brought with it a fresh influx of winter-pale tourists. The Perkery bustled with activity, the air inside redolent with aromas of coffee and fresh baked goods. A burst of laughter came from a group of college students gathered at one end of the room. Two rather weary-looking parents in the opposite corner kept an eagle eye on well-behaved but energetic five-year-old-twin boys munching on oversize cookies.

After passing a plated blueberry scone across the counter to another customer, Elle stepped back to survey her little domain with a rush of pride. The tables were almost all full on this Saturday afternoon. Janet stood beside a table of women as they sipped coffee and discussed an upcoming book club meeting. Charlotte played happily in her corral with her toy cash register. The weather outside was beautiful, the sky clear and blue. Elle could not imagine a more perfect afternoon.

And then a dark-haired man with a self-confident strut and mesmerizing dimples strolled through the door and she knew that somehow the perfect day had just gotten even better.

He wasn't wearing the black leather jacket on this warm afternoon. Elle had been with him the day he'd carefully packed it away for the season. When their eyes had met afterward, she'd known he'd put it away for good, to be cherished with his other memories of the brother he'd stopped trying to replace.

He didn't need the jacket to look sexy enough to make her heart skip a beat, even as familiar as he was to her now.

Shane reached the counter and Elle leaned across to greet him with an unselfconscious kiss as Charlotte shrieked, "Shane!"

Rounding the end of the counter, he swung the child out of the play corral and high into the air, making her dissolve into giggles. Elle was aware that nearly every eye in the shop was focused approvingly on them.

Her mom moved behind the cash register, urging Elle to take Shane into the kitchen where she could greet him properly after his business trip. Elle didn't have to be urged twice. Taking Shane's hand, she tugged him through the swinging door, Charlotte still cradled in his arms.

He gave her another kiss when the door swung closed behind them, blocking them from the shop. From the sink, Amber grinned at them. "Hey,

Shane. I'll, uh, I'll go see if Janet needs help in the front."

Chuckling, Shane watched the young woman hurry for the swinging door. "Thanks, Amber, but you really don't have to run. We're good."

Yes, they were, Elle agreed, her left hand resting on his arm. A diamond glinted on her ring finger, a symbol of the commitment they had made to each other, of the wedding that would take place in the fall when they'd have time for a short honeymoon.

Shane was making arrangements to open a branch office of Scanlon Risk Management, Inc. in Shorty's Landing. In the meantime, they divided their time between Elle's house here and his place in Fayetteville. It involved quite a bit of commuting, lengthy conference calls and computer work for Shane, but he never complained. In fact, Raymond had confided in Elle that he'd never seen Shane happier.

"How was your flight?" she asked him. He'd spent the past few days in Texas with Trevor at the new resort, which was gearing up for its grand opening in two weeks.

He smiled. "No delays and my bag made it back on the same plane, so I can't complain."

Charlotte tugged at Shane's collar. "Shane, Shane."

He snuggled into her cheek. "What?"

"Play with me now?"

"Sure, kiddo. Want to go to the park?"

"Park!" She bounced so hard he winced as he juggled to keep from dropping her.

"Okay, just a minute." He looked at Elle then, and though she knew he must be tired from his trip, he looked perfectly happy about the prospect of chasing a toddler around a playground. So typical of this unselfish, devoted family man she loved with all her heart. Elle couldn't imagine a more dedicated father for Charlotte than the uncle who would spend the rest of his life making sure the ones he loved were safe and happy.

"So," he said, "I just talked to Dottie. She wanted me to remind you to bring her some chocolate-filled doughnuts tomorrow."

Elle laughed softly. "She reminded me herself when I chatted with her on the phone earlier today. Did she think I'd forget?"

Shane grinned. "She just likes giving orders, remember?"

To the family's relief, Dottie had rallied since her health scare five months earlier, and had been feeling fairly well since. Her grateful family had agreed to celebrate every day they could spend with their feisty matriarch without worrying about the future. She had announced her intention to be in the front row at Elle and Shane's wedding—and Elle was confident she would see

Dottie there. Shane had even told Elle that he credited her and Charlotte with giving Dottie a new surge of energy.

Their life wasn't all rainbows and roses, of course. The convoluted logistics of operating two businesses in two different, if adjoining, states sometimes grew wearisome. Parker and Elle were finding their way tentatively toward a guarded friendship. Elle still missed working with Kristen, though she was pleased to say that her friend seemed to be happier in a new job singing on a cruise ship, which gave her a chance to both travel and perform. Yet Elle's new partnership was working out well, and she was excited about preliminary plans for her to take over the existing coffee shop at the Wind Shadow resort. There was even the possibility of opening yet another shop a few miles away in a neighboring resort town.

She'd been hesitant at first when Trevor Farrell had approached her about investing in her business. He'd had to convince her that Shane hadn't been involved; in fact, it had been Kristen who'd gone to Trevor with the idea. Feeling guilty about leaving her friend in the lurch, Kristen had wanted to sell her portion of the business to someone who'd be the ideal new partner for Elle. Trevor had agreed that the collaboration would be a successful one. Elle couldn't be more thrilled with the opportunities being opened to her, as much as she regretted that Kristen wouldn't be taking that journey with her.

"Park, Shane," Charlotte reminded him, pointing toward the door.

He grinned and winked at Elle. "She gets more like her great-grandmother every day."

"Yes," Elle agreed, no longer bothered by such comparisons. "She does."

He pressed a lingering kiss to her lips before moving toward the door. "Love you, Elle. See you at home."

Her smile felt ridiculously happy. "Love you, too. See you at home."

"See you home, Mommy!" Charlotte parroted as Shane toted her out the back door.

"Oh, my goodness, they are so cute together," Elle's mom enthused from the doorway. "You are one lucky woman, my darling girl."

"Yes. Yes, I am," Elle replied contentedly, watching her daughter and her fiancé laughingly chase each other across the back lot.

Her mother wrapped an arm around her waist. "I'd say we're all fortunate that we've got each other. There's nothing more precious than family."

Glancing down at the diamond on her finger, Elle murmured her agreement.

Her mother patted her arm, numerous bracelets jingling merrily. "Didn't I tell you months ago that wonderful things were in store for you? And you said I don't have the gift."

With a laughing groan, Elle shook her head, taking one more lingering look through the back window at the man and child walking toward the park—the man and child who would be waiting for her at home later. And then she turned and got back to work, a smile on her face and happy anticipation in her heart.

* * * * *

*See how it all began in Shorty's Landing
in the first book in Gina Wilkins's
SOLDIERS AND SINGLE MOMS miniseries,
THE SOLDIER'S FOREVER FAMILY.*

*And watch for the next book
coming in February 2018!*

*For another military romance,
check out Amber Leigh Williams's
NAVY SEAL PROMISE.*

Available now from Harlequin Superromance!

Get 2 Free Books,
<u>Plus</u> 2 Free Gifts—
just for trying the Reader Service!

Get 2 Free Books,
Plus 2 Free Gifts—
just for trying the
Reader Service!